Redemption

The Further Adventures of Huck Finn and Tom Sawyer

by
Andrew Joyce

Dedicated to
Louise Maillé Lelièvre
Whose help in producing this book was invaluable.

For myriad reasons, I would like to thank:

Jere Swain

Ben Dorson

Emily Gmitter

Don Myers

&

Mark Gottlieb

ONE

The last time you heard of me and Tom was in that book Sam Clemens wrote telling of when Jim and me flowed down the Mississippi and met up with the King and the Duke. Then Jim got captured, and Tom and I had to set him free. Of course, Jim was already a freed man; Tom just neglected to mention that fact during the planning stage.

Well, we were twelve years of age when Sam wrote about that. Now Tom and I are a mite older, and a lot of water has gone under the bridge since then. One thing is that we're a little bit smarter than we were. We've been reading a lot of books and our English has improved a mite. But it wasn't just books. Both Tom and I have traveled many miles, not always together, and travel broadens one's outlook on life.

We went from being children to men before we knew it. Tom and Becky never married like everyone expected. In the summer of '54, Becky ran off with a drummer. I think he sold women's corsets, but of that, I am not certain. We haven't heard from her since. Judge Thatcher and Tom's Aunt Polly both took sick and died the next year when the cholera epidemic passed through town. Two years after that, the widow Douglas died; the doctor said it was heart failure.

In the spring of 1861, General Beauregard fired on Fort Sumter and the next thing we knew, we were no longer citizens of the United States—we were now proud citizens of the Confederate States of America. Tom and I were then twenty-four years of age, and as soon as we could, we signed up to fight the Yankees.

We were hearty and handsome as we marched out of St. Petersburg wearing our new gray and yellow uniforms. The people cheered as we passed by and every once in a while, a young girl would run out from the crowd and plant a kiss on some fortunate fella. I was lucky enough to get two!

We were off to war or so we thought, but that wasn't the case at all. After three days of marching, we met up with other outfits from around Missouri and set up camp. And there we stayed. At first we were in high spirits; we couldn't wait to get at them Yankees. But after a few weeks of marching back and forth, sometimes through the mud, our spirits started to flag. Around the fires at night, we wondered why we weren't up to Washington burning the place to the ground.

One night, Tom and I were sitting in our tent trying to keep dry after a particularly hard day of marching in the rain when Tom asked me why I signed up. "I thought you didn't cotton to slavery no more?"

I took a pull on my pipe and paused a moment to think before answering, "I don't, not since I seen what it did to

Jim, keeping him from his wife and children until he was freed. Niggers are people too. I'm not a fire-and-brimstone abolitionist, but I just don't feel that slavery is right."

Tom didn't say anything so I went on. "I reckon I signed up because I thought fighting battles and putting my life out there for any Yankee to take, if he could, would be the adventure of a lifetime. But this endless sitting around and marching is wearin' on my soul. Tell me Tom, why did you sign up?"

Tom took out his corncob pipe and filled it with tobacco. After he got her lit, he blew out some smoke and said, "Huck, as you know, I ain't no abolitionist neither, and you know I think mighty highly of niggers, though I don't think they're the same as us white folk, but I wouldn't own one. If other people want to own slaves, I figure that's up to them. I didn't sign up to preserve slavery. Like you, I wanted some adventure, but there was something else. I'm fighting, if we ever get to any fighting, for the Cause. We have a way of life here in the South that is different from that in the North. I don't want us talking or acting like Yankees. So I figure when this war is over, and it should be over soon, then it will be a long time before them Yankees tell us how to live. Now it's about slavery, but how long before they're telling us that we got to talk like them and be like them?" There wasn't much to add to what Tom had said, so I put out my pipe and turned in.

3

It felt like forever, but we were finally told that we were going to move out and get together with some boys from Virginia and other parts of the Confederacy. It seemed the generals thought the Yankees might try to take Richmond. This time we didn't have to march; they put us on a train, and we headed east.

When we got to the Shenandoah Valley, we mixed with other regiments and became known as the Army of the Shenandoah. Our first commander was Colonel Stonewall Jackson, but he wasn't known as Stonewall back then. Later, he was replaced by General Johnston.

After all that waiting and marching, it looked like we were at length going to do some fighting. It wasn't long before Tom and I found ourselves in the thick of it. We were outside a little town called Manassas. It was a white morning, the sun hidden by gray-white clouds. There was a white mist on the fields, about chest-high. Not a sound was heard except the clatter of cannon wagons as they moved through the woods and the thump of the horses' hooves as they hit the ground. The birds seemed to know something was coming because I didn't hear any morning songs as we advanced.

The Yankees attacked our left flank as we were preparing to attack theirs. Confusion was the order of the day with balls whizzing every which way. Within seconds, you couldn't see the enemy for love nor money through the gun smoke. I was firing into a cloud of white smoke and reloading as fast as I could. Standing a little behind me and to my left, Tom was doing the same. At one point as he was reloading, he said to me, "For all I can see of Yankees, we might as well have stayed back in Missouri and shot at trees."

I had just fired and was lowering my gun to reload. Tom was rising after having reloaded when a ball buzzed by my left ear. I didn't think much of it. Balls had been passing by in close proximity all morning, but this one found a home in Tom's right arm. I didn't hear him cry out. I don't think he made a sound, but when I looked over to him, he was on the ground with bright crimson blood soaking through his dull gray uniform. I dropped my gun and went to him, knelt down and asked, I think, the stupidest question I've ever asked, "You've been hit?"

Tom smiled and nodded. I then asked if it hurt. He shook his head and said, "Not yet." Tom had been shot once before when we set Jim free; it was in his leg that time. So I reckoned he knew what he was talking about.

I wanted to get him fixed up before the pain set in. I started to pick him up, but he was having none of that. "What's the matter with you? The ball's in my arm, I can walk. Just help me back to the hospital tent; I feel a bit faint." I helped him up and put his good arm around my neck. Together we retreated through the smoke and clamor into the woods where the hospital was located.

We got to the hospital, and there were many boys already lying about, moaning in pain. I knew we'd have to wait our turn, but I wanted to get the lay of the land. After I had Tom lying comfortable on the ground, I approached the tent, and a man came out carrying the lower part of a leg. I backed up to let him pass and saw him throw it onto a pile of human limbs—arms, legs, feet and hands.

When he came back my way, I asked him how long before Tom could be seen by the doctor.

"No telling, we take 'em as they come." He looked back at the assemblage of men lying on the ground and asked which one was my friend. I pointed to Tom, and he informed me that it would be at least an hour.

I grabbed him by the arm and told him that Tom could bleed to death by then. "Lotta men bleeding to death this day; your friend will be in good company." He added, "Keep some pressure on the wound; he should last until the doc gits to him." As he started to walk off, but before he made two paces, I asked him about the pile of arms and legs.

"When you're shot up like them was, the doctor has gotta cut off the offending limb. Elsewise mortification (nowadays we call it gangrene) will set in and you'll lose your whole body, not just an arm or a leg."

It wasn't an easy thing to do, but I figured I owed it to Tom to tell him what I had just learned. Once I was seated next to him, I asked if the pain had started yet. Then I regretted the question because I could see it in his face. Telling him I'd be right back, I started for the officers' tents. The battle was still raging, and there was no one about. I found what I was looking for in the first tent I went into and brought it back to Tom. It was a bottle, almost full, of good Kentucky sippin' whiskey.

"Here Tom. Drink a little of this while we wait for the sawbones."

He struggled to sit up a ways, reached out with his good arm and took the bottle from my grasp. He pulled the cork with his teeth, spit it out, and took a good pull. He handed me the bottle saying, "I hate to drink alone." I nodded and took a long pull myself. The smooth liquid hit my gullet and its warm fingers spread throughout my being, giving me the courage to tell Tom what was in store for him concerning his arm.

"Tom, the doc is not called a sawbones for nothing. You see that pile of arms and legs over yonder? Well, you just wait, because shortly your right arm is going to be right on top of the heap." Then I went on to explain about mortification and such and handed him back the bottle.

He drank heavily and brooded awhile before saying, "You know, I was readin' about this here doctor fella over in Paris, France. His name is Louis something, like the king that lost his head. Well, this gent was tellin' about these little critters; you could put a million of 'em on the

7

head of a pin. He said that they git into our blood and can kill us. So he was sayin' when you got a wound, it's gotta be washed out good, and then no mortification can set in. Of course, all the other doctor fellas was sayin' he's crazy. But he swears that what he says is true." Tom took another long draw of whiskey and then asked if I had my clasp knife on me.

"Sure Tom, I got it right here," I said as I reached into my pocket and withdrew the knife.

"Then open it and dig the ball outta my arm."

I hesitated for a moment. But after taking another look at the pile of limbs, I opened the knife.

First, I told Tom to take a long, hard swallow of that good Kentucky whiskey. When he had, I stuck a stick in his mouth and told him to bite down hard, which he did. Getting the ball out wasn't easy work. I had to root around in there some. When I finally held the ball in my hand, Tom was passed out. Luckily, he had a firm grip on the bottle, so none of that good whiskey was lost.

My hands were covered in blood, and I wanted to get some water to wash out Tom's wound just in case that gent in France was on the money about them little critters. But I didn't see any water nearby and it looked like it was getting to be Tom's turn with the sawbones, so I poured some whiskey into the wound, figuring that it couldn't hurt.

I wanted to get Tom out of there before he was dragged into the hospital tent. I was sure the doc would cut off his arm if for no other reason than habit.

Tom was still out. I stuck the cork back in the bottle and put it in my pocket. Tom would be needing it when he came round. Next, I picked him up and carried him farther into the woods. Placing him gently on the ground, I removed my yellow sash and dressed his wound. When that task was done, I went in search of a way out of there. Tom's fighting days were over, at least for a while. And mine were over for good. I had never seen such foolishness. Firing into white smoke, not even seeing the enemy!

It looked like a couple of officers bought the farm because I found two saddled horses way back out of the ruckus. They had better sense than most of the men that day. It's probably what is meant by "good horse sense."

I brought the horses over to where Tom lay, sat on my heels, and waited for him to stir. When at last he came around, I asked him if he was able to ride, adding that if we didn't get out of there right away, we'd probably have to fight all through the whole damn war.

He was a bit out of it, but had the presence of mind to say, "I thought that was the idea of going to war, you stuck it out 'til the end."

"Yes Tom, that is the idea. But you can't shoot a gun with that arm. I don't mind dyin'. Hell, I ain't got nothing better to do, but I've got to get you back to Missouri. Then when you're healed up, you can hightail it right back here if you want. But me, I've tasted enough gun smoke to last a lifetime."

Both our uniforms were covered in blood, and it was all Tom's. I knew we couldn't travel in that state. So I went back to the officers' tents and found us something to wear. I promoted Tom to captain and promoted myself to lieutenant. Now, if asked, I could say I was escorting the brave captain, who had been grievously wounded by the damn Yankees, to a place where he could recuperate and then rejoin his regiment.

We started out about mid-afternoon. The battle was still in full force. The cries from the dying and wounded stayed with me long after I could hear them no more.

TWO

We rode until I noticed Tom swaying in his saddle, and seeing as how it was just about dark, I pulled up and told him that we'd stay where we were for the night. While I was helping him off his horse, I saw that he had sweated right through his tunic; he was burning with fever. I was in such a frenzy to get away before we were noticed that I didn't think to secure at least a canteen. Tom needed water, and a blanket wouldn't hurt to help break the fever.

I got him as comfortable as I could and told him I'd be back soon. I started to tell him why I was leaving, but he was in no shape to understand my words. I couldn't leave him for long, not in that condition. I figured I had maybe a half hour to locate what was needed. After it was full dark, I might not be able to find my way back. Before leaving, I unsaddled his horse and covered Tom with the horse blanket.

We were still on the east side of the Appalachians, so I didn't think we'd have any problem wearing the uniform. The western part of the state went with the Union, and we would have to head farther south before we crossed the mountains to avoid that neck of the woods.

I was thinking those thoughts when I came upon a farmhouse. There was a light coming from the windows, and as I rode into the yard, a man came out of the barn wiping his hands on his pants. When he saw me, he smiled, walked over and said, "Howdy soldier, what brings you out at suppertime on a warm night like tonight?"

"Sir, I hope and pray your sympathies be with the South; I need some help. I've got me a wounded man back up the road and he needs some water and a blanket. He's feverish, and I'm hoping I might get such items from ya'all."

He looked at me for a moment. Then without saying a word, he walked to the house and went inside. I thought maybe he was going for a gun, but a second later, the door swung opened, and out ran a young boy followed by the man.

"That's my boy. He's hitchin' up the wagon. Ain't no Son of the South gonna go without as long as I got somethin' to say about it." He smiled and stuck out his hand. "Name's William Lee, no relation to Robert E."

I shook his hand and said, "I'm mighty grateful, Mister Lee."

The short of it is that he drove the wagon and followed me back to Tom while it was still light enough that I could find my way. We got Tom and his saddle in the wagon and tied his horse behind.

When we got back to the farm, the whole family came out of the house while Mister Lee and I lifted Tom and carried him into the barn. He apologized for the barn, but explained that there was no room in the house, what with all his children and such.

"Don't let it worry you none, Mister Lee. The captain and I will be fine out here as long as I can keep him warm and give him water every now and again."

"Call me Will, everyone does. My wife and oldest daughter will attend to your friend." He turned to the woman holding the lantern and said, "This here is my wife Anne, and that pretty young girl standing next to her is my eldest daughter, Molly. They'll see to the captain. The rest of the brood you'll git to know presently." The other children were three in number, two boys and another girl.

Will continued speaking, "Now ya'all git back to the house, and let your mother and Molly attend to this man. You come with me, Lieutenant. We got us some stew in the kettle, and I'm sure a fighting man like yourself could use a little nourishment." I felt bad about letting him think I was still a soldier, but there was Tom to consider.

The stew was good and while eating it, I learned the names of the other children. The boy who had hitched the wagon was sixteen; his name was Caleb. His brother, who looked to be about ten, was named Jacob. The little girl was called Mary; she was six years of age. Molly, who was still in the barn with her mother, was, I reckoned, about eighteen. She was very comely, with long, glossy black hair and bright yellow-green eyes.

13

When I finished my second bowl of stew, I thanked Will and drew the bottle out of my pocket saying, "Care for some sippin' whiskey, Mister Lee?"

Will reached for the bottle and said, "I told you to call me Will, and yes, I ain't had nothin' like this in a coon's age."

After taking a deep swallow, he handed me the bottle, wiped his mouth with the sleeve of his shirt and said, "That's mighty smooth." He then asked me about the battle where Tom got his wound, and who had won.

I was as much in the dark about the battle and its outcome as he was. But I told him we routed them blue bellies and sent them on their way. At the time, I thought it a small deception, but as it turned out, we did win the first battle of the war!

Will was about to ask another question when his wife came in and told me that they had got Tom to drink a little water, and that he was wrapped up in three blankets. "We dressed the wound and put a poultice on it. It has stopped bleeding. That's a good sign; it should start to heal now. Nothing much else we can do until the fever breaks. Molly will stay with him until you go out there, Lieutenant." Seeing the bottle in my hand, she smiled and said to her husband, "Will, what kind of host are you, drinkin' the lieutenant's whiskey? Why don't you offer him some of your mountain dew?"

Will smiled a smile of his own and shook his head. "You married, Lieutenant?"

I informed him that I was not, and he said, "Well, a wife will always tell you to do what you was gonna do anyway. But to keep the peace, you gotta let her think that it was her idea."

Missus Lee laughed and said, "I've gotta put the children to bed. I'll leave you men to gossip 'bout us women. I'll see you in the morning, Lieutenant; maybe then we can get a little broth into the captain."

Before she left, I thanked her for her kindness and her hospitality. She blushed a bit, nodded and left the room, preceded by her children.

When we were alone again, Will got up, walked over to a shelf near the door and picked up a fruit jar. In it was a clear liquid. Handing it to me he said, "I make this myself, and if it's not out of place to say so, I'm right proud of it."

I uncapped the jar and took a pull; it had the kick of a Missouri mule, and I made the appropriate face to be polite. The last time I had anything close was when pap was alive; he had a source of a very similar libation. When Will saw my reaction, he grinned and bid me to have another swallow.

Recapping the jar, I politely declined. "I better get out to the captain so your daughter can come in." He looked a little disappointed. I don't reckon he had too many visitors out where he lived. And fewer still that he could share his moonshine with. We shook hands as I thanked him for his generosity in putting us up and sharing his food and liquor. Then I went out to the barn.

I walked in to see Molly on her knees wiping Tom's brow with a damp rag. As my shadow fell over her, she looked up startled and said, "I did not hear you come in." She was beautiful in the lantern light. Her face was half in shadow and all I could see were her eyes, her deep green eyes. I shook my head to clear it of wayward thoughts and apologized for frightening her. She stood and pointed to a bucket of water with a tin cup lying next to it and said, "If he needs water during the night." She then pointed to a blanket on top of a small pile of hay. "For you," she said as she turned and walked out of the barn. I shrugged and thought, *The man who marries that girl will never have to fear being talked to death.*

Tom was moving around a bit too much and kind of mumbling, but he was well covered, so there wasn't much I could do for him except ask if he wanted some water. His eyes were opened, but they didn't see me. I got some water from the bucket and put the cup to his lips. He wouldn't take any, so I tossed it on the ground and went to lay out the blanket Molly said was for me. I was wore out; it had been a long, hard day. Then my horse, or to be a little more precise, the horse I had appropriated, snorted and it reminded me that I had not unsaddled her.

16

As I loosened the strap, I noticed the saddlebags for the first time. It was funny I hadn't noticed them before, but I reckon I had much on my mind. In the first pouch, I found a Bible and nothing more. In the other was a long-barreled Colt Dragoon revolver with a good sight. It was fully loaded. The pouch also held a sack of ammunition.

I reckoned the owner of the horse and saddlebags went into battle with the two things he thought he'd need the most: a gun to send the enemy to perdition, and a Bible to help him get to heaven, just in case things didn't work out. I guess things didn't work out because he was nowhere near his horse when I found her. He was probably still lying out there on the battlefield. I don't know why, but I took the gun back to my bed and laid it within easy reach. It was crazy. Did I think Molly would come to ravish me in the night, and I'd need the rig to defend myself? Before extinguishing the lantern, I wet the rag Molly had been using to wipe Tom's face and brow, and ministered to him myself.

I must have fallen into a deep sleep because the next thing I was aware of was the clip-clop, clip-clop of horses' hooves. I opened my eyes and saw that it was gray morning. It was light enough to see, but the sun hadn't come up yet.

Pushing myself up, I went and peered out of a space between two of the planks that made up the walls of the barn. I had no idea who the riders might be, but seeing as how Tom and I were now deserters, I was playing it careful. What I saw froze my heart. There were three Yankees coming into the yard. Two privates and a sergeant. They rode three abreast, the sergeant in the middle. The private on the sergeant's left was young; he didn't look old enough to shave. The sergeant was a fat fella with a long black beard. He and the private on his right looked to be about thirty. The privates held long guns resting on the pommel of their saddles. The sergeant held a jug that looked like it contained corn liquor. As soon as they stopped at the front of the house, the sergeant took a healthy swig from the jug, then handed it to the man to his right. Those two looked a little drunk to me.

After getting the jug back, the sergeant took another pull, wiped his mouth with the back of his hand and pointed to the private on his left, the young one, then to the house. The boy dismounted, went up the two steps and knocked on the door. That's when the sergeant bellowed, "You rebs in there, get your carcasses out here!"

After a moment, the door slowly opened, and Will stepped out looking angry and holding a squirrel gun.

The sergeant looked at Will for a full minute before saying, "You rebels are always looking for a fight. We're just peaceful soldiers doing what was asked of us. We're here to commandeer food and anything else that might help us defeat you rebs. You might as well get the rest of the vipers out here, no use getting shot from a window."

He paused in his oration to raise the jug to his mouth. After he consumed a goodly portion of whatever was in the jug, he continued, "Tell the rest to come out unarmed. And private," he said to the one on the porch, "relieve the reb of his gun."

Seeing how the deck was stacked against him, Will handed his gun over, stood a little straighter and said, "There ain't nobody in there but my wife and young'uns. Take what you want and get offa my land, you damn Yankee." He then spat on the wooden flooring of the porch.

To that, the sergeant had a good belly laugh. Then he quieted down, and a mean look came into his eyes. "Private," he said to the man still on the horse to his right, "If that house ain't empty of its occupants in one minute, set it on fire, but shoot the reb first." Will didn't stir, but the front door at his back opened, and his family came out. Farm folk get an early start on the day, so all were dressed.

About then I went for the Colt, stopping just long enough to take a quick look at Tom. He was the same, shivering and sweating. I would have liked to mop his brow and give him some water, but it might not matter. In the next few minutes, we would probably both be dead.

When I got back to my spy hole, the sergeant was just telling the private on the porch to herd the family down into the yard so he could get a better look at them. As they were coming down the steps, he took another pull from the jug. The private to his right reached out his hand, but the sergeant ignored him.

With the family assembled before him, the sergeant said, "Now, as I was saying, we'll take what we want. And the first thing we want is that wagon over yonder. We'll need it for what you folks are going to contribute. And we'll need a horse to pull it. Where are your horses, in the barn?"

Will took a step forward, I think to get his family behind him more than anything else, and said, "I ain't got but one horse mister, and I'll be needing him for plowin', else we'll starve."

The sergeant once again had the jug to his mouth and couldn't answer right away. But when the jug was re-corked and his mouth wiped with the back of his hand, he said, "Don't matter if you and yours starve, just that many less rebs to contend with."

I could see that Will was just itching to have a go at the fat sergeant, but with two guns pointing at him and his family, there wasn't much he could do. I don't know how it would have played out if the sergeant hadn't done what he did next, but he did, and this is what transpired.

For the first time, the sergeant became aware of Molly. Smirking to himself, he got off his horse, walked past Will and stood before her. "Well, what have we here? Aren't you the pretty one?" At his words, Molly shrunk into herself. It looked like she was trying to make herself so small that she would become invisible.

The sergeant took her by the hand and started to drag her toward the barn. "Why don't you show me the horse; we might be able to leave it if you're nice to me." Without turning around, he said to the private standing with the family, "If anyone moves, shoot them, and that includes the children."

That was the pinch in the game for me. With a quick look to Tom, I stepped out of the barn. Now, I've always been a fair to middling shot with a long gun. And Pap always said there was a devil in us Finns. He said we had an Irish temper that couldn't be tamed, but I always thought that was a lot of hogwash. However, on that gray morning, I knew without thinking about it that if I pointed that Colt Dragoon at a man, he'd be dead long before he hit the ground.

I stood just outside the barn door, legs spread. The sergeant was so intent on dragging Molly he didn't see me. The two privates had their attention in the opposite direction, watching the Lee family. Then I saw Will make a run for the sergeant. The private standing with the family raised his gun and took aim, but he did not fire despite the order to shoot. When the sergeant and Molly got to within a hundred feet of me, and before Will caught up to them, I yelled with hatred in my voice, "Let her be, you pig!"

I didn't wait for him to answer or to set Molly free; I raised the Colt and shot him right through the heart. Without hesitating, I pulled back the hammer and squeezed the trigger again, shooting the one on the horse in the forehead. He fell off with a thud as he hit the ground. By that time the other one, the one who had sighted Will but did not shoot, had dropped his gun and had his hands in the air. I walked up to him and said, "Give me one good reason why I shouldn't kill you this very minute." He was shaking from head to foot and didn't say anything. When I got closer to him, I could see that he couldn't have been much more than sixteen. It took everything in me not to pull the hammer back and squeeze the trigger a third time. Instead, I clubbed him behind his left ear, and he kissed the dirt.

From all the commotion that ensued, you would have thought I was Andy Jackson, Daniel Boone and Robert E. Lee all rolled into one. The family crowded round me. Will slapped me on the back and said, "That was some fair shootin'. I want to thank you on behalf of me and my family. If you hadn't been here, I don't know what would have happened."

"I wouldn't have been here if not for your kindness and your Christian charity," I said.

He nodded and called to his children, telling them to go into the house. The younger ones had gathered around the two corpses. Molly was still standing where she had been when I killed the sergeant. She was looking at me kind of peculiar.

But I had no time for any of that. I had to see to Tom. Even though it had been only a few minutes since I last saw him, I needed to know how he was doing. Will took his family into the house and I walked to the barn. The dead soldiers and the unconscious one stayed where they were.

Tom wasn't moving and shaking like he was before; it looked like the fever had broken. I brought him some water and raised his head so that he could drink of it. "Huck," he said, "where you been? I've been dreamin' that I had no arms or legs, and that I was lying in a desert."

"It's alright now, Tom. That ball you took caused you a little trouble, but it looks like you're gonna come through it all right." I then asked him if he felt like he could eat something.

"Yeah Huck, now that you mention it, I do feel a mite peckish. What kinda vittles you got in mind?"

Before I could answer, Missus Lee and Molly came into the barn. When they saw that I was conversing with Tom, they both broke out in big smiles. Missus Lee knelt down next to us and felt Tom's brow.

"Looks like his fever broke," said she.

Trying to be helpful, I concurred. I told her that we were just speaking of something to eat for the "captain."

Tom, for his part, was looking at Molly, and I couldn't blame him.

Then I thought to introduce the women. "Tom, this here is Missus Lee and her daughter Molly. They've been lookin' out after you. This is their barn."

Just then, Will came in and asked if he could talk to me outside for a moment. I looked at Tom and told him that he was in good hands. He looked at Molly and said, "Don't worry none about me, Huck. Take your time, I'm sure I'll manage." I reckoned he *was* feeling a little better.

Once we were outside, Will grabbed me by the arm and steered me to the dead sergeant. "What are we going to do about these dead Yankees?"

It was a good question, one I hadn't thought of because my musings had been about Tom. I looked over to the one I had clubbed; he was starting to move. Pointing my chin in his direction, I said to Will, "That's the one we've got to worry about. We can get rid of the dead ones easy enough."

"Lieutenant," said Will, "that's another question I gotta ask. Why didn't you kill him too?"

"Well Will, you couldn't see what I saw; you were running to save Molly. But from where I was standing, I saw him raise his gun and sight you. He could have carried out the order the sergeant gave him and plugged you in the back, but he didn't. I admit I was a bit wound up, and I was going to shoot him anyway, but when I got close to him and saw how young he was, I didn't have it in me. I figured a good hit to the head might knock some sense into him."

By now, the boy was on his hands and knees with his head hanging down, staring at the ground. He looked up to Will and me with a dazed look, as if he didn't know where he was or how he got there. I said to Will that we could worry about him later, but first we should dispose of the other two before someone else came along. We decided to tie the boy up in the barn while we did what we had to do.

We got him unsteadily to his feet and walked him into the barn. Before sitting him on the ground and tying his hands behind a support, I removed his side arm. It was a Colt Dragoon, just like the one sticking in my belt. Then we set about draping the other two over their saddles. With that done, I asked Will if he knew of a good place to bury them so that the graves would not be found. He replied that he had the perfect place.

We each took a horse by the reins. With Will leading the way, we walked into the woods. It was slow going because the trees were thick. Therefore, we had plenty of time to talk and at one point, Will asked me if I had ever killed a man before. And I had to admit that I hadn't. Then he wanted to know how I felt about killing two men.

"I'm happy to say that I don't feel nothin'." After a few steps, I added to my answer, "It was somethin' that had to be done. When I think of what would have happened if I hadn't killed those two . . . well Will, I get the shakes."

We walked on for a piece in silence.

Following some thought, I decided to tell Will the truth about Tom and me. When I finished my story, he was quiet for a moment, and then he said, "It don't make no never mind to me. But I don't think ya'all should be travelin' in them uniforms. It ain't healthy. What if you was to come upon some more Yankees? And if you ran into some of our boys, you got no papers proving you're officers. Besides, I ain't stupid, you two look a mite young for officers, but I wasn't gonna say nothin'."

He was right and I knew it, so I kept my mouth shut. After a minute he continued, "When we get back, I'll give you some clothes of mine that you can wear."

After a short while, Will came to a halt and pointed before him. "There she is," he said. I looked to where he was pointing and couldn't see anything, so I asked, "Is that where we're gonna bury them?" At that moment, a thought struck me. We hadn't brought a shovel, and I mentioned that fact to Will.

He smiled and took a few steps forward. Pointing to the ground he said, "This here is their final resting place." I walked up next to him and looked into a bottomless sinkhole. We made short work of it. We dragged the sergeant off his horse and dropped him into the hole. Then it was the private's turn, and he followed the sergeant into the earth.

On the way back, I remarked to Will that there were no brands on the horses, so they weren't army issue. They were probably brought from home, therefore it would be safe to keep them. I added, "All in all it hasn't been a bad morning. You started out with one horse and now, you've got three. Maybe four, depending on what we decide to do with the boy tied up in your barn."

We walked the rest of the way in silence. I don't know what Will was thinking, but I was worrying about the complications the Yankees brought with them. It was bad enough Tom got the fever, and we *certainly* didn't need no damn Yankees nosin' around.

So far things had worked out, but what the hell were we going to do with the young Yankee? If we set him free, would he go right back to his outfit and tell them what happened? If he did so, then half the Union Army would descend on Will's farm. But I sure took no pleasure in the thought of having to kill the boy to protect Will and his family. It was a thorny problem alright. Then I reckoned I'd just have to climb that fence when I got to it.

THREE

When we got back at the farm, Will said we should have something to eat before deciding what to do with the Yankee. But first, I wanted to check up on Tom. He was sitting up with his back against the slats of a stall.

"How ya feeling, Tom?"

"A little weak, but I reckon I'm gonna live. Missus Lee redressed my wound and told me that it's healing just fine. She also gave me some broth, saying that anything heartier wouldn't sit well with me at the moment. But she hinted that, maybe later I could have something more substantial."

"That's fine Tom. I don't mind sayin' that I was mighty worried about you. We were powerful lucky that we came across the Lees."

"I reckon we were Huck, but do you mind if I ask you a question?"

"Sure Tom, what is it?"

"Why ya got that Yankee tied up over yonder? He won't talk, and Missus Lee said I should speak to you 'bout him. She acts like he's not here."

"Well Tom, it's a long story." Then I told him what had happened while he was down with the fever.

When I finished my narrative, Tom let out with a low whistle, pointed to the Colt stuck in my belt and said, "You killed two Yankees with that hog's leg?"

"Yes I did, but I had to. Now, if you're feelin' strong enough to walk to the house, let's go up there and maybe we can cadge somethin' to eat." I didn't want to say in front of the Yankee that Will and I were going to discuss whether to kill him or not.

We got to the house, and I introduced Tom and Will to each other.

Missus Lee made a big breakfast of eggs, hominy grits, bacon and coffee. Molly served, but kept giving me a funny look as she did so. The women didn't eat with us. They had eaten earlier with the younger children while Will and I were disposing of the Yankees. I reckon Tom was well on the way to mending because he put away a fair amount of what was placed before him even though he had to use his left hand to do so.

Between mouthfuls, I asked Will about the other children. "They're in their rooms," he replied. "We don't want them out 'til we see if any more Yankees are coming around."

"Speaking of Yankees, what are ya'all going to do with the one in the barn?" asked Tom.

I shrugged. Will shook his head and said, "That's what we're trying to figure out, Tom. I'm afeared of letting him go, and I don't know if I have it in me to walk up and put a bullet in his head while he's sitting tied up in my barn."

By then we had finished eating and the three of us were sipping our coffee while the women were removing the dishes. No one said anything for a while, we were thinking of that Yankee boy out in the barn. Finally Tom said, "Why not talk to the Yankee and get his thoughts on the matter?"

Will and I looked at each other with a look that said, *Why didn't we think of that?* "I reckon it can't hurt none," said Will.

We had been dawdling, but now that we had a plan, such as it was, we rushed to finish our coffee. As we stood to leave, Missus Lee handed Will a plate of eggs and bacon. "Here, take this to the boy. He might be more amiable to talkin' if he had a little food inside him."

Our prisoner was sitting with his back against the post and his legs straight out before him, his arms still tied behind the post. With his head bent down, his chin resting on his chest, he looked to be asleep. However, as we walked in, he looked up at us.

I took out my knife and cut the rope binding his hands. He pulled his arms around in front of him and rubbed his wrists. Tom, thinking it was none of his concern, went to his makeshift bed across the barn and lay down. I reckoned he was still a mite weak.

Will and I sat on our heels in front of the boy, and Will asked if he was hungry.

He looked to Will, then to me, then to the plate of food in Will's hand. His look lingered on the food, then he looked at me again and said, "What are you going to do with me?"

I answered, "That's what we're here to talk about, but we thought that maybe you might want somethin' to eat first."

Will held out the plate toward the boy who cautiously reached for it. We had forgotten to bring a fork, but it didn't matter. He first picked up the bacon and ate it without delay. Then with his fingers, he shoveled the eggs into his mouth. He must have been mighty hungry. While he was chewing the last of the eggs, I went and got him some water from the bucket.

When he had washed down his food and wiped his mouth, he handed the plate back to Will and said, "Thank you sir." Will nodded and put the plate on the ground. We were still on our heels in front of the boy, and he was still seated, legs outstretched. It was time to get down to business. Because I was wearing a uniform, we had decided that I should ask the first question.

"What's your name, son?"

He hesitated a moment before answering. "It's Jed Bevins, sir." He quickly added, "Am I a prisoner of war?"

Will and I looked at each other, and I nodded in Will's direction, meaning that he should take it from there.

"Why did you come to my farm?"

"It wasn't my idea mister. When the rebs routed us back there, Pete and me got separated from the rest. We were kinda lost, but were headed north when we come across the sergeant. He ordered us to go with him and said that as long as we were here, we should forage some and see what we could come up with. Pete was all for it. I wasn't, and I started to say so. But the sergeant cut me off. He said that we were at war, and if I didn't follow his orders, he'd have me shot."

About then the boy's eyes started to get moist and it looked like he was not far off from crying. Will and I stood and walked away a bit to let him simmer down some and collect his thoughts. After a minute, he called to us and asked if it would be all right if he stood up. We both gave our consent by nodding. I said to Will that we should go outside with the boy in case Tom wanted to get some sleep.

Agreeing and pointing to Tom, Will said, "Come on Jed, let's take a walk outside; we might be disturbing the captain." But we weren't disturbing the captain. I looked down at Tom as we passed outside; he was already asleep. We went to the porch, and Will and the boy sat in its shade; I remained standing and addressed our prisoner.

"Alright Jed, now tell it from the beginning. You and the other private, Pete, were in retreat when the two of you met up with the sergeant. Is that right?"

"Yes sir."

"Are there any other foraging patrols out that you know of?"

"No sir, not that I know of. We weren't a real patrol. I think the rest of the army hightailed it right back across the river. We were fairly disorganized, and I hate to admit it, but you rebs sure beat the tar outta us."

"And you did not want to accompany the sergeant but Pete did?"

"Yes sir."

"Is this the first place you came to?"

"No sir. As it was getting dark, we came across a shack back up the road a bit. An old man and woman lived there. Dirt poor they was; there was nothing the sergeant wanted from them exceptin' the man had two jugs of corn liquor.

33

So the sergeant confiscated them in the name of The Army of the Potomac, and he and Pete shared one of the jugs last night."

I interrupted him at that point in his story with a question. "Did you drink any?"

"No sir."

Then I asked Will if he knew the people that the boy was talking about.

"The Sweenys. They live five miles up the road. I'll go over there when we're finished here and see that they're all right."

Looking at the boy I asked, "Are they all right?"

"Yes sir. The sergeant and Pete weren't any too kind to them and tore up their shack some, but they were alive and kickin' when we left this morning."

"Alright son, continue."

"There ain't too much more to say. Early this morning, before light, the sergeant woke me up and said he was hungry, and we was gonna get us some real food to eat, seeing as how the old couple had scant to eat in their shack. We got on our horses and rode 'til we came to this here farm. The rest I reckon you know."

"Just one more question Jed."

He nodded his head eagerly and awaited my query.

"Why didn't you shoot Mister Lee when you had the chance?

"Because of what the sergeant was doing to the girl. I aimed at the gentleman," he said, pointing to Will, "but then thought I'd be better off shooting the sergeant instead. But I was too much of a coward. I knew that if I shot him, Pete would shoot me and then shoot Mister Lee. Pete and me weren't friends; he was much older than me. I mean I seen him around, but we never spoke until we met up after the battle."

When he finished speaking, I turned to Will and said, "You got any questions?"

"Yes I do." Then looking straight into the boy's eyes he said, "If we let you go, are you going to tell what happened here today?"

Hanging his head a little, he whispered, "No." Before Will or I could say anything, he went on. "I am ashamed that I had any part of coming onto your farm. I am also ashamed of the way I let those old folks be treated last night. I never wanted to be in the army. When the war broke out, my father put me on one of his horses, took me to Washington and signed me up. Said it'd make a man outta me. And because I had a horse, they put me in the cavalry. But I hated every minute of it. If you let me go, I'll head out west, and you'll never hear of me again! As far as anyone knows, me, Pete and the sergeant are lying out there on the battlefield, dead. And I'm not going to do anything to change their minds."

When he was done talking, Will turned to me and nodded, and I sighed with relief. It looked like we weren't gonna have to throw him in the sinkhole after all.

"You're kinda young to be going out west all by yourself. Can't you just go home?" asked Will.

Straightening his back and looking directly into Will's eyes, Jed answered him. "Well sir, I figure if I'm old enough to go off to war, then I ought to be old enough to go anyplace else I want to go. Besides, if I went home my father would beat me for deserting, and then he'd take me back even though I'd probably be court-martialed. I don't get along with him all that well, and my mother's dead. There ain't anything back there for me."

"Alright, you go back to the barn and wait for us; you look kinda noticeable. There's no way you'd get far dressed in that blue uniform. You're about the same size as my boy Caleb; I'll fetch you some of his clothes."

When Jed was gone, Will said, "It makes me sad to think of that boy. He's the same age as my son, and I sure wouldn't want Caleb going off to war, or out west for that matter. Both can get you killed."

"Tom and I will keep an eye on him." I said, "We'll be leaving in the morning, and he can ride along with us. Maybe he'll like Missouri. But if not, there are wagon trains leaving from Independence and St. Joe going west. Possibly he can work his way to California." I took out my pipe, filled it, and lit it. After I got a good burn going, I went on, "You know, I once read somewhere that the Chinese believe that when you save a man's life, then you're responsible for him. I didn't actually save the boy's life, but I didn't take it neither and maybe it amounts to the same thing. So I'll look out for him."

While getting a change of clothes for Jed, Will fixed me and Tom up also. And after we were all changed, we went out behind the barn and burned the uniforms—one blue and two gray.

After that, we didn't have much to do. Will was up seeing to the Sweenys, and Tom was sleeping on and off, so Jed and me sat around and talked. About mid-afternoon, Molly came out to the barn and asked if she could speak to me alone. Tom was awake then, and he gave me a wink as I walked out with Molly.

She seemed a little nervous and didn't say anything at first. I kept my mouth shut because I knew sooner or later, she'd get down to what she wanted to say. At length she said, "Do you mind if we walk as we talk? It would be easier on me if I didn't have to look at you."

She blushed, saying she didn't mean it in the way that it sounded. It was just that she was having trouble putting into words what she was feeling. I figured she wanted to thank me for saving her from the sergeant, so I said I'd be pleased to walk with her.

We were walking down the same road that had brought Tom and me to their farm the night before. Only now, the sun was out and it wasn't too hot for being July. Oh . . . and there was one more thing that was different, I was walking down the lane with a pretty girl next to me.

We went on for a ways not saying anything. After about a half a mile, I looked at her and said, "Miss Molly, if we go much farther, I'll be back in Manassas, right where I started from. And there's a whole flock of folks over there that I'd rather not run into." Now, I was only funnin' her, we weren't that close. I was just trying to loosen her tongue a bit.

She stopped walking, told me she was sorry and that she would say what she had to say. But it still took her a minute to get started. "Lieutenant, first of all I want to thank you for what you did this morning for me and my family. It was the bravest thing I ever did see."

I thought I should dispose her of the notion that I was a lieutenant (and that I was brave), but I didn't want to stop the flow.

She went on, "You realize that I don't even know your name. You're the man that saved me from death or worse, and I don't know what to call you."

"The name's Huck Finn. And while I'm at it, I might as well tell you I ain't no lieutenant. I'm a private, or I was a private, but not no more because my friend Tom and me are hightailin' it right back to where we come from. I've had enough of war. I don't know if I'm a coward or not. I reckon not, but I'm not all that brave neither. This morning I was just riled up; anyone would have done what I did."

When I finished with my little speech, she smiled at me and said, "I am so happy to hear you say that. I thought you'd be going back to your regiment after you got the captain back home."

"He's not a captain; he was a private like me."

She paid no mind to what I said. She acted like she didn't hear me and went on, "Now I can go with you when you leave. I won't be no trouble; my father will give me one of the Yankee's horses, and I can cook for you and . . ."

At that point, I held up my hand for her to stop talking. Then I had my say.

"Miss Molly, do you mind if we turn for home? We've come a fair piece, and Tom might need some looking after." I knew Tom was all right; I just didn't want to be alone with this girl when I let her know there was no way, no how, that I was going to take her with me. You just never know how a girl is gonna react. I ain't saying I'm any expert on women, I don't think any man is. In fact, I never had that much truck with 'em. I mean sure, I'd been with the whores at Missus Bradford's in St. Louis, but that ain't like being with regular girls. And Molly was a regular girl if I ever did see one.

We walked along without talking for a spell, and then Molly asked me what I thought about the idea of her going with me. We were still not near the farm, but I had to say something, and this is where I proved I was no coward. I told her the truth.

"Miss Molly, there's something you've got to know about men. I mean honorable men. And that is when a man accepts another man's hospitality, he does not ride out the next day taking that man's daughter with him. Do you understand what I'm sayin'?"

She looked straight ahead as we walked and said nothing for a full minute, although it *seemed* like an hour. Finally she said, "You think I'm ugly don't you? You think I'll be an embarrassment to you. That's it, isn't it? Well, I want you to know that Donny Whitfield thinks I'm beautiful, and he's asked me to marry him."

I kept walking, not looking at her. The farm seemed farther away than ever. Eventually, I noticed she wasn't next to me no more, so I stopped and looked back. There

40

she stood with her head hung low, her shoulders shaking . . . she was crying.

I couldn't leave her there like that. I walked back, took her by the arm and guided her off the road, a little into the woods, where I sat her down in the shade of an old oak. After I settled in next to her, I took her hand and started talking.

"You see Molly, I'm appreciative of you wanting to marry me, but I got places I'm going where I can't take a woman. Me and Tom was just talkin' the other day about signing on to a ship and workin' our way to China when the war was over. And now that it's over for us, that's most likely what we'll do." Actually, we had spoken of no such thing. I was grasping at straws.

She stopped her crying and looked at me with those yellow-green eyes of hers. Right then and there, I thought I'd chuck Tom, Missouri, and the whole kit and caboodle for her. But then she brought me back to my senses. "Huck, you don't have to marry me. I'll go with you to the farthest ends of the earth. Just take me with you. There's those two Yankee horses; I can take one, and we can ride out after everyone goes to bed." *Again with the Yankee horses!*

There was only one way to handle it. She wasn't in love with me; she was in love with being in love. I was the man who had saved her from a fate worse than death, and she was going to give herself to me as payment. I may be a lowdown so-and-so, but I ain't that lowdown as to take a woman's flower if I'm not married to her. And I couldn't marry this girl, as pretty and willing as she was. I had places I wanted to see and many things I wanted to do before I settled down. Besides, she may have been itchin' just to get off the farm and find a little adventure. That I couldn't blame her for, but she'd have to do it with Donny Whitfield or someone else.

Maybe I was part coward after all because I told her that in two nights' time, we would leave together and that she couldn't tell anyone. I said that I was afraid her father would forbid her from leaving with me and because of his hospitality, I would have to abide by his wishes. However, if we left without telling him, then who could know what his wishes were? She wrapped her arms around my neck and gave me a kiss right on the mouth! And let me tell you, her kiss was just as good as any of them whores' at Missus Bradford's.

That night, because there wasn't room at the table for all of us, Missus Lee ate with the children, and then us men ate. Once again, we were served by Molly, and I felt downright uncomfortable because she never took her eyes from me. I was afraid that Will would catch on and know that something was up.

After dinner, Jed was a mite spent and went to the barn to get a little shuteye. Tom, Will, and me sat on the porch smoking our pipes and thinking that the world wasn't such a bad place after all. We sat there without speaking for the longest time. At length Will asked if we'd still be moving on in the morning. "Not that I'm rushin' things. It's just that I thought if you boys would like to stick around for a while longer, me and mine would be mighty pleased to have ya."

"That's right neighborly of you Will, but me and Tom are on our way to China, and we've gotta be movin' on. We'll be outta here before first light, but we need you to do us a favor."

After taking a long pull on his pipe, Will said, "Just name it Huck."

"I don't want you to mention this to your missus or your brood. Tom and me aren't much for good-byes. We want you to tell your missus and Molly that we sure do appreciate all they did for us, especially for Tom, but just hold off until after we're gone."

"Alright," said Will, "if that's the way you want it, that's the way it'll be." When our pipes were out, Tom and I shook hands with Will and said goodnight and good-bye.

On the way back to the barn, Tom asked me what that China stuff was all about. I didn't want to tell him about Molly, so I said I just wanted to get back home, and I didn't want a lot of sentimental good-byes before getting on our way. I know Tom didn't believe me because he said, "Too bad you couldn't give Molly a good-bye kiss." Then he winked at me for the second time that day.

Tom, Jed, and I were long gone before first light. And somehow, I knew that a small part of me would always regret leaving Molly Lee behind.

FOUR

We headed southwest and then rode south along the mountains until we got to Kentucky; then we turned west. Tom got stronger every day. However, with his arm in a sling, he wasn't much use when it came time to hunt our dinner. But Jed turned out to be a fair shot. After the second day, it was his job to procure our evening meal. He only hunted small game—rabbits and such. What we didn't eat that night, we cooked and saved for the next day to eat in the saddle so we wouldn't have to stop until it was suppertime again. We were making good time.

Tom kept to himself. At night around the fire, he only spoke when asked a direct question. I thought that maybe his wound was bothering him, so I didn't press it. Later, as we were crossing into Kentucky, he turned to me and said, "What was that really about back there when you was tellin' Will about us going to China?"

It took a minute for me to know what the hell he was talking about. Then I remembered. I still didn't want to tell him about Molly. Instead, I said, "We did speak of it quite a lot when we was kids. I only said what I said so Will wouldn't push us to stay."

Tom nodded and rode on. I thought that was the end of it. But later, while I was making the fire that night, and Jed was out hunting, Tom said, "You know, I hadn't thought about China in a long time." With a kind of wistful look about him, he whispered, more to himself than to me, "It sure would be somethin' to go all the way to China and sail the South Seas." After that, he laughed out loud, "It's just a downright dirty shame there ain't no pirates around no more."

I agreed with him because I thought that possibly his fever was coming back and I did not want to upset him.

"You know what I'm thinkin' of doin', Huck, as soon as my arm is healed?"

"No Tom, what are you thinkin' of doin' as soon as your arm is healed?"

"I'm going to San Francisco and sign on to one of them sailing ships headed for China."

I let it rest there because I wasn't sure if it was fever or what, that got him talking that way.

We made it to St. Petersburg without any serious mishaps. It was the beginning of August. Jed stayed with me in the house that the Widow Douglas had left me. Tom stayed in his Aunt Polly's house. She had bequeathed it to him and his brother Sid, but Sid was not around. He had gone off to a Yankee college up in Ohio.

Two weeks after we got back home, Tom came over with a bottle of whiskey. The three of us sat out on the porch swatting mosquitoes, sipping whiskey, and telling lies.

"Damn," said Tom, "the bloodsuckers are out in force this year!"

After that, we didn't speak for the longest spell; we just passed the bottle around. Finally, Tom broke the silence, "You know Huck, I made up my mind. I'm goin' to China." Then Jed said he had to be getting a move on too; he was going to California. Jed was young, and I couldn't fault him for itching to get started, but Tom was older. I thought he should let his arm heal first before going halfway around the world, and I told him so.

I slept late the next morning because the whiskey of the night before kinda got to me. When I finally got out of bed and went outside, I found Jed saddling his horse, so I asked him where he was going.

"Hello Huck, glad you're up. I've been dawdling, waiting for you. Didn't want to leave without saying good-bye."

I asked him again where he was going. But before he could answer, my head cleared and I knew where he was off to.

"You're on your way to California?"

"Yep."

"Well, I'll be sorry to see you go."

"I'm sorry to be leaving. I want to thank you and Tom for all you have done for me. There ain't never been anyone who's treated me as fine 'ceptin' my ma."

"Say good-bye to Tom for me. Like you, I ain't much on farewells. Well, I reckon I'll be riding."

As he was putting his foot in the stirrup, I said I'd walk along with him to the edge of town. There wasn't much to say. He knew where to hook up with a wagon train heading west, and it was his intention to try to get work with one of them. However, I was afraid if that didn't pan out, he'd try to make the trek alone.

We came abreast of the St. Petersburg Bank, and I asked Jed to hold up, that I had something to do and I'd be right out.

I'm sure ya'all remember Tom and me finding the treasure and putting it in the hands of Judge Thatcher to invest and handle for us. And if you read Mister Clemens' book, you'd know that I tried to give my share to Judge Thatcher so my pap couldn't get a hold of it. At the time, the judge let me think I sold it to him for one dollar. Later, when we found out that Pap was dead, the judge explained to me that the money and interest was still mine, providing I gave him back his dollar. He was only funnin' about the dollar.

When the Widow Douglas died, she left me not only the house but also some money. I think it was about $800.00. And when Miss Watson, the Widow Douglas' sister, died the year after, having no one to leave her fortune to, she left it to me. It came to almost $5,000.00.

After Judge Thatcher died, Mister Potter down at the bank looked after the money for us. I'm given $362.00 twice a year in interest. That's more money than I could ever spend in a year, my wants being so few.

I went in and asked Mister Potter for the interest that was due in a few weeks, and I asked for it in gold. To say the least, he was a mite put out. He informed me things weren't done that way. But I looked him in the eye and asked, "Is it my money or not?"

I reckon he saw something in my eyes because he said he'd do it this one time, but in the future he'd need some notice. That was fine with me. I walked out of the bank with eighteen twenty-dollar gold pieces and two dollars in folding money.

I took up my place next to Jed and his horse, and we started walking. When we got to the last house on the north side of town, I halted and told Jed that was as far as I was going. He nodded and started off.

"Not so fast Jed. I want you to do me a favor."

At the sound of my voice, he turned his horse. "Sure Huck, what is it?"

I held out the leather pouch that contained the gold coins and said, "I want you to take this. It ain't much, but I'd sleep better at night knowin' you had it." I had kept the two dollars.

He reached out, took the pouch from my hand and right away, he knew what was in it.

"I can't take this from you Huck, it ain't right."

"Damn! I've got more money than I know what to do with, and I didn't work for a single dime of it. Now you take that money because you'll have to outfit for the trail. And if you can't find work, you can pay your way across. If it'll make you feel any better, we'll call it a loan."

Jed saw that I was dead serious. He pocketed the coins, thanked me, turned his horse, and trotted out of town and out of my life for the next twelve years. Yes, I would see him again, but he wouldn't be Jed Bevins no more, he'd go by another name.

A month later, Tom was healed up and ready to get going himself. He asked me if I wanted to go to China with him.

"No, I don't reckon so Tom; it seems a long way to go. To be cooped up on a ship for all that time, I think it might make me a little crazy. But I'd be pleased to go with you as far as San Francisco. Sitting around here and listening to all the talk about the war is already making me a little crazy."

We made our arrangements, bought our outfits, and were on the trail within a week. Because we left so late in the season, we ran the risk of not being able to get over the mountains before the first snows hit. A wagon train could make eighteen, maybe twenty miles a day if everything went smoothly. Traveling light with only our horses and kits, we could make forty or fifty miles a day and beat the snows.

On the way out, I asked Tom if he was going to book passage or go as an able-bodied seaman. I knew he could afford the freight what with his half of the treasure and all, but he said going as a tourist wouldn't be the same.

"What would be the fun in that, Huck? I want to be a sailor, live below decks with my mates, and share the real experience of going to sea. I don't want to sit in a cabin or walk around the deck with nothing to do for all them months it'll take to get to China."

I could see his point, but I had to say, "You don't know nothin' about being a sailor; how will you manage it when the captain gives you an order, and you don't know what in tarnation he's talkin' about?"

Tom smiled his mischievous smile and said, "I'm a fast learner. Anyway, once we're under way, what's the captain gonna do? Heave me overboard and tell me to swim back?"

"He just might Tom, he just might."

FIVE

The second night out, we camped in a ravine using it as a windbreak. We had made about ninety miles in the first two days, but it was clear that neither we nor the horses could stand up to that kind of pace for long. If we were going to make it through the mountains before the passes shut down, we would have to buy extra mounts so we could change horses throughout the day.

We were sitting around the fire feeding sticks into it, drinking good coffee, and discussing our options. Should we go back for more horses or should we go on and hope to buy some along the way? Suddenly, the quiet of the night was broken by a shout.

"Ahoy! Might a tired traveler approach?"

One does not go into a camp without announcing oneself. Doing so could get a man killed.

We didn't think there was another soul within a hundred miles. We stood and turned in the direction from whence the voice had come and could see nothing. We had been staring into the flames of the fire, and when we looked out into the darkness we were blinded. But as our eyes slowly adjusted, we beheld a bizarre creature indeed.

"Come in," said Tom.

The stranger stood well over six feet, had a long gray beard, and he wore clothes made of buckskin. His hat was made out of fur, and he held a gun on us. He was an old man of about sixty, I reckoned. He pointed the gun in our direction for what seemed like a mighty long time before lowering it and smiling.

"Howdy, thought I'd teach you pilgrims a lesson. The name is Daniel Conner, and that coffee smells awfully good."

We invited him to have a cup, but he said he had to take care of his stock first. As we had nothing else to do, we followed him out into the darkness where we saw a saddle horse and five pack horses.

As he loosened the cinch on the saddle he said, "Sorry to put a fright in you boys, but you should never stare into a fire; it ruins your night vision. And another thing, you shouldn't sit so close to it neither. Sit back in the shadows. You never know who might be creepin' up on ya. Ya gotta pay heed to the sounds of the night. I made enough of a ruckus comin' up on you to alert a dead man. You boys ain't gonna last long out here unless you change your ways."

We helped him unload his pack horses and picket them close enough to the small stream that ran though the ravine so they could reach water. Then he said, "You boys might want to move your horses a little closer to the camp; put 'em here next to mine. Your fire can be seen from far off, and nothing an Indian likes better than stealing horses. Remember, a horse will tell you by his manner if a critter—man or beast—is anywhere about. They make good sentries."

Back around the fire, I said, "I'm Huck Finn and this is Tom Sawyer. Where're you headed?"

"Back to St. Louis. Been trapping this past year; got me a nice amount of quality fur."

We asked if he'd like something to eat, but he declined our offer and instead took a piece of jerky out of a pouch hanging from his waist saying, "This will do me fine. I like jerky, and it's good for the teeth."

It turned out Dan Conner was an old mountain man who had trapped with the likes of Joe Walker and Bill Williams—two of the better-known men of that breed.

We were pretty tuckered out, but we had to learn the ropes. We had some questions for Mister Conner. Thus, we talked into the night—him answering our questions. And he had a few questions of his own when we told him about the war. He had heard nothing about it; in fact, he didn't even know we were at war.

He said because we were traveling light, we could make thirty miles a day without killing our horses. That would put us over the mountains before it snowed. He advised us we could run the horses a little in the morning when it was cool, and then as the day heated up, slow them up bit. "Make sure you don't run 'em too far, and always let them walk in between runs," he said while he chewed his jerky. "Doing it that way, you'll make miles each day," he concluded.

Neither Tom nor I had much truck with horses growing up on the River. Therefore, it was good luck that Mister Conner happened along. It was also fortunate because he had been to California a few times and knew the best trail to take, which pass would be the last one to be snowed in, and how to find water on the plains.

"Look for trees. They always grow close to water. There ain't that many out here," he said pointing west, "until you come to the mountains. But the ones you do see will have water nearby."

In the morning, after coffee, beans and biscuits, Mister Conner drew us a map in the sand pointing out landmarks to watch for such as Courthouse Rock, Chimney Rock, and the Republican and Platte Rivers. He finished with, "There's a pile of stones marking the cut-off for South Pass, and if you're on the right trail you should see it. But if you do miss it, you'll end up in the Green Mountains of Oregon and by the time you git there, all the passes will be blocked by snow."

We helped him load up and saw him on his way. Then it was time we made some miles. We crested out of the ravine and beheld a sea of green-brown grass. All of it knee-high, it went on forever. The horizon looked to be unreachable in the far distance. With a smile and a shrug, I said to Tom, "Let's get you to China." I raced my horse down the slope and headed west with Tom following close behind.

We rode for three days without seeing a soul. On the fourth day, with the sun directly overhead, we came upon a small herd of buffalo, about thirty in number. Seeing as how we were low on meat, we stopped to get us some. We hobbled our horses and crept up on the buffalo from about a hundred yards back. Neither of us had ever seen a buffalo before, and we did not know that sneaking up on them was not necessary. We could have walked among them firing our guns at will, and I don't think they would have moved an inch.

When we got close enough, Tom sighted his long gun on a female and her calf. I couldn't tell which one he was sighting, but I put my hand on the barrel of his gun and said, "It don't seem right to kill a mother or her young'un when they're together. There's an old bull over there on the edge of the herd. He's got enough meat on him to last us a while. Why don't you see if you can get him with one shot?"

Tom turned to where I was pointing, squeezed the trigger, and his gun boomed on the prairie. Some quail flew up from wherever they were hiding, but none of the buffalo moved. Not even the one Tom had shot. He just stopped grazing and lifted his head. So I raised my long gun and gave it a try. I don't know which ball did the trick, but shortly thereafter, the buffalo dropped over dead.

Whilst we were walking toward the kill, a bull moved over to the downed buffalo and smelled the pooling blood. He pawed at the ground for a moment, shook his head, then trotted off with the rest of the herd following.

We cut the meat out of the carcass and decided to stop for the day so we could dry it. Besides, the horses needed a rest. About a mile back, we had stopped at a small grove of cottonwoods to water the horses and fill our canteens. That's where we headed with our bounty.

Once we had the meat laid out on sticks, we made a fire. Because we wanted a smokeless fire, we used buffalo chips. Mister Conner had cautioned us to be leery of making a fire during the day because the smoke from it was an invitation to anyone from miles around to come and visit. In Indian country, that's not such a good idea. He also taught us about buffalo chips and their fire-making ability. The only problem was that you needed a bushel basket of them to cook a meal, but there were plenty of them to be had.

As we smoked our pipes, Tom asked me what I was going to do once he was off to China.

"I reckon I'll just go on back to St. Petersburg."

"You gonna cross these plains by yourself?"

"No . . . I don't figure on coming back this way. Remember it's gonna be wintertime, and I won't be able to cross the mountains. I figure to go down south and go through the desert. Anyways, Jed is crossing these plains alone 'cause I reckon he was too late to hitch up with a train, and he's just a boy."

"What are you gonna do in St. Petersburg?" asked Tom.

"Don't rightly know. I'm not really hankerin' to get back there anytime soon, not with the way the town folk looked at me for not being in the war. For you it wasn't so bad because you were wounded. I don't know Tom, I got a feeling that there's something I should be doing, but I just don't know what it is. Maybe if I go back to Missouri, I'll find out."

Tom grinned and said, "Maybe if you go back to Missouri, you'll *never* find out."

Six

We were making good time, but we were getting low on coffee and flour. Mister Conner said there'd be a trading post along the trail, but we'd yet to see neither hide nor hair of it.

On the nineteenth day, we saw the buffalo. This was no small herd. They stretched out before us as far as the eye could see in all directions. They were moving slowly from north to south, and were directly in our path. There was no way to go around them. To the north, south, and west there was nothing but buffalo.

After two hours of anticipating the tail end of the herd, we gave up and moved back a ways to set up camp. There was nothing for it but to wait. All that day the buffalo passed, and as the cloudless sky turned from blue to red in the west, there was still no end in sight of the buffalo.

We pulled up our camp and moved farther back, about a mile. We didn't want to be anywhere close to them in the dark. Tom collected the chips, and I fixed a dinner of pan bread and rabbit. We had killed three rabbits earlier in the day before we came upon the herd. When we were done eating, with the gear stored away, I put out the fire, and we bedded down, hoping that in the morning the buffalo would be gone.

First, we felt it—the shaking of the ground—then we heard it—the pounding of thunderous hooves, millions of them, or so it seemed. It was a stampede! Disoriented, we ran for our horses, jumped on bareback and lit out to the east. It was dark. We had no way of knowing if the great herd was coming our way. If it was, our outfit was gone, but we might get through with our lives if we rode fast enough. We galloped until the deafening noise receded. Our horses were lathered. We were bootless, but alive.

Tom and I waited until daylight and then made our way back. The herd was gone. It had stampeded south, so our outfit was intact. We were well spent and in need of a good cup of coffee. It was the last we had, and we enjoyed it. Then we packed up and once again headed west. Tom and I were tired for lack of sleep, but we had to press on and find that trading post.

We walked our horses because they were as wore out as we were. We traveled for a half a day and still we were in the tracks of the buffalo. Where they had been there was no grass, only the upturned soil. If we'd ridden our horses harder, we'd have been covered in dust. Finally, at about noon, we came to the grass again, and off in the distance, there seemed to be a structure of some sort. It looked to be a sod house, or maybe two.

I was just about to spur my horse onward when I saw something off to my side. Curious as to what it could be, I pulled the reins in that direction. Tom saw where I was headed and followed.

What I had seen turned out to be a child—an Indian child—of about ten years, lying on his back. He was either dead or out cold. Fearing he had been trampled in the stampede, I slipped my horse and knelt down beside him. He was breathing, and he didn't look too bad off. He did have a nasty welt on his forehead, a gash down his right cheek where the blood had dried, and a few scratches here and there. But for the most part, he was in one piece.

By then, Tom was kneeling next to me. I suggested we take the boy to the house, or whatever it was, up ahead. The boy would be out of the sun, and we could attend to his wounds. Tom lifted him while I mounted my horse. Tom then handed him up. Cradling the boy in my left arm, I set out for the structure. Tom rode on ahead.

Tom stood in front of the house as I rode up. He pointed to a sign that read RAWLINGS TRADING POST. I started to smile, but he shook his head and said, "There's another sign on the door that says he's gone to St. Louis to buy supplies and will return in the spring, but the door is open."

Tom took the boy from me and carried him inside while I dismounted. After tethering my horse next to his at the hitch rail, I followed. There were seven steps leading down into the one room that made up the trading post. The room had been dug out of the earth and was maybe seventy feet long and half as wide. The floor was bare earth, but the walls were covered with planks to keep the dirt from falling in. The roof was pitched and covered with sod.

It was dark inside, but there was enough light coming in through the open door to see to the far end of the room where Tom was placing the boy onto one of three bunk beds. In the center of the room stood a circular fireplace with a pipe chimney going up through the roof. Looking around, I saw a coal oil lantern on a counter to my left. Shaking it to make sure there was fuel in it, I lit it and brought it over to Tom. The boy was still unconscious.

I told Tom I was going out to collect chips for a fire. I wanted to heat some water to bathe the boy's wounds. But on my way out, by the door, I saw a bushel basket half filled with chips. Once I got the fire going, I went back to Tom and asked him what he thought.

"Looks like he got in the way of a buffalo or two; he must have been on the edge of the herd when it stampeded. He's lucky to be alive."

"I reckon so." I said, and then I added, "The water will be hot in a minute. Here's a towel I found behind the counter; it looks to be clean. I'm going to check around outside to see what we have here. By the way, I found a note under the lantern that said passers-by should make themselves to home. Mister Rawlings asks only that we leave his establishment as we found it."

"Right neighborly of him," said Tom.

Behind the trading post was another sod house built along similar lines, though a mite smaller. Instead of steps, an earthen ramp led down into it. The place was a stable. Outside, in the back, I found a spring surrounded by a few small oak trees.

Back inside with Tom, I watched as he bathed the boy's wounds. He had discovered another gash on the boy's back that we had not noticed before. It too was caked with dried blood. After the boy was seen to, I covered him with a blanket and then we retreated to the counter.

"You look around for a bottle?" asked Tom.

"All the shelves are empty. That would have been just too kind of Mister Rawlings to leave whiskey for us."

We had a problem to confront. We were about out of food, and we weren't even halfway to California. We could always shoot meat as long as our ammunition held out. There was Fort Laramie, but that was weeks away. A man would like a little coffee in the morning and at the end of the day after a hard ride on the trail. Mister Conner was right; we were pilgrims. And now, there was the problem of the Indian boy. What were we going to do with him? Well, we'd been up most of the night and we were wore out. We would have to worry about things in the morning. Tom went to attend to the horses and I started to concoct a meal out of what we had left, which wasn't much.

After we ate, we checked on the boy; he was the same, but at least he wasn't worse. We were both pretty tuckered out, and it didn't look like he was going to regain consciousness anytime soon, so we thought we'd get a little sleep. Tom took a bunk on one side of him and I took one on the other side. We wanted to be close in case he needed us in the night. I don't know about Tom, but I was out before my head hit the bed.

The next thing I knew, a hand was shaking me awake. "Come on, Tom, leave me be for a while longer." But it wasn't Tom's hand. After another shake, this one harder than the first, I opened my eyes. What I beheld made my blood run cold. Standing over me were three Indians, and one of them was holding my guns. None of them looked too friendly. I turned my head to see Tom sitting up with three of his own Indians standing over him, one of them holding *his* guns.

"Good morning Huck. I hope you slept well," he said with a smile.

There were two more Indians kneeling at the boy's bed who seemed to be examining his wounds. One of them looked at me. Not with hate, but there sure was no love there. The other one lifted the boy and walked out. We were ordered to gather our things and go outside. Of course, the command was not conveyed in words; they did not speak our language. But they made their desires perfectly clear. Without our guns, there wasn't much we could do except go where they pointed.

Once outside, they led us to the stable to get our horses, which was encouraging because it meant they were not going to kill us on the spot. As we saddled up, Tom asked me why they let us come in alone. "Do you think they trust us?"

"They were in here while we were still asleep. They know there is only one way in and one way out . . . and that there are no guns around," I answered.

When we came out of the stable the Indians, astride their ponies, were waiting for us. One of the horses was rigged with a travois on which the boy lay. The Indian that seemed to be in charge said something and we headed out. The horse with the travois led, and the rest of us followed. Tom and I were bunched in the middle, surrounded by the Indians. No one spoke as we rode northwest. The sun was low in the eastern sky. It was easy to tell in which direction we were headed.

At mid-day, we came to a river, and along its banks, an Indian village. There were maybe thirty tipis arranged in circles of five or six each. As we came in, everyone stopped what they were doing and gave our little group their full attention; the only sound, the barking of dogs.

The Indian riding the horse dragging the travois continued on, but the rest of us stopped at a tipi in the middle of the village. With a pointed finger, we were ordered to go inside. An Indian lifted the skin covering the entrance, and Tom and I went in, alone. The light was dim, but our eyes soon adjusted. We stood there looking at each other for a long time, not knowing what to think. Finally, Tom said, "I hope this doesn't make me miss my boat."

That did it for me. I couldn't help myself, I started laughing and then, I couldn't stop. Before I knew it, Tom was laughing right along with me. We were laughing so hard tears streamed down our faces. The laughter slowly subsided, and we got our feet under us, so to speak. At length, I said to Tom, "We've had some adventures, but if this don't take the cake, then I don't know what does."

No one came to check on us. At one point, I lifted the skin and stuck my head out of the tipi. I saw no guard posted and this I relayed Tom. But we decided if we made a run for it, at best it would be futile, and it might even get us killed.

About two hours later, a tall Indian pulled back the flap and came in. He wore only a breechclout and leggings, no shirt; in one of his braids hung a single eagle feather. It was hard to gauge his age, maybe forty. Following him were two comely Indian girls. One held two bowls with some kind of food in them, and the other one carried a skin that turned out to hold water.

The girls put the bowls and skin on a buffalo robe and left. When they were gone, the Indian spoke: "My name is *Skoon Ka Ska*, White Dog in your tongue. You are welcome in our village. I am the chief of my people; the chief of this small band. We are thirty-one lodges of one hundred and twenty people. And as you saw coming in, countless dogs."

Well, that just floored us. We were speechless. A minute ago, I wouldn't have given a treed coon's chance in hell that we were going to get out of this with all of our hair. Now this gent came in speaking better English than Tom and me, welcoming us to his village!

Before we could say anything, he told us to sit and eat the food. "I am sorry that I did not come sooner, but I was worried about my son. You eat now. I will return, and we will smoke the pipe and talk." He then walked out, pulling the flap down after him.

Tom and I, at that moment, were too hungry and thirsty to discuss anything. We shoveled the food—a kind of stew—into our mouths with our hands and gulped water from the skin without a word between us.

After eating our full, we sat on buffalo skins and contemplated our fate.

"Huck, what do you think is happening here?" asked Tom.

"It beats the tar outta me," was my reasoned reply.

Before the discourse could go any further, White Dog walked in.

He came to where we were sitting and sat opposite us. He held a long-stem pipe with eagle feathers hanging from it. There were intricate carvings on the bowl. It was a work of art.

"First, we will smoke the pipe, and then we will talk," he said.

From a pouch hanging around his neck, he drew out a pinch of what I assumed to be tobacco and filled the pipe. Taking a twig lying next to the remains of a fire, he stirred the gray ashes until the embers glowed red. He placed one end of the small stick on the coals and waited a moment. When it was ready, he put fire to the pipe using the glowing red end of the twig.

When the pipe was lit, White Dog took a long pull, expelled the smoke and handed the pipe to Tom. Tom, an old hand at smoking (he'd been doing it since he was twelve), took a pull and immediately he started coughing. Tom held the pipe out to me, but before I could take my pull, he blurted out, in between coughs, "That's not tobacco!"

Smiling, White Dog said, "It is the bark of the red willow tree."

Being forewarned, I did not inhale.

As soon as the ritual was over, White Dog spoke: "I want to thank you for taking care of my son. His name is *Thašúŋke Witkó* or Horse-That-Is-Spirited, as you would call him. The men who brought you here have informed me that you dressed his wounds. Will you tell me how you found my son? He is awake now, but he says he saw no white men."

Before we went any further, I wanted to know how he spoke English so well.

"When I was a child, the Black Robe came to our village. He spent many winters with us, and he taught me your language. The Black Robe was a medicine man; he called himself a priest."

Well, that explained that. Hence, we told him what we knew, and how we found the boy. Afterwards, we asked him what had happened.

"He tells me," said White Dog, "that because he is the son of a chief, he must prove himself at an earlier age than the other boys. He took his pony and his little bow, and went hunting the buffalo. As he was coming up on them, they started to run. He does not know what started them running, but buffalo will run for no reason. He turned for his pony, but she was gone. My son's little legs were not swift enough to get him to a safe place. He tells me two or three buffalo struck him as he was running."

"We're just glad," said Tom, "that he is all right. He must be a scrapper to go out hunting all by himself at that age."

"He is old enough to hunt, but not by himself. In a few winters, he will have his vision quest and he will learn of the animal that is to be his protector. Then he will go on the warpath. I took my first scalp when I was fourteen winters. I have many coup feathers," said White Dog looking rather proud of the fact.

Indians sure do think different from us white folk. According to White Dog, calling coup is what an Indian strives for in battle. First coup is striking an enemy at close range with a coup stick. Second coup is killing your enemy. However, just because a brave has first coup does not mean that he is entitled to second coup. Anyone may rush in, kill the enemy, and claim second coup. First coup feathers are the most desired. For to claim first coup, to attack the enemy in hand-to-hand combat, shows true bravery. When a brave has first coup, he yells his name and says, "I have overcome this one." After the battle, he will need witnesses to claim coup. That is why he loudly shouts his name. If a brave receives a wound or rescues a comrade, he claims third coup, and if he captures a horse, that is fourth coup. The brave is awarded his coup feathers at *Wakté-gli,* which is the Kill Dance, a celebration after a victory.

Sitting in a tipi with a full stomach and listening to White Dog tell of coups was better than riding the prairie, but we had to get moving. Winter was coming on fast, and we had to get to Fort Laramie to replenish our food supply. I explained that to White Dog.

"You are our guests; you may come and go as you please. But I have seen your ponies; they are in need of rest even if you are not. Stay for three sleeps (sleep is Indian talk for days), rest, and we will supply you with all you need. This is my sister's lodge; her husband was killed by the Osage two winters past. Because our father is dead, the men of our village come to me with offers of ponies for her in marriage. But she tells me she does not desire to be a second or a third wife to another man, and that she still laments her husband. I have refused their offers. While you are in our village, she will sleep in my lodge, and you will sleep here. Tomorrow, we will go hunting for deer and antelope. We will smoke the meat, and it will last. We have corn flour and turnips for you. You will take much with you when you leave. Also, I have a pony that is now yours. He is not strong and cannot be used as a war pony, but he can carry the food that you take from here. Your ponies will not have the burden."

There was not much we could say to that. Tom and I looked to each other and both shrugged at the same moment.

"Why not?" he said.

72

"Sounds fine to me," I added.

White Dog smiled and said. "That is good. Now come, I will show you my village."

Seven

White Dog walked us through the village telling us of his people. "We are a band of the Lakota; our enemies fear us. Our nation is made up of many bands like ours—some larger, some smaller. A band is a family. Most of the people you see here are of one family, either through marriage or through birth. The others are close friends."

In the middle of one circle, we saw women kneeling on the ground, grinding corn into meal. Tom asked, "Why are your tipis arranged in circles?"

"Our lodges are arranged as they are to signify the hoop of life. The earth is round; the sky is round, also the moon. Our lives are as a hoop. We come and we go, but there is always another born. There is no end of life. The hoop is the road of life."

After the tour of the village, White Dog brought us to a tipi larger than the others.

"This is our council lodge," White Dog explained. "There will be a celebration here tonight. We are to welcome the two white men who saved my son's life."

Tom hung his head and dragged the toe of his boot through the dust. Me, I looked around for a place to hide. We were both embarrassed. I don't know if we had saved

Spirited Horse's life. Maybe he would have awakened and made his way home even if we had not found him.

That night, Tom and I sat by a large fire outside the council lodge. White Dog sat between us, and Spirited Horse sat next to Tom. All in all, there were thirty Indians at our fire and the several smaller fires burning within the circle. The people were all of White Dog's immediate family. Wives, daughters, sons-in-law and many cousins; his mother was also present. Spirited Horse was White Dog's only son.

Each circle had its own celebration made up of close family members. At one point during the night, White Dog walked Tom and me to the other circles and introduced us around.

Only men sat at our fire, and Spirited Horse was quite pleased to be allowed to sit with the men. He wore the wound on his cheek as a badge of honor. This, his father conveyed to me as Spirited Horse spoke no English. In fact, White Dog was the only member of the band who did speak English.

The mood was festive. Children ran in and out of the circles and around the fires, playing games as children do in all cultures. Song was a big part of the celebrations. Men sang individually of their coups, while the women sang as a group, but only the tone; the women did not sing words. The warriors showed us their war dances, and both the men and women partook in the Sun Dance. We feasted on deer and antelope meat, and concoctions of I knew not what, but it was all good and tasty.

Among the games, the most popular was *Siha*, a wrestling game. Four men from each circle were chosen to form a team and represent their circle. The teams assembled in the great circle of the council lodge; one by one, the teams met in combat until all teams had fought one another. All the people of the band were there to cheer on their teams, and the fighting was quite fierce. Four matches were always going on at any one time. According to the Lakota, four things make a man a man: bravery, fortitude, generosity, and wisdom. And let me tell you— those braves needed a whole heap of fortitude. They'd get each other in headlocks that would turn the man's face redder than it was to begin with. Or they would pin their opponent's arm behind his back and bend it until it was about to break. When the brave could take the pain no longer, he would cry out, *Tawacin mi'yo*, which means *I submit*. There is no word in the Lakota language for "surrender." White Dog stated that in an actual battle, a brave would never submit. He'd rather die. For to submit would bring shame upon himself, his family, and his band.

The score was kept by using a bundle of sticks. Each time a match was won, a point was awarded and the winner removed a stick from the bundle. When all the teams had met, the team with the most sticks was declared the winner. The men at our fire gambled on the teams and on the individual participants. I don't know if odds were given, and I could not understand the conversations, but all the discussions were lively.

When Tom realized there was gambling going on, he wanted in and asked White Dog if he could place a bet. Tom didn't know what the stakes were, but he loved to gamble. White Dog explained that the men were betting ponies. At first, Tom looked a mite crestfallen. But then he smiled and reached into his pocket and withdrew two golden eagles. Holding them in the palm of his hand he said, "These are worth one pony!"

White Dog took one of the proffered coins and looked at it for a moment before saying, "What use have we of these? If a man wants ponies, he will steal them from his enemies."

Tom thought hard for a moment and then said, "With these you can buy ball and powder at the fort's trading post." We had noticed a few of the men carried old muskets as we walked through the village.

White Dog shrugged and said something to the men that were betting, holding the coin up so that it could be seen. Then turning to Tom he said, "I told them what you have said about powder and balls. We are always in need of such things. I think you will get your bets; I will speak for you."

Well, from then on Tom was in the thick of it. At one point, he had won three ponies, but by the end of the competition, he was out six golden eagles and had no ponies. But he had made many friends among the gamblers.

Before the celebration commenced, the pipe was smoked. When the pipe had gone around the fire and come back to us, Tom asked White Dog about the feathers and the work on the bowl. As the others at our fire talked among themselves, White Dog told Tom and me of the sacred pipe and White Buffalo Woman.

"Before we were the Lakota, before we were *The People*, there was a time we were hungry. One day, two scouts were hunting the buffalo when they came to the top of a small hill. A long way off, they saw the figure of a woman. As she approached, they saw that she was beautiful. She was young and wore a white buckskin dress, and she carried a *wakin*. One of the scouts had lustful thoughts and told the other. His friend said that the woman was sacred and he should not have such thoughts.

"As the woman came up to them, she said to the one with the lustful thoughts, 'Come forward.' The brave moved to touch her and a white cloud covered them from sight.

"The woman stepped from the cloud, and it blew away. There on the ground, at the beautiful woman's feet, lay a pile of bones with worms crawling in and among them.

"The woman said to the other scout, 'Good things I am bringing, something holy to your nation. Go to your village and tell your people that I am coming; tell them to build a medicine lodge large enough to hold all the chiefs of the nation.'

"The people heard the scout's story and constructed the lodge. When the woman came to the village, out of the *wakin* she withdrew a pipe with a bison calf carved on one side of the bowl. 'The bison represents the earth, which will house and feed you,' said White Buffalo Woman. On the other side were carved seven circles. 'They represent *Ocheti Shakowin,* the seven sacred campfires of the Lakota nation.'

"From the stem hung thirteen eagle feathers. 'The feathers represent the sky and the twelve moons. With this pipe, you shall prosper. With this pipe, you shall commune with *Wakan Tan'ka*. With this pipe, you shall become *The People*. You shall be bound with the Earth, for She is your mother; She is sacred.'

"White Buffalo Woman filled the pipe with bark of the red willow and lit it.

"'The rising smoke,'" she said, "'is the living breath of *Wakan Tan'ka*.'

"Having given the pipe to *The People*, having said what she had to say, White Buffalo Woman turned and walked four paces from the lodge and sat down. When she stood, she was a black buffalo calf. She walked on, lay down and came up as a brown buffalo calf. Walking still farther, she turned into a red buffalo and finally, she stood upon a hill as a white buffalo calf. She turned, bowed in the four directions of the four winds, and then she vanished.

"Because of what White Buffalo Woman has taught us, the Lakota honor our mother the Earth; we honor our parents and grandparents. We honor the birds of the sky; we honor the beast of the earth. We know that *Wakan Tan'ka* resides in all animals, in all trees and plants and rocks and stones. *Wakan Tan'ka* is in all. We know that *Wakan Tan'ka* lives in each of us. Because of White Buffalo Woman, we have become Lakota."

It was a good story, and I had only one question. Who or what is *Wakan Tan'ka?*

"*Wakan Tan'ka* is the Great Mysterious, the Great Mystery, the life that is in all things. Black Robe called him the Great Spirit," said White Dog.

On the morning of the third day after first coming to the village, Tom and I sat astride our well-rested horses with an Indian pony between us. The pony had two large deerskin bags slung over its back, one on each side. These bags were filled with smoked deer meat and other foods. We were now in good shape. We rode out of the village with White Dog and Spirited Horse by our side. They rode with us for a few miles at which point we shook hands with them in the crosswise fashion that denotes true friendship to the Red-Man. Then we rode on alone . . . heading west once again.

EIGHT

A few days later, we crossed the Republican River. A week after that, we came to the Platte, which meant that Fort Laramie was within striking distance. We still had plenty of food, but we needed ammunition. We would stock up at the fort and then make a fast run for the mountains. November was fast approaching and we had to get over the mountains before mid-October if we were to get over them at all.

We did not dally at the fort. We bought what we needed at the trading post and were back on the trail in a few hours. We had been offered accommodations, but both Tom and I had come to like sleeping out on the prairie. For three hundred and sixty degrees, the stars touched the horizon. There was no light to impede their brilliance, no buildings to block the view of that extraordinary sight. There were only the stars . . . and black sky. I felt as though I could reach out and touch the stars; they seemed that close. I read once that a gent by the name of Ptolemy believed the earth was encapsulated within crystalline spheres. Out on the prairie the stars did indeed look as though they were made of fine, delicate crystal. I saw The Great Bear and Polaris, the only star that does not move. Orion seemed as though he could lower his arm and smite me with his club. Soon we would be leaving the prairie behind and that is why we did not stay at the fort; we wanted to enjoy God's wondrous creation for as many nights as were left us to do so.

Two days after leaving Fort Laramie, we came to the marker that showed the way to South Pass. I don't know why it was called a pass because once we got to the spine of the Continental Divide; it was as flat as a pancake. It seemed as though we were on top of the world.

We hit the pass in the late afternoon and were hoping to descend to the other side by nightfall. However, halfway down, the sky turned gray, the wind picked up, and the temperature quickly fell. A snowstorm was fast approaching. It must have been the first storm of the season because we had seen no snow on the higher elevations. We desperately sought shelter.

Eventually we found a cave that looked large enough to accommodate both the horses and us, but first it had to be explored. Back in Missouri, you can walk a few paces into a cave and then fall hundreds of feet into an abyss. I found a fallen branch that still had some dead leaves on it and lit it. Using the branch as a torch, I entered the cave while Tom stayed with the horses.

I went in far enough to ascertain that there were no open pits. But as I was turning to leave, something caught my eye; a grizzly bear sleeping in a corner of the cave. I had never seen a grizzly before, but this bear was so large he could be nothing else. If he topped off at less than eight hundred pounds, I would have been surprised. I had heard that, aside from a she-bear protecting her cubs, there is nothing more dangerous to your health than awakening a hibernating grizzly. Discretion being the better part of valor, I retreated.

I apprised Tom about the bear. We debated whether to go in and shoot it. But from what we had heard of grizzlies, he would be hard to kill. Most likely, the bear would take a swipe at us and tear off our faces.

With the temperature rapidly falling and the sky getting darker by the minute, we resumed our search for protection from the storm. We finally found it in an outcropping of rock that extended up and out far enough to give us some shelter.

We hastily moved and stacked a few large rocks into place to afford a little protection from the wind. Next, we put the three horses inside the makeshift enclosure and set about securing wood for a fire. We did not know how long the storm would last or if we would be snowed in afterwards. Therefore, we laid in as much wood as we could.

Once we had our firewood, Tom stripped the horses of their saddles, and the Indian pony of his burden. White Dog had given us a supply of corn for the horses and Tom fed it to them as I started a fire. I built it close to the wall so that the heat would reflect back onto us.

The wind was picking up, but it came from behind the outcropping and did not affect us too badly. The temperature continued to fall. Then the first flurries blew into our shelter. It was not long afterward that the snow came down in earnest. There was nothing for it but to wait it out huddled by the fire. We wore buffalo robes given to us by White Dog. He had warned us that if we were caught in the mountains when it snowed, we would need them. And he was right.

It snowed all night; we were too cold to sleep. When morning came around, the storm had passed, and we looked out on a white world. The snow was deep, too deep to travel in. The wind had ceased, and the sun was rising. Perhaps it would not take long for the snow to melt enough for us to get down the mountain. Our first concern was to get firewood to melt some snow. The horses needed water. It would be tough going without snowshoes, but we had to go out. As well as water for the horses, we needed warmth and food. We could have neither without a fire. Thus, bundled in our bulky buffalo robes, we left our refuge.

The snow came up to our thighs, and each step was a chore. Eventually we devised a system to help us make our way. I led and stomped down the snow with my feet, then Tom would step exactly where I had. It was slow going, but at last we made it to the trees. The snow was not as deep and that made it possible to find the dead branches we needed for our fire.

We each collected an armful of wood and brought it back to our camp. It wouldn't last long; we would have to make a few more trips. We decided that I should go back for additional wood while Tom built up the fire, melted snow, and put some coffee on. I followed our trail of crunched snow and made it to the trees in no time at all. I was bending over picking up a good-sized branch when I heard *the sound*—a scratching noise. But who or what would be out in weather like this other than a fool like me?

I straightened and turned to see a sight I hope never to see again. Five hundred feet away stood the grizzly I had seen in the cave. I could tell it was the same bear because of the shock of white fur that ran halfway down his back. I froze, and made not a sound.

He was standing on his hind legs, scratching at the bark of a tree. He stood seven feet tall and had a reach of another three feet; he was marking the tree ten feet above the ground! He must have smelled me or sensed me in some manner because he turned his head, and our eyes met. Right then and there, I knew I was a dead man.

He came down on all fours with his face upturned, but his eyes still held on mine and he let out with a prodigious roar. I had my Colt stuck in my waistband, but it would be of little help unless I shot him in the eye, and it might take more than one shot even at that. I was hoping he would not see me as a threat. I retreated until I backed into a tree and could go no farther. Our eyes still held. Somehow I knew the minute I broke eye contact with him, he would charge.

Moving slowly, I opened the front of my buffalo robe and pulled out the Colt without taking my eyes from the beast. It seemed to me that he was trying to decide if I was worth the trouble of traversing the short distance between us. I did not, with all my heart, want to kill so magnificent a creature. Perhaps both of us would live to see another day. But no . . . he shook his head and started for me.

I brought the Colt up and fired. The bullet just missed him. I took my time aiming the second shot and fired again. The bullet hit him in his jaw and knocked out some teeth, but he kept coming. I ran a few yards, stopped, turned and fired again. This time I hit him in the chest, but it did not slow him down. I had three shots left, and the brute was descending upon me. There was only one thing to do, and in the deep snow, it was not running away. I firmly planted my feet, took careful aim and emptied the Colt into my adversary's head. He still came on and I silently said good-bye to this world. But within feet of me, he stopped in his tracks, stood on his hind legs and looked into my eyes. Then he keeled over dead, knocking me to the ground in the process.

I lay there on my back, next to the monster, looking up through a canopy of evergreen boughs at a patch of blue sky. The sunlight was slanting in through the trees, and not too far off I heard a bird singing its morning song. I couldn't move except to breathe hard. I was panting as though I had just run a foot race. Then I heard Tom shouting my name. It was an effort, but I raised myself to a sitting position, gazing one last time into the bear's eyes. They were open, but they did not see me.

Peering over the mountain of bear flesh, I saw Tom standing not far away, holding his long gun. When he saw me, the relief that flooded his face was evident. He made his way over, stepping carefully in the snow, looked at the bear and then reached out his hand to me. I grabbed it and he pulled me to my feet, saying as he did so, "I declare Huck Finn! Can't a body leave you alone for five minutes without you causing a ruckus?"

I was not in a funnin' disposition, but I did manage to say, "It was quite a ruckus at that." Then added, "I could use some of that coffee you were gonna make, and we should quit this place. The wolves will be comin' around soon for a little bear meat. Let's get us some wood and go back to camp while I can still walk. My legs are a mite rubbery 'bout now."

Of course, when I got outside of some hot coffee, I had to tell Tom what had transpired. When he asked me what had awakened the hibernating bear, I told him that I was no expert on bears, hibernating or otherwise.

"No," he replied, "but I might say that you're hell-on-wheels when it comes to killing 'em."

It took four days for the snow to melt enough so that we could descend the mountain. They were days spent collecting wood, sleeping, and keeping the fire going. We heard wolves in the vicinity; they fretted the horses a mite, but they kept busy with the bear carcass and left us alone.

We came down off the mountain and crossed the Green River. Then we came to the Humboldt and followed it to the Sierra Nevada Mountains where we crossed at Truckee Pass. Coming down out of the pass, we saw a little valley where the grass was green and wild horses contently grazed. We would not have need of a pack horse in San Francisco, and the little Indian pony would not take well to the town. I slipped the lead rope and pack bags off him, and with a slap to his rump, I sent him down into the valley.

We were now in California.

NINE

We hit San Francisco the first week of November, 1861. It was *some* town, bigger than St. Louis even. As soon as we found ourselves a hotel, Tom was down to the wharf going from ship to ship asking where they were headed. After three days, he was feeling pretty low.

"I've talked to every damn captain on the wharf, and those anchored out in the bay. Not one of 'em is going to China."

Trying to make him feel better, I said, "Some ship, at some time, will be going your way. All we have to do is be patient. And whilst we're being patient let's explore the city." Tom was all for that. So that night we went down to the Barbary Coast, a disreputable section of town. We had been informed that The Coast was where we could find almost anything we wanted.

After a night of going from saloon to saloon, we ended up at the Bella Union on Pacific Street. Tom was playing at the faro table and I was drinking at the bar. I was jawboning with two sailors who had been to China; I thought Tom might want to talk with them. I was just waiting for him to lose enough and come back to the bar. Either that or to get thirsty enough to want another shot of rye, our drink of choice that night.

While we were waiting, and because I was buying the drinks, the sailors were talkative and filled me in on something I was not aware of. It appeared that there was this practice down on the Coast known as shanghaiing. I'd never heard of it before, but what it amounted to was just plain kidnapping. When a ship didn't have enough hands, the captain would contract with a local gang to supply the men needed. The method used to deliver the men was to waylay them and knock them out as they left a drinking establishment. Usually late at night because the drunker the man, the less fight he'd put up. When he awoke the next day, he would find himself out to sea, headed for a distant port.

Tom looked as if he was going to play faro for a while, and the sailors had to be back at their ship; it was leaving with the tide. They thanked me for the drinks and departed. I was left alone at the bar with a bottle of cheap rye for company.

Just before dawn, Tom finished up at the faro table and joined me at the bar.

"How much did you win?" I asked.

"I lost four hundred and fifty-three dollars."

"Well, it's a good thing we're rich."

"Yes, that is good," Tom agreed flippantly.

Even for that time of night, the place was still full with noise, tobacco smoke, and laughter. We didn't see many women at the other dives, and the Bella Union was no exception. There were maybe three whores in the bar, but I'm not sure because I didn't pay them any mind. I do know they weren't very pretty. If there were others, they must have been upstairs.

I poured Tom a shot from the bottle and asked him if he wanted to try another bucket of blood.

"I don't think so, Huck. Let's go and get us some sleep. This afternoon we can go down to the wharf and see if any new ships came in. We can start all over again tomorrow night. I'm sure there's a few buckets of blood we missed."

I called to the barkeep and told him we wanted to settle up. He picked up the bottle, looked at the pencil mark he had made earlier and informed me that I owed him four dollars. Which was highway robbery, but not as bad as the four hundred and fifty-three dollars Tom had lost to the house.

Not wanting to push through the mass of men standing between us and the front of the place, we went out the side door. That's where we ran into a little excitement that made the entire evening worthwhile. Tom was pent up because he couldn't find a ship going to China, and I was a little put out because of the two months on the trail. I was saddle sore. I reckon we were both looking for a good scrap.

Tom was in front of me, and as soon as he was in the alleyway, and before I was through the door, I saw a shadow moving towards him. I don't know why, but I instantly thought, *shanghai*, and I yelled for Tom to duck. It was a good thing he had not been drinking for the last few hours because his reflexes were good. The two-by-four that was meant for the side of his head missed completely. By then I was outside and I saw three mean-looking jaspers facing us.

I informed Tom that if he was hell-bent for election on getting out to sea, then these men could aid him in getting his wish. He looked to me and though he said nothing, the expression on his face asked, *"What the hell are you talking about?"*

"Tom, I think these gents want to throw you on a boat going to Boston by way of the Horn. What do you say? You wanna be a Yankee?"

I think the word "Yankee" was all Tom had to hear to set him off. The man who held the two-by-four was the first to go down. Tom hit him with a beautiful haymaker right to his chin. Once down, he never moved again that I saw.

I realized that if I didn't move fast, I'd miss out on all the fun. I made for the man nearest me, and Tom took the other gent. We fought until there was no one left to fight; all three of them were out cold. Tom and I were a little bloodied, but we were in much better shape than the men lying at our feet. It felt good to have let off a little steam. As we made our way back to the hotel, I explained to Tom what being shanghaied meant.

When I awoke later that day, Tom was already gone. I figured he was down at the wharf looking for his ship. I got dressed and went downstairs to the hotel restaurant. I was about to get outside of some ham and eggs when Tom walked in with a big grin on his face and sat down opposite me.

"It looks like our minor tussle this morning brought me some good luck. There's a ship anchored out in the bay by the name of *China Express,* and if it ain't going where I want to go, I don't know what is."

I agreed that was good news indeed, but to be honest, right then and there, I was more interested in my eggs and ham.

It took two days for there to be an open slip on the wharf for the *China Express*. So eager was Tom to get on the ship, that the moment the gangway was lowered, he ran up the plank with no regard for the people trying to come down. He learned from the captain that, yes, they would be making for China, but not for a month. And there probably would be an opening for an able-bodied sailor, but Tom would have to check back just prior to sailing.

"There's always a few who jump ship when we hit Frisco," said the captain, "so don't fret, Son. Come back and see me in three weeks."

The next three weeks were hard on Tom. No other ships came in that were going to the South Seas, let alone China. Trying to keep Tom's mind occupied until it was time to talk with the captain, I took him with me when I rode south of the city. It was good country, a mite dry, but beautiful nevertheless. I liked riding through those brown hills. One day while we were walking our horses, I told Tom that when he got on his way, I would be riding south. "I might even go into Mexico."

The three weeks went by fast for me and slow for Tom. On the appointed morning, Tom was up early and raring to go. "Alright Huck, I'm gonna go see the captain now and see if he'll take me on. If not, then I'll have to go as a tourist."

I was still in bed, but I got up on one elbow and said, "Listen, Tom, it's not even full light out yet. The captain's gonna be asleep. If you wake him, he might not be of a mind to take you along. Why don't you go downstairs and get yourself some breakfast? I'll join you as soon as I get dressed. I'd like to go along and see your accommodations."

He looked pained at having to kill time, but he nodded and said, "I'll wait for you, but don't be all day about it." Then he was through the door. I was able to hold him back some, but at nine that morning we were walking up the gangway of the *China Express*.

The captain was standing on the deck talking with a man that turned out to be the first mate. I held back, but Tom approached them. When the captain saw him, he stopped speaking and addressed Tom. I couldn't hear what was said, but Tom was nodding his head up and down so much I thought it might detach from his body. Then the captain pointed to an open book on the table before him, and Tom wrote something in it, probably signed his name. He shook hands with the mate and the captain then came back to where I was waiting.

"Let's go, Huck. I gotta get my outfit and report back here. They'll be taking on stores and cargo for the rest of the week. I've got to be on hand to help out."

At that point, there wasn't much cause for me to stick around. Tom was on his way to following his dream. I had no dreams to follow and no aspirations to strive for, so we said good-bye at the hotel. Like with Jed, it would be twelve years before I saw Tom Sawyer again. And when I did, he'd be a different man.

TEN

I sold Tom's horse and saddle at the second livery stable I came to. At the first, a man was beating a horse with a quirt as I walked in. I was standing behind him, and as he raised his arm for another onslaught, I pulled the quirt out of his hand. When he turned toward me, I struck him across the face with it, saying, as I did so, "I'll be back, and if that horse or any other horse under your care has one mark on 'im, I'll beat you to within an inch of your life." He backed away from me holding his hand to his face. I asked if he understood what I said. He nodded and rubbed his check. Some things I just can't abide, and beating a horse is one them. Of course, I wasn't coming back, but as long as he thought so, the horses would be safe.

It was about two o'clock when I finally hit the coast road going south. I let my horse have her head. I was in no hurry, had no place to be, and wasn't itching to get back to Missouri any time soon.

I crossed over into Mexico on my thirteenth day out, just before sunset. At the border, I passed through a small town by the name of Tijuana. From what I could see of it, I had no desire to stay any longer than I had to. I rode through as fast as I could and made camp five miles out.

97

The next morning, I got an early start and continued traveling south. At mid-morning, I had some company.

I came around a bend in the road, and there waiting for me was a bandit. I knew he was a bandit right off because he had his gun out and it was pointed in my direction. I didn't want him to think having the drop on me mattered one way or the other. So I maintained my course, ambled up next to him and with a big grin said, "Good morning!"

I don't reckon that he understood English too good because he waved his gun and made a motion for me to raise my hands. Instead of doing what he wanted, I did what *I* wanted. I slapped the gun from his hand and then drew my own revolver. When he saw *my* gun, he started to back up his horse. I shook my head and said, "No!" I reckon he understood that all right because he and his horse stopped right where they were, and he reached for a handful of sky.

He looked dirt poor to me, and I must have looked like a rich gringo to him, which I have to admit I was. But still, you can't let people go pushing you around and robbing you just because they might be hungry. It breeds disrespect, if not contempt, for all us rich gringos.

He was looking mighty forlorn sitting on his horse with his hands in the air. Therefore, I motioned for him to put them down. I shook my head and gave out with a small laugh while thinking, *Huck Finn, you're either a fool or somethin' worse.* I put my gun back in its holster. By now, my bandit was smiling, and I could see that he was missing his two upper front teeth.

Not knowing why, I reached into my shirt pocket and withdrew the few dollars I had tucked in there; I didn't want him to see the roll that I carried in my pants pocket. I held out the bills in his direction. At first, he was hesitant to take them, as if it might be some kind of trick. To hurry things along, I made as if I was going to put them back into their home. That's when he snatched them from my hand. He looked at the money, then at me, and then back at the money. Finally he said, *"Por qué?"*

I did not know what he was talking about. I didn't want to waste any more time, so I took my gun out of its holster and pointed it down the road while saying, *"Vamoose."* That's one word of Spanish I did know.

He pointed to his gun lying in the dirt. I shook my head vigorously and repeated the word *vamoose*. He shrugged, gave me a salute, turned his horse in the direction I had pointed and trotted off, apparently without a care in the world. But he did turn his head to look at me a few times to see if I was going to shoot him in the back.

When he was out of sight, I slipped my horse and retrieved the gun. It was ancient. The hammer had rusted and could not be pulled back. What a pitiful bandit my friend made. I was ambivalent before, but now I was glad I had given him a few measly dollars. I placed the gun on a nearby boulder, in plain sight, so that it would be easily seen when my bandit friend returned to search for it. Then I got back on my horse and continued on my way.

The next day, about the time I was thinking of turning back (by then I had seen all of Mexico that I cared to see), my horse pricked her ears forward; something was spooking her.

As I passed a strand of cottonwoods, two men emerged, one holding a gun. This time the hammer was cocked. *Is everyone in this damn country a bandit?*

I wasn't feeling charitable that day. It was hot and I was sweating. I took off my hat with my left hand and wiped my brow. Then, instead of replacing it, I rested my hand on the pommel of my saddle, partially obscuring my right hand. Next, I tilted my head back as though looking at something in the sky. I wasn't. My eyes never left the man holding the gun.

It took a few seconds, but they couldn't resist. Both of them looked up into the sky to see what was so interesting. I didn't care about the other one, but as soon as the one with the gun took his eyes off of me, I slapped leather and shot him through the hand that was holding the gun. Even before the echo of the shot died out, his friend was beating hooves and turning up dust a quarter of a mile down the road.

At that moment, I was very much inclined to put a second bullet into the man I had shot, but I held back.

What the hell! He was no longer a threat. The gun was on the ground, and he was clutching the wounded hand to his chest with his blood flowing crimson onto his dirty white peon shirt.

I must admit he had a kind of dignity about him. From the way I must have looked (I was not in a good humor), he probably thought I was about to end his life. He stood his ground and waited for the bullet that would take his life. Maybe if the positions had been reversed, he would have killed me, but I couldn't shoot an unarmed man. With a weary sigh, I shook my head and said, "No, not today, friend. You follow your partner, and you'll live to rob another day."

I don't know if he understood me; maybe it was something in my voice or my manner, but he nodded once, took the reins in his good hand, and slowly followed in the wake of his *amigo*.

I should have felt good about averting being robbed and possibly killed, but I didn't. I felt sad. I turned my horse to the northeast, I was going home.

Thus ended my Mexican excursion.

I didn't any waste time. I passed through Sonora and was across the Colorado River and way into New Mexico Territory before my horse could work up a good lather. Once out of Mexico, I again slowed, and because it was wintertime, I decided to keep to the south as I made my way back to Missouri. But sometimes . . . "The best laid plans . . ."

The first town I came to after crossing the Colorado was a town called Lamesa, a mining town. I entered from the west in the late afternoon. The wind was blowing up dust, partially obscuring the sun, turning it a blood red. As I came down the main street, I cast a long shadow before me. I passed a general store, two whorehouses (one on each side of the street), a blacksmith's shop, the town jail, and four saloons. There were more stores and buildings farther on, but I stopped at a saloon called the Cactus Inn. I needed to wash the dust from my gullet.

I pushed my way through the slatted swing doors and was assaulted by raucous laughter and noise. The air was heavy with tobacco smoke and the smell of heated bodies. The place was filled to the rafters with men and a few women. I had to push my way through the throng to get to the bar. Once I got there, I had to yell my order to the barkeep over someone's head. When I secured my bottle of rye, I turned and looked for somewhere to sit and enjoy it.

Normally a crowded environment like that would have made me uncomfortable. But seeing as how I had just spent the last half month alone (except for the bandits), the press of bodies was rather welcomed. As I perused the room, my gaze fell upon a solitary figure sitting at a table off to my right. He sat with his head hung down staring into his drink, unmindful of the people around him.

Right off there were two things that caught my attention; the first and most obvious was that he was sitting alone with three empty chairs at his table. The place was crowded with men pressed together like sardines in a can and yet, here was a man with a table all to himself. Not only that, but it looked like he was being given a wide berth by all those around him. The other patrons were being jostled, but he surely wasn't. The second thing that caught my eye was the size of the man. He was sitting down; consequently, it was hard to judge his height. But if I had to make a guess, I'd say he stood a good six feet, six inches tall. He was big; he had to weigh close to three hundred pounds, and every ounce of it looked like muscle to me.

Pushing through the mass of men, I made my way over to the giant. Without asking permission, I pulled out a chair and sat down. The moment my bottom hit the chair the din around me subsided. There was still talk and laughter on the other side of the room and at the bar, but that too gradually faded away. Slowly, the man raised his head and looked at me as though I was a two-headed calf.

Now, my old pap always said that besides us Finns having a hot and terrible temper, we were also the most sociable people around. With that in mind I said, "Howdy mister, just got off the trail and I'd be mighty proud if you'd allow me to buy you a shot of whatever it is you're drinkin'."

At first, I thought that he didn't speak English because he continued to stare at me without saying a word. His hair was dark as a Mexican's; it hung down to his shoulders and was kinda greasy looking. He had a black beard that hid half his face, and his eyes were black, black as a rattlesnake's. I reckoned that maybe he was a Mexican and didn't understand what I said. But he disabused me of that notion right quick.

Without saying a word, he rose to his feet, picked up one of the empty chairs, and in one fluid motion, smashed it down on the table, splintering it into pieces. If I hadn't been so wore out, I might have jumped an inch or two in my seat. "I drink alone," he said, "and if ya don't want me doing to you what I just done to this here chair, then you best be movin' on." Having finished his speech, he placed both hands flat on the table and leaned into me, his face about six inches from mine. The whole time this was going on, the fifty or sixty people in the room made not a sound.

I noticed he wasn't wearing a gun (he probably didn't need one to kill a man). So I wasn't too concerned. After all, I was heeled. As I was thinking on how best to play the situation, I saw one of the legs of the chair that had just been destroyed. It was on the tabletop and had rolled until it came to rest against my bottle. It was two feet long and thick, about two inches across I'd say.

With a sigh and a slight shake of my head at the foolishness of men, I quickly snatched up the chair leg and brought it down on the head of my would-be drinking companion. And I brought it down *hard*. I didn't want him stirring afterward because then I'd have to kill him.

I must have done it right, because the next thing I knew, he was flayed out. Feet still on the floor, lying on top of the table with his arms outstretched. He had a smile on his face, maybe he liked getting hit on the head.

Slowly, the noise returned. There were murmurs, and a distinguishable word here and there. Then the dam busted wide open and everyone in the place was talking all at once. They still kept their distance, which I didn't mind. I wasn't there to make friends; I had a thirst to quench. Now that I had a place to sit and a little peace, I proceeded to put a dent in the bottle.

I had my back to the room, enjoying my whiskey and looking at my tablemate, who was still asleep on top of the table, when I heard a change in the tenor of the noise. Being a curious type, I turned to see what all the commotion was about, and saw the crowd part as a little man wearing a black, silk top hat pushed his way to the table.

"I would not have believed it . . . not in a thousand years, if I didn't see it with my own two eyes," he said. Turning to the man standing next to him he asked, pointing at me, "Is this here the gent that done it?"

Having been reassured by half the room that I was indeed the gent that had done it, he approached me warily and held out his hand. "Howdy, the name's Maxwell, Herbert T. I'm the mayor of this burg. Do you mind if I sit a spell?"

After shaking his hand, I replied, "No, not at all. Sit."

When he had himself situated, he turned toward the bar and yelled, "Verne, bring me my private stock and two glasses."

"That stuff you're drinking will take the enamel off your teeth. Let me buy you a decent drink, stranger. I'm the owner of this here establishment as well as the mayor. And what's the good of owning a saloon if you can't drink the best?"

By then the patrons were starting to crowd around, getting closer to us so as not to miss out on any of the conversation. As Verne made his way to us, Mister Maxwell pointed to the sleeping giant and asked, "Is he still alive?"

I informed him that, yes, he was alive and that if he looked closely enough, he could see his chest rising and falling. At least he was breathing. After seeing for himself, Mister Maxwell said, "Too bad, if anyone ever needed killing, it's Mac Conroy." Then he poured some of his special stock whiskey into the two glasses, raised one in my direction and said, "Here's to you, stranger. The only man ever to get the best of Mac Conroy."

We downed our whiskey. And as Maxwell was pouring another shot, he asked my name. "Can't keep addressing you as *stranger*," he said.

"The name's Finn, my friends call me Huck."

"Well Huck, if I was you, I'd make tracks outta here and be long gone by the time he comes around. As for myself, the first stirrings outta him and I'm gonna make myself scarce. When he starts to move again, this place will empty out like it was on fire. Even my barmen will find things to do in the back room."

Looking at my empty glass, and then at the bottle, I said, "If he's such a holy terror, why not have your sheriff lock him up?"

Taking the hint, Maxwell refilled my glass to the brim and answered. "We ain't got no sheriff. Mac run off two, and the last one he killed."

I picked up my freshly filled glass. Studying the amber liquid within, I said, "Excuse me for mentionin' it, but here's your chance. He's out cold. You can have him dragged to the hoosegow, try him, and hang him for killing your sheriff."

Just then Conroy moaned, and the crowd around us moved back a few paces. The mayor put his glass down and looked like he was ready to jackrabbit. I hadn't finished my whiskey, and as long as the mayor was buying, I was drinking. I picked up the chair leg and gave Conroy another good whack on top of his head. There was no more moaning after that. I then drained my glass.

Pouring us some more whiskey, the mayor asked where I was headed and if I was in any hurry to get there. When I replied that I was going to Missouri and that I was in no particular hurry to get anywhere, he considered me for a minute. Then he said, "How'd you like to be sheriff? It pays forty dollars a month and there's a lean-to out back of the jail that you can live in. You get three squares a day at Miss Emma's, paid for by the town. Emma, she runs a fine eatery she does."

I had my glass halfway to my mouth when his words struck home. I put it back down, the liquor untouched. Me, a sheriff? It sure was something to think about. But first, I thought I ought to ask a few questions. So I did.

"Mister Maxwell, besides Conroy here, what else would be required of me as your sheriff?"

"Well Huck, we're mining copper here, and the mine runs two twelve-hour shifts, six days a week. The day shift just ended; that's why the place is so full," he said, indicating the room. "Sometimes these miners can get a bit excitable. Your job will be to keep the peace. Mostly you'll be arresting drunks that get out of hand and try to bust up my place or one of the other saloons. "Sometimes a miner will get a snootful and wander down to the residential area, but the citizens that live there have made it plain that ain't such a good idea. Of course it took the shooting of a couple of miners, but the idea eventually sank in."

Then a notion hit me and I asked, "The last sheriff, the one that was killed, how'd Conroy do it? He don't look to wear a gun."

"No, Mac don't carry a gun. You see, a few months ago, Mac was bustin' up a saloon down the street and Ed—he was the sheriff back then, Ed Trask—was gonna put Mac in a cell until he sobered up. But as soon as Ed laid a hand on him, Mac hit Ed with a roundhouse that put him near into the next county. It *did* knock him into the next life."

The short of it is that I decided to take the job.

Once that was settled and drinks hoisted to cement the deal, the mayor excused himself and left the saloon, telling me he'd be right back. Mac stayed where he was and had nothing to say. Of course, he was still out cold, but since I'd become sheriff, he had been a model prisoner.

The mayor returned with a badge and a pair of handcuffs. It was resolved that we'd handcuff Mac while he was still out. The plan was to get him into a cell, but he'd have to get there under his own power. No one was volunteering to help carry him.

We got him cuffed, and a few of the boys helped with lifting him off the table and sitting him in a chair. As soon as he came to, I'd walk him over to the jail. In the meantime, there was still a little of the mayor's private stock left. Things worked out pretty good, because about the time we finished off the bottle, Mac started to come 'round.

As he stirred, the men closest to the table took a step or two back. Even the mayor stood and took a step away from the table. I continued to sit where I was. Mac opened one eye and then the other. He was dazed, to say the least, and it looked like he didn't know where he was. Then I could see the intelligence slowly make its way back into his eyes. He knew where he was all right, and he knew who I was. I was the gent that hit him on the head with the leg from a broken chair. He tried to stand. I think his intent was to come after me, but he fell back into the chair. That's when he realized his hands were behind him and that they were cuffed.

I felt I should introduce myself, so I said in a friendly manner, "Howdy Mac, my name's Huck Finn, and I'm the new sheriff in these here parts. Your hands are handcuffed behind you so that you won't go to breaking up any more chairs, and I won't have to go bustin' you over the head again for doing so."

When I finished speaking, he made an effort and got to his feet, though he swayed on them for a moment. But once he was steady, he took a step in my direction. I was still seated and all he'd have to do is fall on me and he'd win the fight. Before he could take a second step, I brought the chair leg out from under the table where I'd been holding it and brought it down hard on the tabletop. It made quite a noise, and it got his attention. Then I switched the leg to my left hand and drew my gun.

"Mac, I surely don't want to hit you over the head again. I've done it twice now and I promise you I take no pleasure in it. But it's a sight better than having to shoot you. I might be required to remove the body and then I'd have to pay ten or twenty men to assist me."

Unfortunately, he paid no mind to what I said. Instead he put his head down and charged like an enraged bull, but he had to come around the table and that gave me time enough to stand and side-step him. As he went by, I stuck out my foot and tripped him. Because the place was still full, he took three men down with him (nobody wanted to leave until they saw how I'd handle Mac or how he'd handle me).

Without the use of his arms, he couldn't get up off the floor.

With a sigh, I put my gun away and asked two of the men that were standing around enjoying the show to help me get him to his feet. Once we had him up, I said, as I tapped the chair leg against my thigh, "Mac, I know you're a tough *hombre*. Everyone in this room knows how tough you are. But it ain't tough to go up against a man when your arms are cuffed behind your back. That's just plain stupid. Now I'm sure your head is hurtin' from the cracks I gave it. So I'll make you a deal. If you'll walk peacefully down to the jailhouse with me and then go into a cell just as peacefully, I'll share my bottle of rye with you. We'll drink until your head stops hurtin'."

He looked me in the eye for a full minute; I thought I was gonna have to whack him on the head again, but then I saw the slight glint of a smile in his eyes as he said, "You're the first man that ever bested me since I was knee-high to a grasshopper. Let's go and get that drink."

The crowd parted for us as we walked out of the saloon. The mayor declined to accompany me in bringing Mac to the jailhouse, but he did tell me where to find the keys to the cells as he handed me the key to the handcuffs. He then quickly walked off down the street, not looking back. I think he was hedging his bets just in case Mac should somehow get free.

When we got to the jailhouse, I put Mac in one of the two cells without removing the cuffs. As I was locking the door, he asked me how I expected him to drink anything with his hands tied behind his back. I smiled at him and finished locking the cell door. Then I called him over and told him to turn around and stick his hands through the bars. After I got the cuffs off, I said, "I believe you're sincere, but I don't know you that well yet. I think that until I do, I'll play it safe."

He let out with a hardy laugh, and I slipped the rye from my pocket and handed it over. "You need that more than me, so enjoy. Anyway, I've got a job to do, I gotta keep the peace, but it shouldn't be too hard now that you're locked up." He laughed again, pulled the cork and took a deep pull. I said that I'd be back in a while and that he should make himself to home. In response, he shrugged and said that I could take my time because he wasn't planning on going anywhere.

The first place I went was back to The Cactus Inn. It had thinned out a mite. I stood at the bar waiting for one of the barkeeps to slow down in his duties long enough so that I might have a word with him. At length Verne approached and asked what I was having.

"Nothing to drink, only some information."

Looking at the badge that I'd pinned to my shirt, he said, "Sure Sheriff, whatcha wanna know?"

I asked about the time of the shift changes, how many saloons in town; things of that nature. I needed to get a sense of the place. When he had answered all my questions, I told him that I needed to speak with the mayor, and to please relay that information to His Honor at his earliest convenience.

I took a walk around town. It wasn't much of a walk because it wasn't much of a town. Next to Maxwell's saloon, on the east side was a livery stable; that was the dividing line. The western half of town held the saloons, whorehouses, and a few stores. Oh yes, and the jail. The east side of town was where the decent folks lived. That side of town consisted of houses, a small church, a boarding house, a general store, and Miss Emma's. The miners, I found out later, lived in a mining camp about a mile out of town to the north.

On the way back to the jail, I stopped in at Miss Emma's to introduce myself and to cadge a meal. The introduction wasn't necessary; she took one look at the star on my chest and told me that the whole town was talking about the man who slugged Mac Conroy and took him to the calaboose. When I left, I took along a plate of grub for Mac, but that wasn't necessary. Mac was lying on the bed, on his back, snoring rather gently for such a big man. The bottle lay on the bed next to him, empty. I laid the plate on the floor just outside the cell so he could reach it, and went to find a bed for myself. It had been a long day. I had about eight hours before the next shift change at the mine.

The lean-to out back had no windows, just a door and a dirt floor. Inside was a bed, a table and one chair. The bed looked mighty good from where I stood. I went to it and lay down, not even taking off my boots. The next thing I knew I was being shook awake by a man in a white apron.

"Sheriff," he said, "you gotta come quick. There's two drunks fightin' and tearin' up my place."

It took me a few ticks to realize that he was talking to me and that I was the sheriff. I nodded, got up and followed him out the door. I didn't even have to put on my boots.

It was still dark, and as we walked down the street, I reckoned I must have slept through the shift change because the saloons were full like they had been the evening before. Presently, we came to a building with a sign over it that simply read "Saloon."

"This is my place," said the man. Pointing to a broken window on the left side of the door, he added, "You see? They done that!"

I heard a lot of noise coming out of the open door, but nothing that sounded like fighting noise. I took two steps inside, and as I stood perusing the room, the noise and conversation slowly died away. Everyone was looking in my direction. The owner came up beside me and pointed to two men at the bar. "That's them, Sheriff. Them's the ones that broke my window and trashed my place."

His place, except for the window, didn't look all that trashed to me, but I said nothing. Instead, I walked up to the two men and asked them what the fuss was about. One had a cut lip and the other the beginnings of a beaut of a black eye. The one with the cut lip stood a little straighter and said, "Just a minor misunderstanding Sheriff, but we got it worked out. I was just buyin' Jim here a drink and then he's buyin'. Won't you join us?"

I didn't address his query, but I did speak out so that everyone in the room could hear what I had to say. "From now on, any ruckus that gets my attention will result in a fifty dollar fine and a few days in jail." I knew that fifty dollars was a lot of money to those miners. And they couldn't earn any money while sitting on their backsides in jail. I was hoping that the fine was steep enough to keep the peace. Then I dealt with the two combatants.

"You two are gonna pay for any damage you caused tonight. The owner will tell you the amount, and you'll pay it, fifty-fifty. If you don't, then you'll be fined and put in the hoosegow until you do pay. Do you understand what I'm sayin'?" I was assured that they both understood and that they would settle up the damages right away.

I went from saloon to saloon making the same speech about the fifty dollar fine and jail time for disturbing the peace. The last place I hit was The Cactus Inn, and Maxwell was there. He offered to buy me a drink, but I declined. "Heard you wanted to talk to me. What can I do for you?" he asked.

"It's about Conroy. What are we gonna do with him? Do you have a judge here in town?"

Maxwell looked a little sheepish and hesitated for a moment before saying, "I might have put the cart before the horse last night. But when I heard that Mac was breaking up my place and a stranger stopped him, all I could think of was to get him locked up before he could do any more damage." Maxwell stopped talking and reached for his glass, but seeing that it was empty, motioned to Verne for a refill. Once Maxwell had a full glass, he took a long swallow and then continued, "To answer your question, no, we ain't got a judge, never had need of one before. And to answer your other question, I don't know what the hell we're gonna do with Mac. I reckon I could appoint a judge, but there ain't no one around with any legal learnin'. I don't think we'd get twelve good men and true to serve on any jury that was tryin' Mac Conroy. Every jasper in town, including me, is afraid of him."

I sighed, "This is your town. If you want, I'll let him go, but then I'll have to resign and move on. I ain't never been a sheriff before, but if I'm gonna be your sheriff, then there's gotta be some rules. And the first rule in my book is that you don't go around killin' sheriffs."

Maxwell's eyes grew wide. He hurriedly said, "No, don't do that. Give me a few days to figure somethin' out. I liked what you said just now to the boys. I mean about keeping the peace and fining them if they don't. It's what this town needs. Hell, maybe we need a judge too. We're growing every day, but we won't grow for long if we don't have some law and order."

I told him I'd wait and see what he and the town wanted to do. "But I wouldn't take forever in deciding if I was you, because as long as Mac is a prisoner, the town's responsible for feeding him. And from the looks of him, ya'all go broke in about two weeks." He smiled at my little joke, but it was just a polite smile. There was no humor in his eyes.

When I walked outside, the sky was just turning from black to gray in the east and I realized that I was hungry, so I headed to Emma's for some breakfast.

After eating, there was nothing to do until the next shift change. Things were quiet; the miners were all either digging copper or back at their camp sleeping. So I went to the jail to see how Mac was fairing. He was awake, lying on the bed staring up at the ceiling. The plate of food I had left last night had been eaten; all that remained was the bare plate. When he heard my footfalls, he asked for some water without taking his gaze from the ceiling.

I got him fixed up with a bucket and a tin cup just outside his cell where he could reach it, then asked him if he'd like a game of checkers. (I had found a set and a board in the outer office.) Neither one of us had anything more pressing to do, so I set up an old apple crate for a table and dragged a chair in from the office. With me sitting outside the cell, and Mac sitting on the bed inside the cell with his arms through the bars, we played checkers until it was time for me to make my rounds at the afternoon shift change.

When things quieted down and the saloons were mostly empty, I stopped by Emma's to get two plates of grub and went back to the jail where Mac and I dined together. Him in the cell, me outside.

For the next two days, when I wasn't working or sleeping, I spent my time with Mac playing checkers. Of course, we did a whole heap of talking.

About an hour before the afternoon shift change on the seventh day of Mac's most recent incarceration, we were playing checkers, and I felt that I knew him well enough to ask him a question that I'd been thinking on for a spell.

"Mac, there's somethin' I've been meaning to ask you. How do you feel about killing Ed Trask?"

Had I not noticed his left eye twitch slightly, I would have thought he hadn't heard me. He was about to make a move when I proffered my query. Without missing a beat, he jumped my piece and removed my red checker. Then he slowly leaned back some, looked me straight in the eye and said, "I feel bad about it. Hell, I didn't even know I done it until the next day in the mine. Men were talking about it when they thought I couldn't hear 'em."

After having said his piece, his very big shoulders sagged and he hung his head.

Thinking it was best to leave him to himself for a while, I started to walk out, but his head came up fast, and he asked me to stay. He said he wanted to talk about it. So I sat back down and waited; there was nothing for me to say. After a minute or two, he stood and started to pace back and forth as much as the small cell would allow.

"You know, Huck, since I found out I killed Ed, I ain't been right. I liked Ed. It's just that when I git to drinkin', I git a mite ornery. But I never did kill a man before."

He stopped his pacing, came over to the bars and grabbed one in each hand, a little above his head; there were tears flowing down his cheeks and into his black beard. He stood there and cried like a little child. Then I knew what he wanted . . . he wanted forgiveness.

Because Ed Trask was sheriff before me, I wanted to know as much about him as I could find out; I wanted to know how he did the job. Maybe he made mistakes and maybe he didn't, but whatever he did, I could learn from him. In the course of one of my many talks with the mayor, I found out that Ed had sent half his pay back east to his mother. According to Maxwell, he had no other kin. Maxwell had been the one deducting the twenty dollars from Ed's pay and sending the money to his mother each month. My point being that Maxwell knew Missus Trask's postal address.

I had come to like Mac or else I would not have done what I did next. I told him about Ed's mother and the monthly contribution that he made to her well-being. I told him that she probably needed the money or else Ed wouldn't have sent it. I asked him what he thought might become of her now.

He shook the bars with his large hands and shouted at me, "Nothin' gonna happen to her! I got me a grubstake rolled up in my bedroll back at camp. It's almost a thousand dollars. I've been savin' up nigh on four years now. I want you to send it to Missus Trask, but don't tell her where it come from; I don't think she'd accept it. Tell her that the town thought so much of her boy that they took up a collection. Then you can hang me, and I'll die a happy man."

The upshot was that I retrieved Mac's poke and gave it to Maxwell to send to Missus Trask along with a letter telling her how much the town liked and respected her son and that the money was their way of showing it.

When that was taken care of, there were two more things to be done. The first, buy a horse, a good, big strong horse, and a saddle. I found a nice looking bay at the livery stable and hitched it out back of the jail by my lean-to. The other thing that had to be done was set Mac free.

He had the checkerboard all set up when I walked in. I looked at it and then at him and said, "Not tonight, Mac. Tonight I thought you might like a little exercise."

I took him out back and showed him the horse. I told him there was a canteen and some jerky in the saddlebags and that I wanted him to get on the damn horse and ride west. "Go to California," I said, "and be careful of your drinkin' from now on."

He stood where he was and made no move for the horse. "I ain't never run from a fight in my life, and I ain't about to start now. I'm ready to take my medicine for what I done."

"This ain't a fight," I said. "It's what's best for you *and* the town. Hell Mac, they don't know what to do with you. They ain't got a judge, and no one wants to serve on your jury. They either have to let you go free or lynch you. Now, you done right by Missus Trask or as right as you can make it. You got a life ahead of you, and you might just do some good with that life. But you sure as hell ain't gonna do any good kicking air from an old white oak."

He still didn't move. I had to push him toward the horse. Finally, he took a step on his own and put his foot in the stirrup. But before mounting, he turned to me and said, "I ain't about to forget you Huck Finn. Someday, I hope our trails will cross agin, and I want you to know, as of now I ain't drinkin' no more. I'm gonna make up for the life I took." With those words, he mounted the bay and rode off into the night. I had forgotten to tell him of the hundred dollars in gold coin also in the saddlebags.

When 4:00 a.m. rolled around, I did my rounds of the saloons. You know, it was funny; there was never any trouble at the whorehouses. And even the saloons were peaceful now. I was told that no one wanted to have truck with the sheriff that locked up Mac Conroy. Things were just too peaceful to suit me.

At eight that morning, I met the mayor at Emma's for what was to be my last meal in Lamesa. I handed over my badge and told him that he didn't have to fret about Mac anymore. I confided to him what I had done and that I'd be riding out too. He tried to talk me into staying, but I told him the town couldn't have a sheriff that let prisoners go, and besides, I was looking for more of a challenge.

After saying good-bye to Miss Emma and thanking her for her fine food, I saddled my horse and headed north, but I never did make it back to Missouri. I got other jobs as a lawman over the years. I even worked for Bill Brady for a spell; he who became famous—or infamous—in the Lincoln County War. Sometimes I was a sheriff or marshal, and sometimes I worked as a deputy. I did time in Abilene, Dodge, Ogallala and Durango to mention just a few. Not all towns had need of my services, but I honed my skills a little in each place I found work. My reputation grew, but I wish it hadn't because the more well-known I became, the harder it made my job. There was always some young gun slick who wanted to make a name for himself by killing the fast gun Huck Finn. Then, in the summer of '73, all that I had learned through the years was put into play when I rode into Redemption, Colorado.

ELEVEN

The boy rode north, headed for the jumping-off town of Westport, Missouri. From there he hoped to hook up with a wagon train going to the Promised Lands of California. However, he did not know that it was too late in the season. The trains had to leave in the spring if they were to make it over the mountains before first snow, and here it was the end of summer. Without a train to attach to, he outfitted and hit the trail by himself.

The trail was easy to track; all he had to do was follow the wheel ruts of the wagons. He had heard that if he stayed on the trail, he would find a few trading posts along the way. He had his sacks of beans and coffee with him, and some dried fruit to ward off scurvy. For meat, he had to depend on his long gun. There were jackrabbits, prairie chickens, and once he shot a buffalo calf and cut out a slab that lasted him four days. His horse dined on the sage and grass of the prairie. At night, he would hobble his horse, lay out his bedroll in the tall grass, and fall into an exhausted sleep under uncountable stars.

On the fifteenth day out, he turned seventeen years of age. On the nineteenth day, he crossed the South Platte River headed for Fort Laramie. He never made it. Twenty miles north of the river, he came across a watering hole. He should have filled his canteen when he crossed the

South Platte, but it took a long time to find a place to ford. His mind was on putting miles behind him before dark, which made him forget about his canteen. The small cottonwoods that surrounded the water hole drew his attention; he knew he would find water there and it looked like a good place to bed down for the night. Thus his fate was sealed.

He unsaddled his horse and filled his canteen. Taking a long pull from it, he sighed with satisfaction. It had been a long, drawn out day. He had covered many miles; there would be no hunting this night, he was too tired. He settled for some cold beans and bedded down. Unbeknownst to him, the deadly cholera bacteria had contaminated the water he drank.

A few hours later, awakened by violent pains in his stomach, he turned on his side and vomited. That was all that he could do; he vomited until there was nothing left to regurgitate. He then fell back, drew his knees to his chest, and wrapped his arms about them. The pains were getting worse and he cried out. Feeling cold, he drew his blanket tight about him. It was the last conscious thing he did. The next morning when the sun slanted through the cottonwood trees and the shafts of sunlight fell on the boy, he was still alive, but barely.

The land along the Sweetwater-Platte plain and along the north fork of the Loup River belonged to a band of the Pawnee Nation known as Republicans, though they referred to themselves as *Chaticks-si-Chaticks* or Men-of-Men. On that morning, as the boy lay dying, a small hunting party was passing the grove of cottonwoods. A single brave saw the hobbled horse among the trees. With a whoop and a holler, he spurred his pony in that direction. Of course, the others in the party looked to see what all the fuss was about; when they saw the horse, they too trotted their ponies over to the trees.

An Indian family's wealth is measured by the number of ponies they own. To find a tamed horse, and a good-looking one at that, was good fortune indeed. The brave that first saw the horse stood on the ground and inspected his find. The other braves, still on their ponies, spoke of their friend's good fortune. One brave, the youngest of the lot, noticed the boy curled up on the ground, off to the side. With a stammering exclamation, he informed the others of *his* discovery. The horse was forgotten, and all crowded around the boy.

After an initial hesitation while they looked the boy over and prodded him with the toes of their moccasins, the discussion began. Some were for taking his horse and guns and leaving him where he lay. Two of the braves wanted to kill him right then and there, saying that all white men were bad medicine.

The young brave who had first spotted the boy said nothing as he listened to the talk; his name was Gray Wolf. He was of fourteen winters, three years younger than the boy lying on the ground. Finally, Gray Wolf spoke, "He is mine as the horse is Black Bear's. No one will kill him, and I will not leave him here. I will make a drag for my pony, and will bring him back to our village. He may die before I get him there, but if he does not, Running Fox, our medicine man, will save him if *Sakuru* wills it." That was the end of all discussion. Black Bear unhobbled the horse. Two braves fought over the boy's guns, but finally settled the matter by each taking one. No one wanted the saddle. The hunting party rode off to the northeast, leaving Gray Wolf with the nearly dead Jed Bevins.

Before the braves made a mile, Gray Wolf had a branch cut from a tree and in short time, he had his pony drag. He put Jed onto it and started for his village.

As Gray Wolf entered the village, the women stopped working and stared at him; the children ran alongside his pony asking questions about the white man. The men, for the most part, ignored him. He rode to the medicine man's lodge. Running Fox was standing outside waiting for him.

"I have been told of your white man and that you have said I would save his life if *Sakuru* wills it. Is that not so?"

Gray Wolf hesitated before answering. After all, he was of only fourteen winters, and the man who stood before him was the much-respected medicine man of his band. Running Fox had cared for his people for many winters, even before Gray Wolf was born. Then Gray Wolf remembered something Running Fox had told him when he was but a child.

"Yes, Running Fox, I did say that you would save this man. I want you to save his life, if it can be saved, because of what you have taught me."

Running Fox was taken aback by Gray Wolf's statement and asked, "What have I said to make you think I would save a white man's life?"

"When you prepared me for my vision quest, you taught me that *Sakuru* lives in all. He lives in the animals, in the trees, in the blades of grass. You told me he lives in the rocks and the dirt of the earth. He lives in all men, you said, even our enemies the Blackfeet and Crow. If he lives in all, then he must surely live within this white man."

Running Fox had lived many winters, and it had been a long time since he felt shame. But here was this boy reminding him of his beliefs. One either walked the path of one's beliefs, or one was not a truthful man.

"I do not know if he can be saved," said Running Fox. "He looks to have a white man sickness that I know nothing of, but we will take him to your lodge and see what can be done." As it turned out, there was nothing Running Fox could do. It was Jed's own young, strong body that shook off the disease at Death's door.

Two days later, Jed opened his eyes for the first time since being brought into the village. He was weak and disoriented. Lying on his back, he looked around the tipi trying to figure out what had happened to him and where he was. The last thing he remembered was bedding down for the night under the cottonwoods. Just then, Gray Wolf walked in. He smiled when he saw that Jed was awake. "Would you like some water?" he asked.

Jed did not understand what the Indian had said; he just lay there befuddled. Gray Wolf went to the skin holding the water, poured some into a small wooden bowl, and handed it to Jed.

Up until that moment, Jed did not realize how thirsty he was. He took the proffered bowl and gulped down the water. Handing the bowl back to Gray Wolf, he said in a hoarse voice, "Thanks." Which, of course, Gray Wolf did not understand, but he assumed the meaning and smiled as he received the bowl.

Jed made a slow recovery, but two weeks later, he was out walking in the village, nodding to people as he passed them by. He was living with Gray Wolf and his mother. Gray Wolf's father had been killed two winters past when a war party of Blackfeet raided their village.

During his third week among the Pawnee, Jed found out what had happened to him, and how he had ended up in an Indian village. An old French fur trapper by the name of Henri Lelièvre who had traded with the band for years was passing through on his way to Fort Laramie, and had acted as an interpreter. Jed also learned about his horse and outfit and what became of them. While Lelièvre was in the village, Jed was invited to stay for as long as he liked.

Thinking he would stay for a short period while he recuperated, Jed accepted the offer. It was then that his horse and guns were returned to him. The Pawnee stole from their enemies, never from friends. The next day, he and Gray Wolf went to retrieve his saddle. Jed wanted the saddle for more than the obvious reason. Hidden within it were the remaining gold coins his friend, Huck, had given him.

With the saddle on his horse and the gold in his pocket, Jed, accompanied by Gray Wolf, went up to Fort Laramie where he bought a goodly amount of ammunition for his long gun and his six-shooter.

"You planning on starting a small war with all this ammunition?" asked the fort's trader.

Jed liked being with the Pawnee and decided to stay as long as he was welcomed. He had a good ear for their language, and in a short time could converse in it fluently. Moreover, his hunting skills with his long gun made him popular when he accompanied hunting parties.

Jed had been with the band five moons when he was asked if he'd like to go on a raiding party. He readily accepted. By that time, his clothes had turned to rags, and he had discarded them for a breechclout, leggings, and a deerskin shirt. His hair, which was the color of corn, had grown out and was plaited into two braids with strips of rawhide.

The band, and Gray Wolf in particular, had saved his life and given him a home; he was not about to disgrace himself in his first battle. He charged right in with his six-gun blazing, killing three enemy braves right off. When his gun was empty, he attacked with a tomahawk, killing another two braves before the Blackfeet retreated. That night his coups were talked about in hushed tones around the fires. After that the years slipped by.

Six years, almost to the day, that Jed had first come to the village, he walked into the lodge to find Gray Wolf packing for travel. Jed still lived with Gray Wolf and his mother; they had become a family.

"Are you going somewhere?" Jed asked.

"Yes, I am going to visit relatives over to the Platte. My uncle and my cousins live there. Do you want to come along?"

"I would like to, but I just came back to get my guns. I promised Two Bear I would go hunting with him today." Jed retrieved his guns and wished Grey Wolf a good visit.

The hunting went well and that evening Jed and Two Bear brought back a good-sized buck deer. Being tired, they decided to skin and dress it in the morning. Jed returned to his lodge as Gray Wolf's mother, Moon Woman, prepared the evening meal.

"Hello Mother," said Jed.

"How was the hunting?"

"We will be eating deer meat for a while."

They ate a simple meal that night while Jed told of the day's hunting. Then they lay on their buffalo robes and slept, one of them for the last time.

TWELVE

The next morning, an hour before sunrise, thirty-one men assemble three miles from the Pawnee camp. The leader of the group sits astride a white gelding. He wears the uniform of a colonel of the Confederate Army, although General Lee had surrendered two years before. His name is Zacharias Cantry, formerly of Savannah, Georgia. Before the war, he served as a captain in the Union Army, but resigned his commission after Fort Sumter. Now that the war is over, he has come west to start a cattle ranch. His brother is collecting stray longhorns down in Texas and will be driving them up the trail; they are to rendezvous on the Platte. There is only one problem. A small band of Pawnee occupy the land where Cantry wants to establish his ranch.

The morning star and a crescent moon hang low in the eastern sky as Cantry speaks to his men. "Most of you rode with me during the war, so you know what I expect from you. We are here to build an empire and to do so, we have to be tough; tough as the country is big. There is an Indian camp where we are going to graze our stock. They think it is their land, but we white men have a manifest destiny to civilize this continent. To do so, the savage Red-Man must be driven from this land. In a few minutes, we will ride out and attack the Indian camp. We will kill every damn Indian in the village, and anything of value that you men find you may keep. Call it the spoils of war. Now, are there any questions?"

There are no questions. The men had followed Cantry west after the war because things just weren't the same. They had become enamored with the fighting and the bloodshed. They are violent men who enjoy killing. For his part, Cantry recruited his men one by one in the final months before Appomattox. Even then, he held a vision of an empire. An empire built upon the ownership of vast tracts of land. His family's plantation had been ransacked and then confiscated by Sherman's army on their march to the sea. Cantry has vowed never to be without land again, lots of land. Hence, he came west with his men to a place where land was ripe for the taking . . . if one was strong enough to take it.

Three miles to the west, the Pawnee sleep. The first sign of trouble is the sound of hoof beats heard through the ground. The sound is faint, but a few are roused from their sleep. As the hoof beats become louder, they can be heard through the air. Those who are awake rouse the others. It must be an attack from an Indian foe, perhaps the Blackfeet or maybe the Crow.

Before anyone is fully awake or can take action, the bullets come ripping through the skins of the lodges, killing many people. Cantry's men ride into the village firing from horseback at the people as they flee their tipis. A few of the attackers jump from their horses and butt children in the head with the stocks of their rifles, splitting the children's skulls.

The colonel sits his horse at the edge of the village with both hands on the pommel of his saddle watching the slaughter with a smile upon his face.

Torches are lit and passed around. Five men are detailed to set fire to the tipis while the others go about the business of exterminating anyone within sight. A few braves are able to get off a handful of shots. More than one of the attackers has an arrow sticking out of him, and a few have bullet wounds. However, the meager defense is to no avail. The band consists of sixty people, mostly women and children. Of those in the camp that morning, all are slated to die. All save one.

• • • • •

Jed awoke with the sound of the first gunshot; he thought the Blackfeet were attacking. He grabbed his long gun and strapped on his six-shooter, but before leaving the tipi, he turned to Moon Woman to tell her to stay inside. The words were barely out of his mouth when a bullet smashed into the back of her head and exited through her right eye. She was dead before she hit the skins on the floor of the tipi. Jed went to her. He had no doubt that she was dead, but it was something he had to do.

Going to the entrance of the lodge, he pulled back the skin and raised the long gun to his shoulder. He sighted a raider, fired, and saw the man stiffen in his saddle then fall to the ground. Before he could reload and fire again, a bullet creased his head and he fell backwards into the tipi. As he lay unconscious, the tipi was set afire, but luck was with him that day. Well, if not luck then it was something. The fire had been set at the base of the tipi and had burned only halfway up before going out. The burnt lodge poles collapsed, toppling the upper portion of the tipi onto Jed's recumbent form, thus saving his life.

When all the Indians were thought dead, the raiders went from body to body, disfiguring each one because Indians believed you traveled into the next life with your body looking as it did when you left this life. Cantry was sending a message to other Indians in the vicinity. *Stay off my range.*

Though all the people had been killed, their dogs had been spared. At first, the dogs were under foot as the men went from tipi to tipi looking for plunder. However, no plunder was to be found. There were a few old muskets, a ring here and there taken from a dead woman's still warm finger. What is valuable to an Indian—things like blankets, metal tools and cooking pots—are worthless to a white man.

When it became evident that there was nothing of value, and seeing as how the dogs were making a nuisance of themselves, one man—out of frustration more than anything else—took out his revolver and shot two dogs.

When the other men saw what he had done, they too took to shooting dogs. When they had finished, more than one hundred dogs lay on the ground dead or dying.

As the sound of the gunfire faded, Cantry rode up and said, "Now that you men have had your fun, let's ride back to camp. You've done a good morning's work. The drinks are on me." He was pleased that he lost only one man, the one Jed had shot. A few were wounded, three by gunfire and four with arrows. The raiders had been there less than two hours, and now sixty Indians lay dead before them. Cantry was a very happy man.

One of his men asked about the Indians' horses. The horses had scattered when their rope corral was torn down, but a few were still within sight. Cantry said to leave them be. "They're Indian ponies; they don't take to white men."

The thirty-one rode east . . . one slung over his saddle.

Jed came around in the late afternoon; the skins of the tipi covered him. At first, he thought it night. He tried to get up, but the lodge skins impeded his movement. Then the horror of the morning came back into his memory. He got out from under the collapsed tipi and looked around. He beheld dead bodies and a destroyed village. His head hurt where the bullet had cut a furrow. Dried blood covered that side of his face. He knew white men had done this terrible thing, but he knew not why. He could not think straight, it made no sense. Nevertheless, he had things to do. Soon it would be dark, then the wolves and coyotes would come. He had to protect the dead from being torn apart and disfigured more than they already were.

Jed collected all the lodge poles that had not burned completely and put them in a big pile. Then he dragged the dead and placed them around the pile of wood. He did not drag Moon Woman; he carried her in his arms and laid her gently on the ground by herself, away from the others. When dark came, he would build a great fire and tend it throughout the night. No wolves would touch his people this night. But he would bury Moon Woman before doing anything else. There was a shovel and a pickaxe in the village that had been community property. First with the pick and then with the shovel, Jed dug Moon Woman's grave. It was only four feet deep, but deep enough to keep the wolves from getting to her.

Afterward, Jed walked the edge of the village looking for the raiders' tracks. When he found them, he saw that they had come from the east and went back the same way. He then went to collect as many of the ponies as he could before dark.

Jed sat at the fire that night surrounded by death; he had nothing to do but think. As the night wore on, he came to a decision. He was going to track down every last man that had anything to do with the slaughter. He didn't care if it took him the rest of his life. When the dead were buried, he would cut his braids and go to Fort Laramie to buy clothes with his last gold eagle. The one he had kept for luck, and as a remembrance of his friend Huck Finn. For what he was about to do, he had to do as a white man. But first, the dead had to be attended to.

The next morning Jed set about his sorrowful task. He put two bodies in each grave. The children were buried three or more to a grave. He had to do it that way or else he would not finish by nightfall.

Gray Wolf returned the day after the burials, and Jed told him what had happened. He told Gray Wolf he was going to track down the murderers and kill every last one of them. Gray Wolf said he was going along too.

At first, Jed tried to talk him out of it. "I'll most likely have to go into the towns of the white men, mix with them in their saloons, and listen for talk of what has happened here. Men who could do something like this are men who will like to talk of it. You can't go into a saloon with me. And if you killed a white man, for whatever reason, they'd hang you before you could say a word." But Gray Wolf was insistent; these were his people that were killed, and with or without Jed, he was going to track down the killers. Jed was thinking that they were his people too, but said nothing. He knew that Gray Wolf was distraught.

In the morning they rode north to Fort Laramie.

They did not report the massacre to the soldiers at the fort because they knew no action would be taken. That was all right, Jed and Gray Wolf would take whatever action they deemed necessary. Once outfitted with clothes for Jed and ammunition for the two of them, they rode east to pick up the tracks of the killers.

About the time Gray Wolf and Jed reached the fort, Cantry and his men were tracking south. The plan was for some of his men to rendezvous with the drive coming up from Texas. The rest would go into Colorado Territory. Cantry wanted to scout a location for a second ranch just in case there were repercussions from the slaughter. Besides, he didn't want to be in the vicinity when the bodies were discovered. Even though he believed there were no survivors, it would be known that white men were to blame because of the tracks of their shod horses. The Indians might have relatives that would want to avenge the deaths of their people.

Gray Wolf and Jed picked up the trail just east of where the village once stood. They followed the tracks until they came to where the murderers had camped. There they found tracks that showed the raiders were headed south. They tracked them until they came to a place where the trail split in two. Still going south were ten horses. Going off to the southwest were the tracks of the others. Jed could not read sign as well as Gray Wolf, but he could see that the leader was with the ones going southwest. The tracks showed that one man rode alone at the head of the column. Jed and Gray Wolf talked it over and decided to follow the ten going south. They would take care of them and then catch up with the others.

Jed and Gray Wolf traveled south. Near dark, they saw a campfire in the distance. It was the camp of the men they sought. Jed and Gray Wolf held back until full dark and then approached on foot. Both men wore moccasins and made no sound as they drew near the campfire. Just outside of its light, they halted and listened to the conversation. If there was any doubt that these were the men they were after, it was then dispelled. The murderers were talking of the horrors that were perpetrated at the Pawnee camp. It was a good thing Gray Wolf could not understand their words or he would have opened fire right then and there. Eight men sat around the fire. Two others were in their blankets, seemingly asleep.

Jed whispered to Gray Wolf, "Stay hidden and cover me with your long gun." Then Jed stood, took his six-shooter from its holster and walked into the firelight.

"Good evening, gents. What brings you to this neck of the woods?"

The men around the fire were startled; Jed had appeared out of nowhere, like a ghost. One of them went for his gun, but before he could touch leather, Jed raised his six-shooter—it coughed flame. The man took a step backwards, fell to his knees and pitched forward, face down on the ground, dead.

"Raise your hands slowly, boys. I've come all the way from Fort Laramie to talk to you. There are others out there in the dark that have you covered. If you want to live a while longer, you'll do as I say, but I'd like you to try something. Go for your guns, if you're feelin' lucky."

The men did not know what to make of the situation. One minute they were swapping stories and the next, one of their own lay dead. And a boy with a crazed look in his eyes was taunting them to draw on him.

Jed, standing there with the nine men covered, smiled. Hate was in his heart. Such a hate he never knew could exist. He wanted to cut them down where they stood. He had five rounds left, and Gray Wolf had a single round in his gun. If he and Gray Wolf hit all their targets—which wasn't likely, even though they were both good shots— that would leave three men standing.

One of the men looked to the ground. Jed noticed he was longing to get to his rifle, a Spencer repeater capable of shooting eight rounds a minute. He knew about the Spencer, but had never fired one. Jed called to Gray Wolf to come into the firelight. When the murderers saw the Indian, they knew what this was all about.

Gray Wolf covered the men while Jed walked over to the owner of the Spencer. Keeping his six-gun trained on him, he asked, "Is that your gun?"

The man was afraid to say anything, fearing that whatever answer he gave would be the wrong answer. He was right. Jed took a step closer to him and shot him in the chest. Before he hit the ground, Jed had holstered his gun and had the Spencer in his hands, pointed at the remaining eight men.

"My friend here," motioning to Gray Wolf with the barrel of the Spencer, "just had his mother killed and his whole village wiped out. You boys wouldn't know anything about that, would you?"

One man broke and ran. Jed got him in the back before the night swallowed him. The others went for their guns and Jed swung the rifle on them, levering a round as he did so. "First man that touches leather dies."

It was a stand-off. Jed figured he could get two, maybe three of them, and Gray Wolf would get one. But by then the others would have their guns out and lead would be flying. Jed could tell that the men were thinking along similar lines. The only reason bullets weren't flying already was that none of them wanted to be among the two or three that were going to take a bullet from the Spencer.

As Jed mulled these things over in his mind, he noticed that two of the men weren't wearing gun belts. That brought the odds down a bit. It would take a few seconds for those two to dive for their guns. So he had five heeled men to contend with. Before too much more time elapsed, there would be gunplay and everyone knew it.

144

With a sigh, Jed took a step backward. In Pawnee, he told Gray Wolf to take the six-shooter out of his holster. That would give Gray Wolf four shots. He had seven left in the Spencer. At least he hoped he did. A man who didn't keep his gun fully loaded was a fool. Jed would try for the four bunched together on the other side of the fire. He told Gray Wolf which three he should take.

Jed started the shooting, and Gray Wolf followed suit. Their targets were too close to miss and the men they were shooting at weren't gun slicks; they fired in haste without taking aim. As Jed shot his third man, the man's gun went off. A bullet plowed into Jed's right shoulder and spun him halfway around, but he kept on his feet. When he turned back, he was looking into the barrel of a six-shooter. When Jed heard the click of the hammer being cocked, there was nothing to do except wait for the explosion. It didn't matter, his home had been destroyed. Everyone he knew, with the exception of Gray Wolf, was dead. He did not care if he lived or died. He had come a long way in miles and in time from the boy who, at the Lee farm, shook with fear of being shot, back those many years ago.

The explosion—when it came—did not come from the gun he was staring into as he had expected; it came from behind him. The man standing before him had a surprised look on his face. He dropped the gun, and clutching his chest, he fell to his knees and then backward, dead.

Jed turned to see Gray Wolf holding in his hand a six-shooter he had taken from one of the dead men. Gray Wolf had emptied Jed's gun. Jed smiled and waved, then turned back to assess the situation. First, he opened his shirt to check on his wound. It was bleeding, but it didn't hurt too badly. It was a clean wound. The bullet had passed through his shoulder without hitting bone; he would attend to it in a minute.

Jed surveyed the camp. The dead littered the ground. One man had his hand lying in the fire and it was starting to burn. Jed left it there; the man would not be feeling anything. Then a thought struck him. They had tracked *ten* men. There were only *nine* bodies.

He turned back to Gray Wolf to ask if he knew where the tenth man was. Gray Wolf was lying on the ground, covering his stomach with his hands, blood seeping through his fingers. He had been belly shot.

Still holding the Spencer, Jed went to him and knelt down on one knee.

"I reckon you've been shot."

Through gritted teeth, Gray Wolf tried to smile, but the pain was too great. "I see from the blood on your shirt that you also have earned yourself a bullet."

"I have, but it's nothing. Let me take a look at your wound."

146

Gray Wolf shook his head and said, "No, we both know what a wound like this means. Do not waste your time. You have much to do. When the shooting started, one of the men ran away, the one wearing the red shirt. You must track him down and kill him. Then you must track down the others and figure a way to kill them. I suggest that you not walk into their camp as we did here. We both could have been killed, not just me." Again Gray Wolf tried to smile, and this time he did manage a slight grin.

Jed told Gray Wolf that he would not let him die. "You have saved my life twice now. Let me see the wound; I will take out the bullet and when you are healed, we will track down the killers together." Before Gray Wolf could say anything, they heard the beat of hooves. A horse was being ridden hard.

"That must be the one who ran," said Gray Wolf. "You cannot follow his tracks until morning when it is light. That will give you time to bury me so the coyotes and wolves will not eat me."

Jed shook his head. "I told you, I will not let you die!"

"I am already dead and we both know it. I am in great pain. It will be hours before I leave my body. Hand me that gun over there," said Gray Wolf, indicating a six-shooter nearby.

147

Jed did not move. He knew what Gray Wolf said was true. If he were really Gray Wolf's friend, he would accede to his wish. It took a few minutes for Jed to come to that conclusion, and when he did, he bent over, picked up the six-shooter that Gray Wolf had indicated and flung it out into the darkness. Only his own weapon would serve the purpose for what he had to do. Then Jed said, "You have my word that I will hunt down those who killed our people, no matter how long it takes. After I bury you, I will go on the trail of the one who just left. Once I have finished with him, I will go after the others." With a smile, Jed added, "I promise you, I will not walk into their camp without a plan."

Gray Wolf nodded. "I can now die knowing that my enemies are marked for death. But I will need the gun. I do not want to lie here and die slowly."

With tears running down his cheeks, Jed said, "My friend, what I owe you, I cannot repay. This is all that I can do." Jed picked up his six-shooter from the ground where it lay and slowly filled a chamber with ball and powder. Then he placed it against Gray Wolf's temple. Gray Wolf smiled and nodded. The gun bucked in Jed's hand, and Gray Wolf was at peace.

Six years later, the trail of the killers would lead Jed to Redemption.

THIRTEEN

I was sitting outside my office in Redemption, Colorado on a cool September morning. The chair was tilted back, my feet rested up on the rail. It had been a hot summer, and the cool morning air felt good. I like sitting here in the mornings when things are quiet. We're not a big town, only the main street, two side streets that run parallel, and four cross streets. We have some rough edges and there's a range war brewing, but I'm paid to keep the peace.

I was admiring Miss Jenny as she walked down the other side of the street. She had her shopping basket on her arm, so I reckoned she was on her way to Jim Niles' general store. She sure is a pert and pretty young thing. She has quite a following. Half the cowpunchers, when they come into town, go right over to the eating house where she works. The other half head straight for the saloons.

Jenny had just turned the corner when Johnny Davis came running up. "Marshal Finn, Marshal Finn!" he was yelling. "Pa wants you to come over right away. He says to tell you that the Laramie Kid is in town." Johnny's the ten-year-old son of Mike Davis who runs the largest saloon in town, The Silver Dollar Dance Hall.

I knew the morning was too nice and peaceful to last. The Laramie Kid was supposed to be bad news. I'd heard

149

tell of him, most folks have. They say he's a killer, that he has thirty notches on his guns and when he rides into a town, the first thing he does is go to a saloon and picks a fight with the fastest gun in town. In this town, that would be me.

Of course, I didn't put much stock in all that talk. A real gun slick doesn't notch his gun, and he doesn't go looking for fights. About the only thing I believed in all that talk was maybe he headed for a saloon right off. I mean, where else is a man supposed to get the dust of the trail out of his throat if not at the first saloon he comes to? But seeing as how I was the town marshal, I figured I'd better go and brace him and see what he was doing here.

I walked into The Silver Dollar and saw only three men, two at a table on the left and a single man standing at the bar. He wore two crossed gun belts and the holsters were tied-down. He had his elbows on the bar and held his glass with both hands, studying the liquid within. His back was to the room, but I could see his face in the mirror. It wasn't a mean face like I thought it would be. He was tall and thin, and he wore a drooping mustache the color of his hair, yellow.

We were both looking in the mirror and our eyes met. I was ready for something, but I didn't know what. He smiled and turned around fast, facing me. My hand went to my gun, but I did not draw. I was waiting for him. Then he did the dangest thing; he let out with a whoop and said,

"Huck, you old sonavabitch! I've been on the lookout for you nigh on three years now. I just kept missing you."

My first thought was that he was searching for me so he could add to his reputation. He wouldn't have been the first. But there was something not right. Over the last few years, I've had to face men who wanted to kill me just so they could say they were the one that killed Huck Finn. But this man was smiling and acting like I was a long lost friend.

Keeping my hand near my gun I asked, "What brings you to my town?"

He kept his hands far from his guns as he answered, "Don't you know me Huck? It's me, Jed, Jed Bevins formerly of the Union Army," and then he laughed.

You could have said that General Lee really did win the war, and I wouldn't have been any more surprised. I relaxed and walked toward him, and he took a step towards me. When we met, we shook hands instead of slapping leather like I figured we'd be doing a few minutes earlier.

When it became apparent that there was to be no shoot-out, Mike Davis came down the bar from where he was standing. I reckon he was staying out of the way of stray lead. "Morning Marshal, didn't know you and the Kid were friends."

"Mike, you got it wrong this time. This ain't the Laramie Kid; this here is an old friend of mine, Jed Bevins."

"Marshal," said Mike, "I was in Dodge when he shot it out with two saddle tramps. He goaded them into it, like he wanted to kill them and knew that he could. They all three drew at the same time, and when the smoke cleared, only the Kid was left standing. It was the dangest thing I ever saw, and I ain't likely to forget a man that can outdraw two men."

I looked over to Jed for an explanation. I was waiting for him to deny what Mike had said. Instead, he said, "Some call me the Laramie Kid, but it's not what I call myself. And there was a reason those two men had to die, but it's a long story. Let's get us a bottle of something decent and I'll tell you all about it."

After Mike gave us some of his private stock, and once we were seated at a table, I poured out two glasses and we toasted to old friends. Then he asked me about Tom; I told him of our going to San Francisco and Tom going on to China. He asked if I had heard from Tom since. "No, not since we said good-bye at the hotel."

"Huck, that was twelve years ago! You ever wonder 'bout him?"

"Yes Jed I have, like I wondered about you. You ever make it to California?"

152

He shook his head sadly and began telling me his story.

By the time he got to the part where he had to shoot his Indian friend, the saloon was filling up fast. It wasn't even noon yet, but the place was almost full. I reckoned word got around about the Laramie Kid being in town. At least it was good for Mike's business, and it was most likely him that passed the word around.

Because of the crowd, I suggested that we go over to the eating house and get some food into us to counteract the whiskey we'd been drinking. Jed thought it a good idea.

When Jenny had taken our order and placed two cups of coffee before us, Jed continued with his story, but only after watching Jenny walk back to the kitchen.

"After I tended to my wound, buried Gray Wolf, and set the murderers' horses free, I lit out after the one that got away. His trail was easy to follow, and I was about eight hours behind him. Late that afternoon, I was resting my horse on a bluff overlooking the trail when up from the south comes a herd of longhorns. I don't know why, but I backed into the trees so they wouldn't see me. I watched them pass, and dang it if I don't see ol' Red Shirt riding the chuck wagon just pretty-as-you-please. I reckon he thought he was safe among the drovers."

Jenny came with our food, and Jed again had to watch her walk away before he went on.

"I followed them for two days, stayin' out of sight. Once I got their routine down, I just waited for the man I was after to ride drag. It was easy to come up behind him and get a rope over him. I didn't want to use a gun and start a stampede. Well, I lassoed him right around the chest and pulled him from his horse. With all the ruckus the cows were making, no one heard him when he yelled. I took off due south dragging him behind my horse. I dragged him for miles. I would have gone right into Texas if my horse hadn't gotten tired. I slipped my horse and went back to check on him. There was very little left that resembled a man. But I didn't care; all I could see were those sixty bodies that I had to bury, mostly women and children, massacred and disfigured.

"Well, that's about it, Huck. After that I went back to try to find the trail of the twenty other murderers, but I couldn't find their tracks. I knew what direction they were headed and I went the same way. Before too long I needed money, so I took a job punching cows, and when I saved a small stake, I set out again to keep my promise to Gray Wolf. It's been like that for the last six years, work for a stake and then go hunting again. Every once in a while, I'd come across someone in a saloon telling of how he had helped massacre an Indian village. Sometimes there was only one, sometimes two. Once, there were three of them. Before they knew my intent, I always bought them a drink tryin' to get them to talk more. I wanted to know who was in it with them and who the leader was. That way I got me a few names."

Jed stopped talking for a minute to finish his food and ask Jenny for more coffee.

Before he could continue I said, "I reckon that's how you got your reputation. The word is that you go into a town looking to shoot it out with anyone with a fast gun. Now I see that you're hunting men, particular men, and *that* I can understand. But how'd you get the handle 'The Laramie Kid'? And how'd you get so fast?"

"Fort Laramie was the closest place to the village that white men would know. So when asked where I hailed from, I always said Fort Laramie. I got fast because I practiced a lot at night when I was punching cows. There was nothing else to do out there on the range unless I wanted to listen to the same old stories around the campfire."

We were both quiet after that. Until Jenny walked by and Jed asked her if she had any apple pie.

"Sorry mister, it's a mite late in the season for fruit pies. But the cook just brought some cinnamon muffins out of the oven and they're still warm."

Jed looked to me, but I shook my head. He asked Jenny to bring him two and added, "I don't get good home cookin' like this very often."

I smiled, remembering the boy that he was when we first met. Then I got down to business. "What brings you to my town, Jed?"

"I could say I was huntin' you. I've heard tell of the famous lawman, Huck Finn. I've asked about you in every town I've come to. Once or twice I missed you by days."

I replied, "Is that why you're here, to look up an old friend?"

Jed sipped his coffee, holding the cup in both hands, and smiled. "No Huck, I didn't know you were here. I have finally come to the end of my trail. Of the thirty-one men who attacked my village, I've killed twenty-six. I'm told four of them, when they heard I was hunting 'em, left the country. They could be in California or New York for all I know. But that don't matter at this stage in the game. Last winter I learned the name of the man who gave the orders. He's here abouts and I aim to kill him."

Jed had his say, now I would have mine.

"What's the name of this man?"

"His name is Cantry. I'm told he has a spread west of town."

"Yes, I know of him. His brand is the Slash C, and he's a bad actor. He's runnin' his herd on government grazing land, but he acts as though it's his land. He's run off more than one homesteader, but because he hasn't done anything in town, there's not much I can do. The range is on county land and we don't have a sheriff. There's a federal marshal that works outta Durango, but he only gets up here once or twice a year."

Jed was enjoying his cinnamon muffins and nodded as I talked. He wiped his mouth with a napkin and looked me dead in the eye.

"Don't need no sheriff, Huck. I'm ridin' out to his ranch when I'm done with these here muffins, and I'm gonna kill him." He smiled and went back to his muffins.

I was thinking the boy sure had come a long way since I'd seen him last. But he didn't know what he was up against. If he could ride out and kill the sonavabitch, I wouldn't mind. But he didn't know there were more than twenty gunmen on Cantry's payroll nowadays, the meanest of them, Tuck Cole.

"You know Jed, you told me about the men that came out here with Cantry after the war. And you killed most of 'em. But they were just men who thought they were tougher than they were. They could raid a sleeping Indian village and kill women and children. But when it came time to run men off their land, men who had fought in the war and knew how to use a gun, they drifted. When the

157

real fightin' started, they pulled out one by one and were replaced by some bad jaspers.

"And there's more going on here than you know. We got us a three-way tussle. There's Cantry, the sodbusters, and a man by the name of Bob McNally. He ranches to the south, and his cattle graze on the same range as Cantry's. It's Cantry's intent to run 'em all off."

By now Jed had finished his muffins and sat, arms folded, listening to me. So, as long as I had his attention, I went on.

"McNally's not a bad sort. I think he'd make peace with the homesteaders if Cantry was out of the picture. But I heard him say he'd be damned before he'd let Cantry make off with all the range land. And Cantry, he's gonna set his hired guns onto McNally *and* the homesteaders."

When Jed finished his coffee I said, "It's getting nigh on lunchtime, and this place will be fillin' up. Why not go to my office and continue this talk."

I insisted on paying because it was my town. Jed, after a brief argument, agreed to let me pay. We walked outside where there were a few gawkers in the street waiting to get a look at the infamous Laramie Kid.

Once I was comfortably installed behind my desk with Jed seated before me, I put into play something I had thought about while we ate.

"Jed, I've been at this marshal job in this town for only three months. I came here because I heard about Cantry and what he was doin' to the homesteaders. Someone tried to hire me to side up with Cantry; he wanted to hire my gun. But when the play was explained to me, I refused to sign on. I made up my mind then that I was gonna put a burr under Cantry's saddle and foil his plans."

Jed started to say something, but I cut him off. "Listen to me Jed. Cantry thinks he's the big bug in this neck of the woods. Now you ain't gonna get nowhere near him. He always rides with four or five hired guns. And he never goes no place without Tuck Cole. Cole is as fast as greased lightnin', maybe faster than you, maybe faster than me. Why not use your head? Get the lay of the land and then attack. Didn't they teach you at least that much at Yankee cavalry school?"

With a short laugh, Jed said, "They didn't teach us nothing; they just put us on our horses, pointed us in the right direction, and ordered us to go kill us some rebs. Like you Huck." We both laughed at that.

Then I got back down to business. "I don't care where the town limits end. I came here to fight Cantry because I don't like mudsills like him. I've been biding my time until I could figure a play. Now that you're here, I have an idea. Do you want to hear it?"

"If your idea ends up with Cantry dead, then I wanna hear it."

159

"Well, it's just this. I want you to be my deputy. Hold on Jed, hear me through. As lawmen, even if we're off our range, we can get Cantry. Remember, there's just the two of us and twenty of them. We're gonna have to outthink them if we want to make the prairie safe for the homesteaders."

Jed averted his eyes and said, "Who said I was in this for the sodbusters? I'm out to kill Cantry!"

"Jed, think back to how you felt when you rode into Mister Lee's yard that morning we met. That fat sergeant was the same type of man as Cantry. You have my word that Cantry is yours, but to get near him, we're gonna have to whittle down the odds some. Savvy?"

Jed looked like he was running it around in his head and then after a while he said, "Alright Huck, I'm your deputy. Now, what's the plan to whittle them down some?"

"We wait and see what develops."

"That's it?" he said, "All we do is wait and see what develops?"

"Yep, unless you got a better plan," I said.

"Nope, so I reckon I'll go along with yours."

"Then let's get started. Raise your right hand."

FOURTEEN

The seas were rough. The rain and sea spray were blowing in his face. He was cold and miserable. And to top it off, he was seasick. This sure was not what he envisioned when he set sail. They'd been out of San Francisco for ten days, and he had not seen the sun since day two. But Tom Sawyer did his work. It was not that hard except for the long days, twelve hours on deck and twelve hours below, every day, seven days a week. By the third day, he wished he had sailed as a tourist.

He'd been told by his fellow sailors that it would take sixty-one days to reach China. That was counting a three-day stopover at Hawaii in the Sandwich Islands to replenish drinking water and pick up some cargo. Sixty-one days if they had fair winds and a following sea, but the winds had not been fair, and there was no following sea. They'd been beating into the wind since they left San Francisco. At this rate, it would take six months to get to China. Tom had also been informed that it would take twenty days to reach the Sandwich Islands, but that wasn't going to happen either. Well, whenever they did get to Hawaii, Tom Sawyer had decided that he was going to jump ship and catch the next boat back to California.

Battered, with torn sails, the *China Express* limped into Honolulu Harbor thirty-seven days after leaving San

Francisco. Because of the damage to the sails and the depleted stores due to the storm, the captain announced that the ship would lay over for ten days, not the three originally planned.

Tom had to time his departure exactly right. If he jumped ship too early, men would be sent to bring him back, and if that happened, the remainder of the voyage would be more dismal than anything he had experienced thus far, if that were possible. Tom didn't think the crew would be allowed to leave the ship during the last twenty-four hours in port. The captain would not want to delay sailing to have to round up stragglers. So Tom chose to take his departure two nights before the ship was scheduled to leave. He would hide out in the hills until the ship was well on her way.

Luck was with Tom that night. As he had one leg over the gunwale preparing to slip into the water, the man on watch—for some inexplicable reason—went below decks. Tom, seeing his opportunity, scurried down the gangway and was out of sight and into the town before anyone knew he was gone. And he was dry to boot!

His plan was to hide out in the foothills of Leahi, the mountain he saw when they first entered the harbor. Even though he had almost four hundred dollars left in his poke despite his gambling losses in San Francisco, he could not stay at a hotel. It would be the first place they would look for him. Also, he had to get supplies. Not much, just a blanket and enough food to last him two days, food that would not have to be cooked.

Walking through the town, he came to a general store that was still open for business. It was late, but the store accommodated the ships that had to leave with the tide regardless of the time of day. Tom purchased his provisions and proceeded to find a suitable camping site, suitable meaning a place where he would not be seen. He found what he was looking for in the Nuuanu Valley. There was a gibbous moon that night and it gave off enough light for Tom to make his way through the woods and set up his camp. After living with twenty men below deck, he enjoyed the solitude.

The first day of hiding out, he walked a little ways up the mountain and sat on the trunk of a fallen tree. The view of the blue Pacific was extraordinary and wondrous. Tom sat there for hours until he became hungry and returned to his camp. After he had eaten, Tom wished he had a book to read, but as he did not, he lay down and went to sleep.

He awoke a few hours later as the sun kissed the horizon. He was lying on his back looking up at the branches of the tree under which he had made his camp. He turned on his side, and there stood a beautiful girl! She looked to be eighteen or nineteen years old, certainly no more than twenty. Her skin was light brown, her hair long and black. When she moved her head, her hair shone with waves of light like waves of wind traveling over prairie

163

grass. Her face was the face of an angel; she had high cheekbones and a strong chin. Her eyes were slate gray. Tom had never before seen such striking eyes on a girl. He thought that he must be dreaming and said so aloud, "Am I dreaming?"

The girl smiled at Tom and answered, "You are not dreaming. My uncle has sent me to invite you to our house for dinner. He says it will storm soon, and you would be unhappy out here huddled in the rain. My name is Kalei O'Day. In your language Kalei means flower, and remember, it's pronounced *Ka-Lay* not *Kay-Lee*. I don't like being called Kaylee!"

Tom stood up, and as the fog of sleep dissipated, he took in what the girl had said.

"How did your uncle know I was here? I have seen no one."

"You are on our land. We live to the east of here. We heard you when you passed close to our house last night. You are welcome to stay if you like, and we would not have intruded except for the storm."

Tom started to say something, but Kalei cut him off. "Come, I have been gone long enough. I stood watching while you slept because I did not want to wake you, but now that you are awake, we must go. My uncle will worry, and the storm fast approaches."

Tom shrugged, collected his kit, and followed the girl. It was good of her and her uncle to allow him on their land, and it was good of them to offer shelter from the storm. He would go with her without further comment; he was sure his questions would be answered in time. Questions such as what did she mean by "your language" when she spoke English better than he did? And how did she and her uncle know a storm was coming? There were only a few clouds in the sky, and they were off to the west where the sun had just slipped into the sea.

Presently Tom saw a light through the trees. "We are here," announced Kalei.

The house was rectangular, a little longer than a train car and wider by half. There was a small porch attached to the front, the front being the end facing the sea. At each end was a door that stood open. The doors were aligned with one another. There were three windows on each side with no glass, but each had an awning that was propped open with a stick. When the stick was removed, the awning fit tightly into the window. At a later time, a house of that sort would be known as a *shotgun house*. One could stand at the front door and fire off a shotgun and the buckshot would go through the house and out the backdoor without hitting anything.

They entered by the front. To his left Tom saw a man at a counter cutting up something and putting it into a pot. To his right stood a stone fireplace; a little further along

165

sat a round table with four chairs arranged around it. Beyond that, a curtained partition that Tom later learned separated the front of the house from the sleeping quarters.

When they came through the door, the man stopped what he was doing. After wiping his hands on the apron he was wearing, he stuck out his hand to Tom and said, "Hello, my name is Makaio. Welcome to our humble home."

Introducing himself, Tom shook the man's hand and said that he was very grateful for the invitation to dinner.

Makaio turned to Kalei and said, "Make our guest comfortable at the table, and pour him a little wine to work up his appetite."

Tom was looking around for a place to store his kit when Makaio told him to put it against any wall where there was space.

After he was ensconced at the table with a strange but good-tasting wine of a golden color, Tom saw something that had initially escaped his notice. Both sides of the room were lined with bookshelves, and they were filled to capacity with books of all sorts. Tom stood, with wine in hand, to peruse the selection; Kalei and Makaio were in the kitchen area preparing the repast. There were a few books whose titles he recognized, such as *Count of Monte Cristo* and *Robinson Crusoe*, two of his favorites. However, most of the titles were unfamiliar to him.

"You enjoy reading?"

Tom turned to see Makaio smiling at him, with a glass of wine in his hand.

"Yes I do," answered Tom.

Makaio went to a shelf and took down a volume. "I just got this a month ago. I'm pretty lucky in that I have a few captain friends that bring me books when they come to our island. That is how I built up my library." He handed the book to Tom saying, "This one was published only two years ago, and I already have a copy. It's a wonderful world we live in."

Tom read the embossed cover aloud, "*A Tale of Two Cities* by Charles Dickens."

"He wrote *Oliver Twist*. You ever read it?"

Tom was about to reply in the negative when Kalei came in and placed a platter of food on the table.

"Let's sit down and eat," said Makaio. "We can talk books later."

The storm broke before they were finished eating, and it reminded Tom to ask Makaio how he knew it was coming.

"When I was a young man, I broke my right leg. Now, when it is going to storm, I get a misery right where the bone knitted together. It works better than a barometer."

167

Tom remarked that it was lucky for him Makaio had the talent, because instead of sitting in a dry house eating a fine meal with pleasant company, he would be out in the rain with a sodden blanket wrapped about him.

"We are happy to have you here with us. Are we not, Kalei?"

Kalei shyly smiled and nodded her head. It was then, in the candle light, that Tom first realized how truly beautiful she was. If he was not careful, he might find himself falling in love.

After dinner, while Kalei cleared the dishes, Tom and Makaio sat on the porch and watched the rain come down. Tom had his pipe going and Makaio sipped wine. They sat in silence, each lost in his own thoughts. At length Tom cleared his throat and said, "I reckon you're wondering what I was doin' on your land?"

Makaio finished the wine in his glass and answered, "No, I haven't given it much thought. I figured you had your reasons for not staying in a nice dry hotel room with a comfortable bed."

Tom shook his head and said, "Well, I didn't reckon on it raining like this, that's for sure." Then he told his story about starting out for China, jumping ship, and hiding out until the ship left. He concluded with, "Tomorrow the ship should be gone, and I plan on buying passage back to the States on the first boat that will take me. That is if I can afford it; if not I'll work my way back."

Makaio said nothing, but being a good host, he offered Tom another glass of wine.

"Thank you, Makaio. I would like some more wine. It's mighty good and it has a particular flavor, though I can't seem to place it."

"It's tomato wine. It takes me two months to make. But I always make enough for the year."

When Tom had his refilled glass in hand, he held it up to the light coming through the door and said, "You would think that tomato wine would be red in color."

"That," replied Makaio, "is why it takes two months to make. It's the racking, or refining as you would call it."

After sitting in silence for a while, Tom asked the questions he had wanted to ask since he first met Kalei. "Kalei said her name was O'Day and that English was *my* language, I reckon meaning that it wasn't hers. How did she come across a name like O'Day? She's not married is she? Is your name O'Day too?"

Smiling and keeping his eyes toward the sea, which was not visible through the rain, Makaio spoke. "No Tom, she is not married, and my name is not O'Day. You will not be able to pronounce it, but it's Kamehameha. Kalei's father married my sister. His name was Mike O'Day, a big

Irishman with an infectious smile who jumped ship about twenty years ago, like you did. But unlike you, he fell in love with the islands and wanted to spend the rest of his life here. He had no plan, but then he met my sister; they fell in love and they got married.

"I'm a fisherman, and Mike worked with me for a year. In his off hours, he built a house for him and his wife. But after Kalei was born, Mike wanted to branch out, you know, make his own way. They scrimped and saved for two years and finally had enough to purchase a boat that was big enough to make it between the islands and carry cargo and passengers. She was only fifty feet long, but she had a wide beam and she was yare. Mike named her the *Kalei*.

"The business grew slowly at first, but within a few years of ferrying people and goods between the islands, he had all the business he could handle. In fact, he could have used another boat, but Mike didn't want to be rich. He just wanted to be his own man doing what he loved. Next to my sister and Kalei, Mike loved the sea the most.

"When Kalei was seven, she started school, and sometimes when Mike had a short haul, he would bring her over here for me to look after so Halina, that was my sister's name, could go with him. They were never gone more than one or two nights."

At this point Makaio stopped speaking to sip some wine. Tom, not wanting to break the mood, said nothing.

Without looking at Tom, and with a heavy sigh, Makaio continued, "On a bright summer morning—I'll never forget it—Halina brought Kalei over and said that she and Mike were making a run over to the Big Island to pick up a load of coffee beans. They were to be gone only two days. An hour after they left, my leg started to hurt. It pained me like never before. I knew a hell of a storm was coming. When it broke, they would have been half way to Maui. Mike knew his boat and he knew the waters, so I wasn't too fearful for them.

"The next word I had of them was a week later. The boat washed up on the southeast shore of Lanai; their bodies were never found. Kalei has been living with me ever since. We are all the family either of us has."

Makaio had finished speaking, and Tom did not know what to say. As he was thinking of something appropriate, Kalei walked out onto the porch. Looking at the two silent men, she addressed Makaio, "Uncle, it is time for bed. I have fixed a place for our guest in the kitchen where he will be warm." Then turning to Tom she added, "I am sorry that you have to sleep on the floor, but we do not have an extra bed."

Tom grinned, and looked out at the rain before he said, "Your kitchen floor will be fine. I thank you for your hospitality, and you too Makaio. I will leave early in the morning and get myself a hotel room. Then I'll try to find a ship to take me back to the States. If I do not see you before I leave, I thank you again."

Makaio herded Kalei and Tom into the house and shut the door. He and Kalei walked to the partition, and Makaio pulled the curtain aside for Kalei. She bade Tom a good night and Makaio said, "As long as you are on the island, feel free to come and visit us. We still haven't had our discussion about books, and I'm sure Kalei would be pleased to see you again." Kalei flushed a deep crimson and retired. For his part, Makaio grinned and said, "Goodnight."

The place Kalei had prepared for Tom was next to the fireplace. After taking off his boots, he lay down and pulled the blanket over him. His last thoughts that night were of Kalei O'Day.

FIFTEEN

The next morning, Tom was up and out of the house before daybreak. He wanted to be away before he saw Kalei again; he did not trust himself where she was concerned. But it would not matter in a day or so. By then he would be on the high seas and headed for home.

Home? What home? He was never that close to his half-brother Sid. The house he lived in and owned in partnership with Sid, while comfortable, was too big for his taste. He would have sold it long ago if not for his brother, who, for his own reasons, did not want to sell. *Hell,* he thought, *When I get home I'll deed my half over to Sid. I should have done it long ago!* These were his thoughts that morning as he made his way down to the harbor to find a hotel room for himself.

After getting a room at the American Hotel and storing his gear, Tom set out for the wharf. He saw that the *China Express* was no longer in her berth and went about looking for a ship heading east. The first ship he approached was going to Boston by way of the Horn. At the second ship, a deckhand informed him she was leaving for San Francisco in two days' time. However, the captain had gone ashore and would not return for another three hours. Tom thanked the man and said he would come back then.

Tom returned to his hotel and seated himself in the lobby thinking he would wait out the time reading old newspapers from the States, but after ten minutes, he decided to take a tour of the town. As he walked, his thoughts kept returning to the night before and to Kalei. He remembered how beautiful she looked with the candle light reflected in her gray eyes. The way she laughed made him feel warm inside. He just could not get her out of his mind, try as he might. He was going home and he would never see her again. But why was he going back? What was there for him? Then a thought struck him that would change his life. *You know something, Tom Sawyer? You don't really want to go back to Missouri. This is a beautiful land and there is a beautiful girl a ways up that mountain. Where in tarnation do you think you're runnin' to?*

He turned around and went back to the hotel where he secured an envelope and some writing paper. Sitting in his room, Tom wrote to Mister Potter of the St. Petersburg Bank instructing him to forward his interest payments for the foreseeable future to him in care of the hotel whose address was on the letterhead.

With that task accomplished, Tom set out to explore the city. He had time to kill because he could not go back up the mountain until after sunset. He did not want to arrive before Makaio and Kalei had finished eating. That would not be polite. His Aunt Polly had taught him, if nothing else, that you do not go visiting people at suppertime.

That evening Tom went up the mountain bearing gifts: a bottle of good whiskey for Makaio, and for Kalei, flowers that he had picked himself.

They were happy to see him and bid that he enter and make himself to home. That is what it felt like to Tom Sawyer; he was coming home.

Tom and Makaio spoke of books well into the night. Makaio ran back and forth to the bookshelves grabbing volumes to show Tom a sentence or a passage that he thought Tom would enjoy or to make a point about something they were discussing.

Though Tom's mind was on the discussion, his eyes tracked Kalei as she tidied up the house and moved about. When she was through with her work, she sat down next to him at the table; that's when he had trouble following what Makaio was saying.

Makaio saw where Tom's true interests lay and stopped making his point about the book he was holding. Instead he said, "So Tom, you tell us that you are going to stay awhile, and I think that is good, but have you given any thought as to what you are going to do?"

"No Makaio, I haven't. I have a small income, but it's not enough for a man living in a hotel."

Makaio looked over at Kalei who seemed engrossed in the book she was reading, but he knew she was taking in every word. Speaking to Tom, Makaio said, "Let us go outside on the porch. You can smoke your pipe, and we can have a little talk." He wasn't sure, but Makaio thought he saw a tightening around Kalei's mouth when he made the suggestion.

Seated on the porch, Makaio came right to the point once Tom had his pipe going. "Tom, you remind me a lot of Mike O'Day in more ways than one. Why not throw in with me as he did until you get your bearings? I'm getting a little long-in-the-tooth to be hauling in those nets every day. At night, my shoulders are sore as the dickens. I'm not talking about wages either. You come in as a partner. If you work out, and I think you will, I'll cut you in for forty percent after expenses. And expenses aren't that much, just the upkeep of the boat and the nets."

Tom did not say anything right away. Not because he was hesitant to take the kind offer, but because he could not believe his good fortune. This would allow him to see Kalei every day, and she, if he was honest with himself, was the reason he was staying.

Makaio, mistaking Tom's silence for something other than what it was, hastily added, "You don't have to decide now. Think it over; sleep on it for a day or so. Then you can tell me of your decision."

His words brought Tom around and he said, "No, I don't have to think it over. I'd be proud to work with you. And if you'll have patience with me until I learn the ropes, I'll work for you like there's no tomorrow."

That is how Tom Sawyer became a fisherman. Makaio made the offer because being the wily old man that he was, he knew of Tom's interest in Kalei and thought she might also be attracted to Tom. Besides, she was nearing nineteen—it was time she was married. So Makaio thought he would throw them together and see what developed.

Tom moved into the house that Mike O'Day had built. It had not been lived in since Mike and Halina were lost, and it needed a little fixing up, but Tom was handy in that way. Tom would see Kalei every morning when he stopped by for Makaio. Then at night, after they sold the day's catch, he would eat with them. Sometimes, after dinner, Kalei and Tom would take walks, long walks. She would tell of her island and of herself. As time went on, she shared with Tom her innermost thoughts. And he would regale her with his adventures on the Mississippi, stretching the truth a little. On the nights when there was a full moon, or near to it, they would sit on a hill overlooking the Pacific and watch the waves roll in from the silver sea. On more than a few occasions, they held hands. Makaio had wanted to see what would develop between Tom and Kalei if they were cast in close proximity to one another. What developed was love. Still, it took Tom almost six months to work up the courage to ask for Kalei's hand in marriage.

Her answer, of course, was yes. "Uncle and I were beginning to despair of you ever getting up the nerve to propose. I knew I was going to marry you that second night you came back and said you were not leaving for the States. Uncle knew it too. You were the only one not sure." Then she kissed him. It was their first kiss, but it was all right because now they were engaged.

On a fine, sunny June day in 1862, in a little white missionary church overlooking the Pacific Ocean, Tom and Kalei were married. Kalei moved into the house of her youth and set up housekeeping. Tom would go fishing with Makaio six days a week. They would have their catch by noon and then spend the afternoon selling it. They never caught more than they could sell that day.

The next years were happy ones for Tom and Kalei. That is until the winter of '65 when Kalei gave birth to a stillborn girl. The doctor said she would not be able to bear any more children because of complications during the birth. But their love of each other soon brought the happiness back into their lives.

In the winter of '68, Makaio turned the business of catching the fish over to Tom, though they were still partners. At sixty-one, Makaio had gotten too old to fight the weather and the nets. However, he did meet Tom at the dock every afternoon, and together they would sell their fish.

The three of them, Tom, Kalei and Makaio, ate together most nights. Usually Makaio would visit his niece and her husband, but a couple of nights a week, Tom and Kalei would go to Makaio's house. Tom enjoyed those visits because there was always tomato wine on hand. Makaio still added to his book collection whenever he could, and Tom never knew when he might find a real gem on Makaio's bookshelves.

It was on a warm night in '72 while Tom was perusing Makaio's shelves that a certain book caught his eye. Pulling the book from the shelf, he saw that it wasn't a real book, one with a bound cover. This book had a paper cover, but that is not what caught his notice. It was the title: *Huck Finn in Six-Gun Justice.*

Immediately Tom turned to Makaio, who was seated at the table with his ever-present glass of tomato wine, and asked where he had obtained the book.

"A friend of mine off a ship gave it to me. He said it was called a dime novel. According to him, they're something new and they are very popular. Why do you ask?"

"I know this man Huck Finn; at least I think I do. There can't be two Huckleberry Finns on this man's earth. Do you mind if I borrow it?"

"Of course not. You know you always have access to my books."

Tom took the book home with him that night, and while Kalei slept, he sat at the kitchen table and read by lantern light. It was the dangest thing. The hero, Huck Finn, was a lawman taming the west single-handedly, at least according to the book. He would ride into a town that was almost as bad as Sodom and Gomorrah. The next thing you knew, the bad men were pushing up daisies on Boot Hill, and decent women could walk the streets again without fear of being molested, all thanks to Huck Finn!

It took Tom two hours to read the entire story, and when he was done, he sat back and smiled to himself. He didn't know if they were writing about his friend, it was a novel after all, but he sure would have liked to know how such a thing as Huck being the hero in any story had come about. He resolved to write to Mister Potter first thing in the morning asking for word of Huck. Huck had his money in Mister Potter's bank, so if anyone knew the goings-on of Huck Finn, it would be Mister Potter.

Because the States were now linked from coast to coast by the railroad, an answer to Tom's query arrived in record time, three-and-a-half months! In his letter, Mister Potter said he had not heard from Huck since the two of them left in '61. However, he knew Huck was in good health as of a few months ago. He enclosed the source of his information, a clipping from the local newspaper. It read as follows:

Local Boy Hero of the Dime Novel

By Edward Judson

(Abilene, Kansas) This reporter spoke today with former St. Petersburg resident, Huckleberry Finn. We spoke on the occasion of his being appointed town marshal after the unfortunate killing of Mike Williams by former town marshal, James Butler Hickok, also known as Wild Bill Hickok.

Mr. Hickok was defending himself from an assassination attempt by the gambler Phil Coe. Mr. Hickok returned Mr. Coe's fire, killing him instantly. However, one of Mr. Hickok's bullets went wide, hitting his deputy Mr. Williams, killing him also.

The town fathers, wanting a marshal who is quick with his gun but can also shoot straight, terminated Mr. Hickok from his position of town marshal and replaced him with Mr. Finn. Said town council member, Mr. Conrad Lebold: "If half of what we read about Mr. Finn in those dime novels is true, then we will have a safe and secure town where decent folk can walk the streets without fear of being shot down by one of their peace officers."

Approached for an interview, Mr. Finn was at first taciturn in his remarks. When advised that the reporter was from his hometown, he opened up a bit and answered a few questions.

As to what Mr. Finn thinks of his fame vis-à-vis the dime novels, he said, "I never read that kind of trash." Referring to the author of the dime novels, Mr. Finn stated, "I wish Mr. Buntline would mind his own damn business."

Responding to a question about his future plans, Mr. Finn said, "I just got this job. I plan to make this town safe for God-fearin' folk, and then I'll move on. There's a little town in Colorado that may have need of my services, but that will have to wait until I'm finished here."

Asked the name of the town, he enigmatically answered, "When I go, I'll go seeking redemption." Then he stood and withdrew his six-shooter from its holster and spun the cylinder to make sure there was a bullet in every chamber. There was. Replacing the gun in its home, he said, "Now if you'll excuse me, I have a town to protect."

Tom finished reading the newspaper account, leaned back and smiled. Who would have ever thought that his friend, Huck, would have ended up a famous lawman? But it was getting on to dinnertime and he was to meet Kalei at Makaio's house where they were eating that night.

Kalei and Makaio prepared the meal; Makaio liked to cook. Tom was relegated to the table where he kept up a running conversation with the two cooks. He took great delight in telling them about his friend Huck. He even interrupted their preparations to have them read the clipping for themselves.

After dinner, Makaio mentioned that his leg was hurting him something awful. "I'm afraid we're in for a big storm. I think you two young people should head for home now and batten down the hatches."

The storm, spawned by *El Niño,* the warm waters of the Pacific, would have been called a hurricane in the East. In the South Pacific, such storms were known as typhoons. This particular storm would have winds exceeding one hundred and fifty miles per hour by the time it hit the island.

As Kalei and Tom left for home, the first mild winds were coming ashore. There was no rain as of yet, and the two enjoyed the walk. They held hands as Tom told Kalei of his boyhood adventures with Huck. She looked to her husband as he spoke and realized, not for the first time, how very much she loved him. As for Tom, he never looked at Kalei that he did not thank his lucky stars she had consented to be his wife.

Just before they arrived home, the wind picked up and the first soft raindrops fell.

SIXTEEN

It has been a long day. Both Tom and Kalei are tired. As Kalei prepares for bed, Tom checks the doors and windows, making sure that everything is buttoned up tight. The wind has picked up and with the increased winds comes the rain.

They lie in their bed listening to the storm build in strength and fury. Kalei reaches out for Tom. She takes his hand in hers and says, "Tom, I'm worried."

Tom squeezes Kalei's hand and says, "It's just a summer storm. It'll be gone and out to sea before you know it."

"That's not what is bothering me, Tom. I've had this premonition all day that something terrible is going to happen. If anything happened to you, I wouldn't want to live anymore."

"Don't worry about me. When I'm out fishing, I'm never far from land; if there's trouble I can always swim in."

That is not what she means, but she does not know how to put into words the apprehension she is feeling. Instead, she strokes Tom face with the back of her hand

and says goodnight. Despite the storm, they are asleep in minutes.

A short while later, they are awakened by the sound of breaking glass. Tom sits up in bed and in the ambient light he can see Kalei's face, her eyes wide with fear.

"I'll see what happened," says Tom, "you stay here." He slips into his pants and lights a lamp. It does not take long to find the cause of the disturbance. A large branch from a tree has crashed through the parlor window and the wind and rain are blowing in through the open space. There is no way to board it up with the branch sticking through; it is too big to remove without going out into the storm and dragging it back outside. When Tom thinks of going outside, he realizes that the storm has more than doubled in strength since they fell asleep.

Then he hears other noises . . . creaks and groans. Holding the lamp over his head, he looks around the room. What he sees makes him go cold inside. The roof is rising an inch or two with the wind. It looks as though it could be torn off at any minute. Running into the bedroom, he tells Kalei to get dressed fast. He puts on his shoes and grabs two coats from the wardrobe. Throwing one to Kalei he says, "Here, put it on. We might have to go outside."

They go to the kitchen, sit at the table and hold hands while they listen to the storm rage. That awful noise. The rain beats upon the roof, and wind coming in from the broken window is blowing throughout the house. There is a loud CRACK! and then a tearing sound; the roof is gone! The full force of the storm now enters their home.

For a moment, Kalei and Tom are stunned. One minute they are sitting in their house and the next, for all intents and purposes, they are outside in the storm. The walls are still standing, but Tom is worried that if one or all of them should fall, they could be caught underneath and crushed to death.

As Tom is pondering if they should leave the house or not, the decision is taken from him. The far wall blows away. Tom grabs Kalei by the hand, and together they run out the kitchen door and into the full fury of the storm. The wind is so intense that Kalei is blown off her feet. If Tom had not had a firm grip on her hand, she would have been blown away.

Next to the house is an old banyan tree. Large and solid, it has withstood many typhoons and it will survive this one. Tom, dragging Kalei, seeks shelter from the wind in and among the crevasses of its mighty trunk. There they hunker down wrapped in each other's arms while the storm rages around them.

After what seems like days but is only hours, the storm abates. All is calm and the sun is shining. Tom takes his arms from around Kalei and stands. Reaching down, he extends his hand to his wife and helps her up. Together they stare at the devastation. Trees are blown over, branches litter the landscape and where their house once stood, now only a bare wooden floor exists. Their home is gone as well as everything else they owned.

They are thankful to be alive, but still—to lose everything. They walk over to the house or what is left of it. The house that Kalei's father built. The house that Tom has restored. The house that Kalei has made into a home. They walk up the three steps that used to lead into their home and step onto the bare wooden floor. There they hug and realize that as long as they still have each other, that is all that matters for the moment.

However, there is one thing that Tom and Kalei do not know as they stand out in the open. The storm that they thought gone out to sea is not a summer storm; it is a typhoon. As with all typhoons, this one has an eye. Unbeknown to them, they are standing in the eye of the storm as it passes. Soon, the inner wall of the storm will hit them with a vengeance.

Tom is telling Kalei that they will rebuild, trying to lift her spirits. He tells her of the enjoyment she will have in decorating their new house. "I have plenty of money in the bank; you can buy whatever you desire."

Those are the last words he will ever speak to her.

The wall of the eye hits them unawares. The wind and rain are back with a vengeance. Kalei is swept off her feet; she reaches out her hand to Tom and he grabs for her. Their fingertips touch and then she is gone. A gust of wind almost two hundred miles an hour has taken Kalei from Tom.

Tom runs after her. However, the wind is too much for him. It blows Tom along as it has Kalei. He cannot stay on his feet. He is blown into trees and dragged along the ground by the wind. Try as he might, he cannot stand. By now, his flesh is ripped and blood pours from the wounds. Then the wind picks him up and smashes him into a large tree. Just before losing consciousness, he whispers . . . "Kalei."

First one eye opens, then the other. There is a bird singing close by and the sun is warm upon his skin. He moves to get up and that is when the pain shoots through him. What is wrong? It looks like a beautiful day. Why is he racked with pain? Then the memory of the storm comes flooding back.

THE STORM! KALEI!

Despite the pain, Tom stands up. There seems to be no broken bones, but it hurts to breathe, maybe a cracked rib or two. The first order of business is to find Kalei. He sets out looking for her. The wind has ripped his shirt and coat from him and taken his shoes, but he walks on, calling her name. He makes his way over and around fallen trees. He walks in the direction the wind had been blowing, still calling her name. He is afraid Kalei is lying somewhere injured as he is injured, only far worse.

Eventually, he comes to a cliff. If she had been blown along in a more or less straight line, she would have been carried over the precipice. It is a fifty foot drop to the beach below. Tom does not want to think of that. Instead, he veers to the north, then inland, then south . . . all the while, calling Kalei's name.

After hours of searching, Tom works his way back to the cliff. He does not want to, but he has to go down to the beach. He knows if he finds her down there, she will be dead. He sees a path that leads down, and he follows it. Kalei is not there. He starts to make his way back to where their house once stood. Every inch of every foot of every mile along the way, he hopes and prays that Kalei will be there waiting for him.

She is not.

Totally spent and exhausted, Tom makes his way to Makaio's house. Maybe she'll be there.

She is not.

• • • • •

Makaio's house looked undamaged. He was outside dragging debris and placing it in a pile that he intended to burn later. When he saw Tom coming toward him, he dropped the large branch he held and ran to him. "I'm so glad to see you. I was over to your house, and when I saw what was left, I thought the worse had happened. I looked

190

for you and Kalei everywhere. I thought that you might have gone down to the town for shelter. By the way . . . where *is* Kalei?"

When Makaio asked about Kalei, Tom fell to his knees. He feared that she might be dead. That she had been blown over the cliff and out to sea. It was the first time since he started his search that he admitted to himself the possibility of not finding her alive. After a moment to collect himself, he said to Makaio, "I don't know where she is; I was hoping that she would be here. I've been searching for her all day. I'm going back to look some more. She might be lying somewhere injured. I just can't stop looking."

Tom asked for a pair of shoes and a shirt. When they were provided, he and Makaio set out to search for Kalei. They separated to cover more ground and searched until nightfall, but they did not find her. Tom wanted to continue in the dark, but Makaio persuaded him that such an endeavor would be fruitless. Besides, Tom was dead on his feet. His ribs hurt, and his wounds had not been attended to. So Makaio led him to his house, bandaged his wounds, and fed him. Tom fell asleep at the table before he had finished eating.

The next day, Tom and Makaio broadened the search. It wasn't until the sun was going down that Tom finally came to the realization that he was not going to find Kalei, alive or dead. She was gone, and all Tom could think of was that Kalei was lost because of him. He should have been faster reaching out when the wind caught her. He blamed himself for her death.

The town of Honolulu was badly damaged by the storm. There were many dead to be buried, and Tom volunteered for the burial detail. He could not sit and do nothing. Remembering the look in Kalei's eyes as she was taken from him was driving him mad. He had to do something. For a week, he buried the dead and helped with the search for survivors among the collapsed buildings. When everyone was accounted for, everyone, that is, except Kalei, Tom came to a decision. He was going to leave Hawaii. The memories here were just too painful.

Tom was living with Makaio and at dinner that night, he told Makaio of his plans. Their boat had been lost in the storm so there was no way for Makaio to make a living, even if he had been young and strong enough to haul in the nets every day. Tom said to Makaio, "I'm leaving the island, Uncle, to see my friend, Huck Finn. And I've made arrangements with Mister Dolan at the bank. I get three hundred and sixty dollars twice a year; that's seven hundred and twenty dollars every year. Because I could support Kalei and myself on what I made fishing, I never had to spend any of it and it's been building up for over ten years. There was over eight thousand dollars in my account. I took out two thousand for my passage to the States and to buy a horse and outfit once there.

"All the money left in the account is yours. Mister Dolan will give you whatever you need whenever you want it. Also, when I reach the States, I'm sending a letter to my banker in Missouri to continue to send the interest payments to the Honolulu bank, and Mister Dolan will deposit them into your account."

Makaio started to say something, but Tom interjected. "There's nothing to say, Uncle; Mister Dolan has his instructions. I cannot stay on this island, and I think you know why. I'm going to hunt up my old friend; the one that book was about. I'm not going to need much money to do that. Besides, I couldn't leave unless I knew that you'd be all right. So let's not have any talk about anything. Let's just enjoy your tomato wine. It's probably the last time I'll ever have any."

What Tom did not say was that he was going to Huck Finn because he wanted to be in a dangerous land where a man could be killed for looking at another man the wrong way. Tom Sawyer did not want to live very much longer, but only a coward would take his own life. However, there are many ways to die. A week later, Tom was on a ship, headed for Redemption by way of Abilene.

SEVENTEEN

Jed and I meet every morning at the eating house. It's the best place in town for a good meal, but I think Jed is more interested in Jenny than anything on the menu. This morning he was there before me and when I walked in, he and Jenny were talking.

"Howdy Jenny . . . howdy Jed, think you two could put off the confabulation long enough for Jenny to get me some coffee?"

Jenny flushed a mite then she smiled at me. "Sure, Marshal, we wasn't talkin' about nothing particular."

After I was comfortably seated and Jenny had left to get me some coffee, Jed said, "She's a fine girl; make some man a good wife."

I shook my head. "Jed, you've been my deputy for nigh on a month now. Every morning and most nights, we're in here eatin'. You see Jenny every day, and not once have you asked her to go for a buggy ride or anything. You know she's popular with the young studs in town and the cowpunchers too. But she hasn't taken up with none of 'em. Maybe she's waiting for you to ask her out."

"No woman wants a gunfighter for her man. And even if she did, I couldn't do it to her. I could be shot and killed at any time. There were a few men I had to kill who weren't on the raid that Cantry staged. They were just young cowpokes who thought they were fast and wanted to make a reputation for themselves by killing the Laramie Kid. No Huck, I think I'm destined to ride my trail alone."

"Well, if you think different in the next week or so, Hollister is having that dance over to his barn in two weeks. I know a number of punchers have asked Jenny to go to the dance with them, and she has turned them all down. I'm a mite older than you Jed, and though I might not know the way of women folk any better than you, I got me a feelin' Jenny's just waiting for you to ask her to the dance."

The subject of the conversation brought my coffee and took our order. They had eggs that day so we both had us some eggs and bacon. Eggs are hard to come by in a town like ours. When they're available, that's all you want to eat.

When we were alone again, Jed sipped his coffee looking at me over the rim of the cup. At length he said, "Huck, I know I've been here a month. And I know I gave you my word I wouldn't go up against Cantry until you gave the go-ahead, but I'm getting mighty tired of sittin' on my backside and playing at being your deputy. Things are too peaceful. Hell, you had things well in hand long before I showed up."

I took my time in answering. It ain't polite to speak with your mouth full. Or maybe I was just prolonging what I had to say for my own personal amusement. After swallowing my eggs I said, "You know, it's funny you should say that. I had a visitor last night, nigh onto midnight. It was Bob McGuiness; he's got him a homestead about five miles out. Seems like he had a visit yesterday from some jaspers that work for the Slash C. They told him he'd have till noon today to move off his land or be buried under it. It took him that long to come in because he was talkin' it over with his wife. Finally the missus said he should come in and speak with me."

Jed lost all interest in his food. He pushed his plate off to one side, leaned forward, and folding his arms on the table said. "You ain't funnin' me, are you, Huck?"

"Well now, you can see for yourself. I told him we would be out there well before noon. Thought we might try to reason with whoever the Slash C sends out."

"Then let's get us a move on!"

"Hold on young fella, I'm aimin' on finishing my eggs and I suggest you do the same. It might be weeks before we see their like again."

196

Jed and I rode up to the McGuiness homestead about eleven that morning. He was sitting on the porch with a Winchester across his knee and as we rode in, he stood. He saw who we were, turned his head a bit and said, "It's alright Martha, it's the marshal and his deputy."

By the time we reached the yard, they were both standing there shielding their eyes from the glare of the sun. Missus McGuiness was holding a scattergun.

I touched my hat, pointed to the gun she was holding and said, "Morning ma'am, you know how to use that thing?"

She didn't answer, but McGuiness said, "If any of that Slash C outfit comes within range of it, they'll find out if she can use it or not."

Jed laughed and said, "I'm glad we don't ride for the Slash C." Then we dismounted and walked to the shade of the porch. McGuiness pointed to a bench, telling us to take a load off. Then he asked his wife to get us some water. "Ya'all must be parched after the ride out here."

We drank the water and got down to business. We put our horses in the barn to get them out of sight. We decided that I would sit out on the porch and talk to the riders when they came; the others would stay inside. Then, just before things got serious, Jed would come out, and we'd play it by ear from then on. I didn't want the McGuinesses in the picture because then I'd be worrying about them. If too many riders showed up, well, they could cover us from inside.

We didn't have long to wait. Presently I saw the dust swirls, and soon four riders came into sight. They walked their horses up to the porch and the one on the far left spoke. "I see that badge, Marshal, but it don't hold no sway here. You're off your range. We're here to move some squatters offa Colonel Cantry's land."

I pushed my hat back and wiped my brow saying, "I didn't know it was his range, thought it belonged to the government. But it's kinda hot, boys. You wanna sit and talk a spell?"

The man who had first spoken turned, and to his companions he said, "Looks like the marshal's tryin' to be hospitable. But I reckon we don't need no talk; all we need is for them damn squatters to leave."

I figured I tried. "You gents mind tellin' me what you plan to do about the lady if she don't want to leave? You gonna plant her in the ground too?"

I got no response to my question, so I tried another. "You, the one that's doin' all the talkin', what's your name?"

"My name is no concern of yours, Marshal. And what happens here don't concern you none neither. Now why don't you ride off while you can? There's four of us and just you and that badge, and I don't reckon that badge is gonna be much help when the shootin' starts."

"I reckon you're right, but my deputy might be a small help." That's when Jed stepped out onto the porch. He was wearing both guns and they were tied down.

One of the men, the one farthest to the right, jerked back on his reins when he saw Jed, but his horse stayed in place. Then the talker said, "We're still four to two, and any way you slice it, you're gonna be dead if you don't drift now."

Jed took a step forward and looking the speaker square in the eye said, "It ain't gonna matter to you if we're dead or not because when the ball goes up, you're the first one I'm gonna kill." Then turning his head ever so slightly he said to the other Slash C boys, "I reckon I could get the rest of you coyotes by myself, but I should save at least one of you for the marshal. What you do you think, Huck? Can I have three of 'em?"

At the mention of my name, the man on the right backed up his horse a bit and said to the leader, "Stacy, this here's Huck Finn, and the other one is the Laramie Kid. I seen him in action up in Ogallala. I don't want no part of this. The colonel ain't payin' me enough to git shot up and killed."

Jed and I stood there waiting for them to make their play. You could see that Stacy, their leader, hadn't figured on us. He thought he'd just be running a farmer and his wife off their land. If they fought him, he'd probably kill them without too much thought to it. But now that it was his rear end on the line, he was having second thoughts.

I figured I'd help him reach a decision one way or the other. "Stacy, don't think otherwise; when the shootin' starts you will be the first to go down. Then my deputy and I will kill your partners at our leisure. So what's it gonna be? Make your play or ride outta here alive?"

You could see he was tryin' to find some way to save face, but in the end, his shoulders sagged and he said, "Reckon we'll ride."

He and the others started to turn their horses, but before they made the turn, I quietly said, "Stop." And as one, they froze, half turned.

"When I said ride outta here, I meant the country and without your guns. If you ride outta here alive, it's without your guns, and you keep going because if either me or my deputy see you again, we'll kill you on sight. So either shuck your guns or pull iron—I don't much care which." They were beaten and they knew it. They unbuckled their gun belts very carefully, and let them fall to the ground. Then Jed walked out and took the rifles from their scabbards.

When they were out of the yard and on their way, Jed asked me if I thought they'd go back to Cantry. I answered that knowing what I knew of Cantry, he'd have them horsewhipped for not moving the McGuinesses off their land. "No Jed. I think they're gonna hightail it outta this country. That will make sixteen hired guns that we're up against, not counting Cantry."

The McGuinesses came out of the house with big smiles on their faces. McGuiness said he was surely grateful and invited us to stay to dinner. I told him we couldn't stay; we had to get on back to town. I also informed him that the fight wasn't over yet, and it wouldn't be over until Cantry saw reason or was run out of the country . . . or he was dead.

On the way back to town, Jed asked if I thought any of the other homesteaders might be getting a visit from Cantry's men.

"I don't think so. I've studied on it some and talked around. Cantry runs 'em off one at a time. He won't move against anyone else until McGuiness is gone. If those men don't report back, then it'll take him a few days to figure out what happened."

"Why does he run them off one at a time? You'd think if he wanted the range so bad, he'd swoop down with his twenty riders and do in a day what he did up north to the Pawnee."

"If he did that, he'd have a war on his hands and a lot of sodbusters would be killed. Not that he cares about killin' a few, or all of 'em for that matter. It's just that if he did it that way, word would get back east, and he'd have the army out here investigating in two shakes of a lamb's tail."

"Alright," said Jed, "that makes sense. But now that we saved the McGuinesses for a few days, what's our next move?"

"I reckon we'll go pay Colonel Cantry a visit tomorrow. Get the lay of the land. When I was back in the army, the officers were always goin' on about reconnoitering. So that's what we're gonna do. Then we'll come up with a plan."

We rode up to The Silver Dollar and hitched our horses to the hitch rail out front. When we got inside, I saw that Mike Davis wasn't behind the bar. Henry was holding down the fort. Henry was Mike's head bartender. We ordered two beers and when Henry had them before us he said, "Marshal, there's some dude lookin' for you, looks like he's from back east. He's been in here twice."

"Was he heeled?"

"No, at least not that I could see."

He could be some drifter looking to make a reputation, but if he wasn't heeled, then probably not. Maybe he had some marshal business for me. There was only one way to find out.

"He say where he'd be?"

"Yeah, second time in he said he was gonna check down to the Last Chance and for me to tell you he'd wait for you there."

I finished my beer and headed for the door with Jed right beside me.

"Jed, this ain't a job for two men. He's most likely a dime novel reader. I get 'em every once in a while. Why don't you go over and see Jenny. It's nigh on two o'clock, and things should be slowin' down over there. Get yourself somethin' to eat and talk with Jenny. I'll be over presently."

I could tell he was torn between wanting to go with me to brace the stranger and going over to see Miss Jenny. I took the decision from him by telling him I was the marshal and he was the deputy, and I expected him to do as he was told.

The Last Chance Saloon is the second largest saloon in town and almost as well run as Mike Davis' place. I pushed through the swing doors and stood a minute to let my eyes adjust to the gloom. Looking around, I saw it was pretty busy for a weekday afternoon; it was half filled with men. I didn't see none of the whores; they usually worked only at night, which was good, seeing as how some of them looked in the daylight.

I heard a shout from across the room and then someone yelled, "Huck Finn, you old reprobate!"

Whoever it was had to push his way through some men, and I couldn't get a good look at him until he was right before me. Well, you could have blown me down, there stood Tom Sawyer!

We shook hands, clapped each other on the back and then hugged. It had been twelve long years since we had seen one another. There was a whole lot of catching up to do.

We pushed our way back to his table and sat down. He had a bottle of house rye sitting there, but that wouldn't do. I called to the barkeep and ordered a bottle of his best whiskey and two glasses.

I poured a liberal amount of the amber liquid into each glass and then we raised them. We didn't say anything; we knew each other too well to have need of words. We both nodded and downed the whiskey.

"So tell me Tom, how did you find me, and how did you like China?"

Tom smiled and said, "I have a few questions of my own. But I'll answer your two first and then you answer mine. I found you because I read about you in a clipping from the St. Petersburg Advertiser; it said you were the marshal of Abilene. So, when I hit San Francisco, I took a train there and found out you had resigned and gone to a town called Redemption in the Colorado Territory. I bought a horse and headed west and here I am. As to China, I never did make it. I got to the Sandwich Islands, jumped ship and stayed there until a couple of months ago."

Tom insisted I tell him how I became the famous Huck Finn of dime novel fame. Of course, I told him that was all a bunch of nonsense. But I did tell him how it all began down in Lamesa, and how one thing led to another until I ended up the marshal of Redemption. I did not tell him *why* I had come to Redemption.

Then Tom shared his tale. When he was done, I refilled our glasses, raised mine and said, "Here's to Kalei."

Tom raised his glass and said softly, "To Kalei."

As we downed the contents, Jed walked up to the table. "When you didn't show," he said, "I thought you might need some help. But it looks like the only help you need is finishing that bottle." He looked over to Tom and broke into a big grin.

Jed had done some growing since Tom had seen him last. And Jed didn't have the mustache back then, so Tom failed to recognize him, but Jed knew Tom right off.

"Howdy Tom, don't ya know me? It's me, Jed Bevins!"

It took Tom a moment or two, but then his eyes widened. He got to his feet and shot out his hand. "I sure do remember you! How are you doing, Jed?"

Jed took Tom's hand, and they stood there pumping each other's hand until I said, "Excuse me gents, but Jed, if you will fetch yourself a glass from the bar, then the three of us can get down to some serious drinkin'."

They seemed to like that idea because they stopped shaking hands. Jed got himself a glass and we got down to some serious drinkin'.

We had to have something to talk about, so in the course of the afternoon, Jed and I told Tom about Cantry, his gun slicks and his plans for the homesteaders. Jed talked about the raid on the Pawnee village, but he kind of soft-pedaled what he did about it. Never once did he mention the Laramie Kid.

The more Tom listened to us talk about Cantry, the more sober he became. Not that any of us were drunk, but when you split a bottle three ways, you're bound to feel it a little. Tom asked some sharp questions about Cantry, things even I hadn't thought to ask myself. Like where was the brother, the one that brought the original herd up from Texas? And were the gun slicks cowpunchers too, or were they on the payroll only for their guns? Sharp things like that.

Tom said if the gun slicks had to punch cows, they'd be out on the range scattered and would be easier to pick off; we could corral them one or two at a time. Then he said the dangest thing. He said he wanted in on it. He wanted to be a deputy and go up against Cantry with us. Maybe he wasn't as sober as I thought he was.

I explained, "Tom, I've been doing what I do for nigh on twelve years, and Jed has been doing what he does for six. And we're both good with a gun, six-shooters in particular. Besides, the town fathers will not go for another deputy on the payroll. Things in town are quiet, and that's all they care about. If I told 'em we were going up against Cantry, well, I'm pretty sure they would fire me and Jed in a heartbeat. Cantry draws a lotta water in this part of the country. His spread spends more in town than all the nesters combined. The town council is made up of men who make their living, or a good part of it, from Cantry."

I knew that Jed was going to kill Cantry no matter what, so I couldn't fool myself into thinking that I only wanted Cantry to leave the sodbusters alone and then we'd leave him alone. When the smoke cleared, there was going be some dead bodies lying about. Maybe among those bodies would be me and Jed. I didn't want to bring Tom into something like that, and I told him so.

Tom nodded and finished his drink. Putting down the glass he said, "It's been a long ride and I'm kind of tired. Where can I find a place to bed down?"

Jed went to make his rounds while I took Tom to the boarding house where Jed and I lived and got old lady Burnett to fix him up with a room. Before leaving, I had to ask one question. "You know, Tom, you don't sound like you used to. You kinda sound like a Yankee. Not that there's anything wrong with that, but I mean, what happened?"

"Huck, I've just been reading a lot of books, and it kind of rubs off on you. Besides, Kalei and her uncle spoke better English than you and me put together. And it was their second language! I reckon I just picked up on the way they talked."

"Well, it's good to see you Tom. I'll come by in the morning, and we'll have breakfast together. Then me and Jed have business to do. We have to go and pay a call on Cantry. Goodnight."

The next morning when I went to get Tom, he wasn't there. When I inquired as to his whereabouts, Missus Burnett relayed the message that Tom had left for me. "He said he'd meet you and your deputy at the eating house."

I was working my way through a slab of beef and some beans when Tom came in. Jed, he was watching Jenny as she served the other tables. Tom sure didn't look like a dude no more. He wore hand-tooled black boots, black jeans, and a red shirt. He had a blue kerchief tied around his neck and his hat was a flat brim, flat-crowned affair. It was black also. In his hand was the biggest damn shotgun that I ever did see.

Looking up from my beef and beans, I asked, "What's that, Tom?"

"It's a Colt revolving shotgun, ten gauge. It holds four rounds. I may not be the gun slick you boys are, but I betcha if I aimed this gun in the general vicinity of anything, I'd hit it."

I just wanted to know where he got the damn thing. "Picked it up in Abilene with the rest of my outfit. I came here for a reason Huck, and I'm not gonna be denied."

What the reason was he didn't say, and I didn't ask.

Jed said, "I reckon you would hit anything you aimed at, but how about some bacon and beans and a few biscuits?"

Tom told us he was up early and had already eaten. "I'll just have some coffee and wait for ya'all to finish. Then we can go and brace Cantry."

I looked at Jed; he just shrugged his shoulders and said nothing. I sighed, and told Tom, that if he was hell-bent on coming along, he might as well go as a deputy. "An unpaid deputy," I hastily added.

As we rode out to Cantry's ranch, I let both Jed and Tom know that I'd do all the talking. I was afraid that Jed might say something to provoke either Cantry or Cole into making a move. If we had to kill them, I wanted it to be on our own ground where we were the law.

We rode west toward the hazy, purple mountains. The prairie stretched out before us. Green-brown grass rippled like waves on the ocean as the wind moved across it. The sky went on forever, its blueness interrupted only by white, cottony clouds.

We walked our horses into the yard as two men came out of the house. One was tall, as tall as me, and I'm an inch over six foot. He had gray hair, a full head of it. He was clean-shaven and stood with a military erectness. He looked to be about fifty years old. This had to be Cantry. He wasn't wearing his colonel's uniform; I reckoned it must have been a mite moth-eaten by now. The other one was thin and kind of short—maybe five-seven—and I reckoned him to be on the north side of thirty, but not by much. He had a pinched face that sported a droopy, black mustache, and he wore one of them English Bowler hats. He also wore two crossed gun belts tied down with bone handled Colt .45s in the holsters. He had black, dead eyes.

The older man walked into the yard and said, "What can I do for you men?"

"Mister Cantry, we haven't met before. My name is Huck Finn; I'm the marshal of Redemption. I thought me and my deputies would come out and get acquainted with you. There's been a little trouble, but I'm sure everything can be worked out with a little palavering."

Cantry took a moment; he looked from me to Tom, and then to Jed, and then back to me. He took his time. Cole, if that was Cole, didn't move. He hadn't left the porch. He was leaning his left shoulder against a support post, his right hand hanging loosely by his gun. Finally Cantry said, "First of all, Marshal, I prefer to be addressed as Colonel. And second, you and your deputies are a bit off your range; this here is county land."

"Well Colonel, you see, we're not here officially. It's just that we heard four of your riders went missing and we thought we might be able to help out."

At the mention of the missing men, Cantry's mouth tightened, his eyes became slits. But then he smiled and said, "Where are my manners? Musta been a thirsty ride out here. Why don't you men come on inside, get outta the sun, and have something cool to drink?"

Tom and Jed were to my right, and I turned to them and nodded. We slipped our horses, tied them to the porch railing and followed Cantry inside. Cole stayed where he was and did not move until we were all through the door. Once inside, Cole went to a corner of the room and leaned against a bookshelf, folded his arms, and looked at us from under hooded eyes.

By the look of it, we were in Cantry's study. He motioned for us to take a seat in one of the four chairs arranged on one side of his desk. Tom and I sat; Jed remained standing looking at Cole. Cantry sat in a big chair behind a big desk.

"Cole," said Cantry "would you be so kind as to ask Chang to bring us some refreshment of the liquid sort?"

Cole didn't look like he wanted to leave Cantry alone with us, but he pushed himself straight and left the room. He was back in a few seconds, followed by a Chinaman with a pigtail down his back that almost reached his waist. He wore a white housecoat and carried a silver tray. On the tray was an array of bottles, and lo and behold, a bucket of ice!

Cantry saw me looking at the ice and boasted, "Just completed the ice house last month. Don't know how I lived so long without it." He was showing off, but that was all right. It had been a while since I had had a drink with ice in it. Tom and I had whiskey, good Kentucky whiskey, over ice. Jed refused a drink.

Once we were all seated comfortably with our whiskey, all, that is, except Jed and Cole (they stood eyeing each other like two stallions getting ready to fight to the death for the mares of the herd), Cantry asked me what I knew of his missing men.

"To be honest with you Mister . . . I mean Colonel Cantry, we rode 'em off. Warned 'em if they showed their faces in this country again we'd kill 'em."

Cole straightened up a mite, and Cantry choked a little on his whiskey.

Before he could say anything, I asked Cantry about his brother. "Word around town is that he is partnered with you, but no one ever sees him."

"Not that it's anyone's business, but my brother is in Chicago. I raise the beef and ship it to him. He sells it. No middle man."

By the way he said it, and the fact that he let the matter of the missing men alone for the moment, I could tell he was proud of the arrangement—he thought it pretty slick. Then he got down to business.

"What gives you the right to run off my cowhands, Marshal?"

"We didn't run off no cowhands, Colonel. We run off some murderin' skunks that was fixin' to run Bob McGuiness and his wife off their land."

Cantry freshened his drink, but he didn't offer any to Tom or me. Then, through clenched teeth, he said, "It ain't their land; it's mine. I was here long before them damn sodbusters. This is grazing range, always was, always will be. Before cows, it was the buffalo. I got eight thousand head out there that's gotta eat. Them sodbusters plant a few measly crops, then fence them off to keep my cows away. If I allowed the sodbusters to stay, before long that's all there would be, piss-ant little farms and no more grazing range!"

When he finished talking, I looked at my empty glass and rattled the ice around a bit. Cantry sighed and offered to freshen up our glasses because he thought himself a southern gentleman. Tom and I accepted his offer; Jed and Cole continued to stare at each other.

I took a sip of that fine Kentucky whiskey before saying, "Alright Colonel, you had your say. Now I'll have mine. This is not your land, it's government land and those sodbusters paid for their one hundred-sixty acres. How much did you pay for your twenty thousand acres? You run off some people before I got here. But you ain't gonna do it no more. If Bob McGuiness or any of them nesters have any more trouble, you'll have the same trouble they have and more. We came out here to put you on notice. One more incident with the nesters and I'm gonna let my deputy here kill you." I pointed my glass at Jed, then stood up.

By now, Cantry was furious. Good, because that is just what I wanted. He threw his glass against the wall where it shattered, and, sputtering and spitting, he screamed, "Who the hell are you to come into my house and threaten me? I

214

could have you killed at the drop of a hat. You get outta here, and if I see you again, I'll have Cole kill you."

I gently put the glass on his desk and said, "Mighty good whiskey, and it sure does go better with ice." I started to walk out, but stopped and turned back to Cantry. "You want to know who the hell I am? I'll tell you who the hell I am. I'm the man that saved your life. My deputy here, the one that seems so interested in your man Cole, he came to town to kill you. But I asked him as a favor to me, not to . . . at least not yet. You might have heard of him; he's the Laramie Kid, and he's killed all but four of the men that were with you when you raided that Pawnee village up north where you killed men, women, and children. Then you didn't move onto that range because you found better land down here. So, sixty people were massacred for nothing, just on the whim of a greedy old man playin' soldier. That's who I am and that's who you are. Now, thank you for the drink, but I think it's time we drifted."

Cantry stood there, his face ashen, and his mouth hanging open. Cole hadn't moved. I let Tom go out first, and then I walked out. Turning his back to Cole, Jed followed us.

215

EIGHTEEN

On the way back to town, I told Tom that I noticed he had left his shotgun in the saddle boot and did not take it into the house. "That's right Huck, but there were only two of them and I was with two of the fastest gun slicks in the west. I felt safe."

"Well, from now on, no matter how safe you feel, keep that gun close by."

"Did you happen to notice anything else besides me not carrying the gun?" asked Tom.

"You mean that there were no horses outside of the bunk house and no men loitering about? If that's what you mean, then I did notice it."

Tom smiled and nodded. "Reckon that means his gun hands are also cowpunchers."

"Reckon you're right," I agreed.

Jed rode up next to me with a big grin on his face and said, "So you thought *I* might say something that would start a ruckus?" Then he spurred his horse and rode on ahead. I knew it took all he had not to draw and kill Cole and then Cantry, but I also knew he was a man of his word.

It didn't take long for things to get moving. The next morning Tom and I went into the eating house and saw Jed at a table in the back, talking to Jenny. Tom started off in that direction, but I held him back saying, "Let's leave the young folk to themselves. There's a dance comin' up, and I think Jed is workin' up the courage to ask Jenny to go with him. Let's sit by the window; I want to keep an eye on the street."

Tom stood his shotgun by the door, and we grabbed a table. We wouldn't be getting any service for a while, at least not until Jenny and Jed exhausted things to talk about. So Tom and I looked out the window at the street traffic as it went by—a few saddled horses, their riders looking neither left nor right; some freighters with teamsters on them, prodding their horses forward. The morning stage went by in a hurry to be out of town, as it always is. Then things quieted down.

I was thinking what a nice, peaceful morning it was when I saw six riders coming up the street. Four of them stopped in front of The Silver Dollar and hitched their horses. The other two men continued on and went down the alley that runs alongside the saloon. I noticed all the horses wore the Slash C brand.

"Tom, go and get Jed and bring him here."

Tom didn't hesitate or ask fool questions; he did as he was told.

When Jed and Tom were sitting on the bench opposite me, I told Jed what I had seen. Then I asked him, "If you wanted to ambush some real good-lookin' fellas, say like us three, how would you go about it?"

Jed rubbed his chin and looked thoughtful before saying, "What I'd do is go into a drinking establishment and make a ruckus until the law was called. Of course, I'd have a couple friends go up the back stairs and get to the balcony overlooking the saloon. Then, when those three good-looking fellas came in, my friends could shoot 'em in the back whilst their attention was on me."

I looked at Tom. "Is that what you'd do?"

"If two of those good-looking fellas were fast guns, I'd have a whole slew of back shooters up in the balcony. But seeing as how I don't know any real good-looking fellas, why are you asking me?"

We all laughed. Tom stood to retrieve his shotgun, and Jed and I met him at the door. When we went out, we made sure not to look toward The Silver Dollar. I directed Tom to go 'round back, find his way up to the balcony, and take out the back shooters when Jed and I made our play. "And Tom, don't hesitate to shoot 'em in the back."

Next, Jed and I walked down the street a ways and waited for things to start up. We didn't have long to wait. A few minutes later, Henry came running out onto the street. He looked both ways and when he saw us, he hightailed it on over.

When Henry pulled up, I said, "What's the matter Henry? You look like you're bein' chased by the devil hisself."

"Marshall, there are some cowboys in the Silver Dollar breaking it up pretty bad. Mike ain't around, and they look kinda mean. There's four of 'em and there was nothing I could do."

"That's alright Henry; we'll come along with you. Anyone else in there?"

"No, Marshal, just the four cowboys."

"That's good Henry. When we get there, I want you to stay outside until I tell you otherwise. And don't let nobody else come in. You understand?"

"Sure Marshal, whatever you say."

Jed and I pushed through the swing doors; Jed went left, I went right. We didn't walk out onto the middle of the floor. We kept back a ways under the balcony, waiting for the blast of Tom's gun. Before we went in, Jed and I agreed on who we were going kill. He'd get the ones on the left, and I'd take care of the two on the right.

When the Slash C boys saw us, they stopped what they were doing—breaking up chairs and throwing the pieces against the mirror behind the bar. The tallest one took a step toward Jed and me before he said, "Howdy Marshal, you and your deputy care to join us in a drink?" He was trying to get us to walk out onto the floor.

I nodded and said, "Sorry boys, but you're a mite too rambunctious for this time of the day. I'm going to have to ask you to accompany us to the hoosegow until you pay off the damages."

The tall one said if we'd come over and have one drink with them, then they'd go anywhere we wanted. It was then we heard the first BOOM of Tom's gun. Before we heard the second, Jed and I had our guns out and cut down the four Slash C gunnies.

As we were reloading our guns, I called up to Tom. "You alright up there?"

He leaned over the railing, answering, "These are the first men I have ever killed."

"Don't let it bother you none," I said. "They were hired guns; it was their fate to die young. Come on down here and we'll have us a drink." Next, I called to Henry and told him to go and fetch the undertaker.

NINETEEN

Now I know from the way I've been going on that you might think my only concern was with Cantry and the Slash C. Well, that's not true. I came to Redemption because of Cantry, but the town was in need of a marshal about then. The Slash C ain't the only cattle ranch in this neck of the woods and Cantry ain't the only rancher.

Of course, the other ranchers don't have big outfits like Cantry except maybe McNally; he comes close. But they do have cowboys and on payday, there ain't nothing more high-spirited than a cowpuncher with a snootful. All the ranchers know the times are changing. They don't like the nesters being on the range any more than Cantry does, but they realize there's nothing they can do about it. If they ran one off, the next day there'd be two more trying to take his place. Some ranchers are even talking of fencing off their land. So the only problem I have with the other ranchers is when their cowpokes come into town for a good time.

That's why Jed and I have to make sure we're seen walking the town and making our rounds from sunset until around three in the morning. The saloons never close, but about then, things quiet down a mite. We never have trouble at the whorehouses. Once in a great while a puncher might think he was shorted on his time with a girl

221

and raise a ruckus, but all the whorehouses have their own bouncers. That leaves me and Jed free to patrol the saloons.

When I first took over as town marshal, I thought of having everyone check their guns at the jail, but that's a headache because you're always running down there to give someone back his gun. At the time I didn't have a deputy, but even if I did, I'd rather he be walking the streets keeping trouble to a minimum than playing at being a hat check girl.

I reckon I took the long way round just to tell you that because Jed and I work late, we sleep late. That's why we were asleep when the bank was robbed and Hoyt Baxter was killed.

The first I knew about it was when Tom shook me awake and told me there had been a bank robbery and that a man had been shot. I told him to go wake up Jed and for them to meet me at the bank.

When I arrived, I had to push my way through the crowd to get inside. Once I was in, I saw Doc kneeling over Baxter. He stood and shook his head before saying "Didn't have a chance, Marshal. I figure he was dead before he hit the floor."

Jed and Tom made their way in and I told them to push the sightseers out onto the street. Then I collected everyone who was in the bank at the time of the robbery and questioned them. They all had the same story. Three men came in right after the bank opened for business and demanded all the money from the safe and teller cages. Hoyt was the manager and when he was a little too slow in opening the safe, one of the robbers shot him. Because the safe was still locked, and no one else had the combination, the robbers had to be satisfied with what they got from the teller cages.

Jed said to me, "Doesn't look like those three are the brightest boys around. I mean killing the only man that can open the safe before he opens it . . . well, you see what I mean." Yes I did, but now Jed and I were going to hunt them down, bright boys or not.

I asked Jed to get us an outfit together with enough supplies to last a week and said that I'd meet him at the livery stable in an hour. But first, I had to find Jim Niles, the head alderman, and tell him that Tom would be in charge of keeping the peace while Jed and I were away. Niles balked at the idea. "Who is this man? What's he gonna cost us? Why don't ya git a posse up and leave your deputy in charge?"

I patiently explained to him that Tom was my friend and could be counted on to do the job; that it wasn't going to cost the town anything because Tom did not want to be paid, and that a posse of shopkeepers would get in my way and slow me down. I told him that I needed Jed because he was the best white-man tracker I ever knew. I didn't have

223

to explain *anything* to Niles because I was the law, at least until they fired me, but there's a certain amount of politics in any job.

I met up with Jed at the livery stable. He had my blue roan gelding saddled, and he was seated on his lineback buckskin holding the lead line to a pack mule.

"We ready to go Jed?"

"Just waiting for you Huck."

"Then let's get this show on the road."

I took the line to the mule so that Jed could look for sign. We left town in a column; Jed, followed by me, and following me, the pack mule.

At first, their trail was not hard to follow; it looked like they were heading for the mountains. That was the smart thing to do seeing as how there aren't too many places to hide out on the prairie. After a couple of hours, Jed got down from his horse and walked around a bit to pick up their sign. At one point, he knelt for a few minutes, staring at something. Even from atop my horse, I could see they were hoof prints. I asked Jed what he was doing. He said that he was memorizing the prints of the three horses because if we lost the trail, he wanted to know those particular prints when he saw them again. Jed had learned his tracking skills well when he was with the Pawnee.

We rode until the sun dropped over the mountains. When we reached the foothills, we made a dry camp. We ground-staked the horses and the mule, and rubbed them down with grass.

The animals grazed on prairie grass and some nearby sage while we made a fire. We didn't care if the men we were tracking saw it. In fact, we wanted them to see it. We figured they were above us, up on the mountain and could look down on our camp. Jed said they were only two, maybe three hours ahead of us, and if they knew we were tracking them, they might stop moving and try to dry-gulch us. If they weren't moving, then we could get our business done all the sooner. Well, we would see tomorrow what transpired. In the meantime, Jed made some pan biscuits and fried us up a slab of salt pork. As Jed cooked, I asked him if he had the presence of mind to bring along a little whiskey.

"Knowin' you Huck, I wouldn't dare not bring some. In one of the saddle bags from the mule, you'll find a bottle."

After getting the bottle and sitting back down, I pulled the cork and took a good swallow. It wasn't smooth, but it was warm going down. Handing the bottle to Jed, I asked him if he'd asked Jenny to the dance. He didn't answer me; he just took a pull from the bottle and handed it back. I reckoned he didn't want to talk about it. I mentally shrugged, re-corked the bottle, and leaned it against my saddle. As he handed me a plate of salt pork he said, "I sure did ask her, and she said she'd be proud to go with me."

He wasn't smiling when he said it. I thought he'd be a mite happier about the whole thing, so I asked him if anything was wrong.

"It's just this, Huck. She's always asking me why I'm a killer and if I can change my killin' ways. I never thought of myself as a killer or even a gun slick. I just set out to avenge a terrible wrong and to keep my word to my friend. I plan to maybe go to California as soon as I'm finished here and Cantry's dead. But now she's got me thinking that maybe I am a killer and I like killing." Having had his say, Jed sat back and started to eat his salt pork and biscuits.

I finished my plate, set it aside, and reached for the whiskey. This was going to take some thought. I took a few pulls from the bottle while Jed ate. At length I said, "Jed, I know you're no killer. Tell me, how many times did you ride into a town, and when you couldn't find any of the men you were hunting, kill someone else just for the sake of killing? And I'm not talking about those few times you was braced because of your reputation and had to defend yourself."

Jed was thoughtful while he chewed his pork. He said nothing as he cleaned up the cooking things. His silence went on for a long spell. I thought he might be finished talking for the night. But when things were packed away, he sat on his heels by the fire and reached out his hand for the bottle. After taking a good long swallow, he finally answered my question, "I don't reckon I ever went looking for a fight with nobody 'ceptin' those murderers. I took no joy in killing them. It was just a job, just something that had to be done."

He took another pull and went on, "When I first came to Redemption, I was itching to have a go at Cantry, but not so much because I wanted to kill him. There was that, but once he was dead, the long haul would be over and I could have my life back. Does that make any sense to you, Huck?"

Of course, it made sense to me, and I told him so. I also told him it was my belief that Jenny, thinking he was a killer, was trying to reform him because she had some plans of her own. Jed didn't get my drift right off, so I spelled it out for him. "She thinks you're husband material, and she has set her cap for you."

"I find that hard to believe, Huck." But as he said it, a smile came to his face. It was the first time he had smiled all day.

I took the first watch, and Jed relieved me at midnight.

The next morning we were up, ate a cold breakfast, and were on the trail before the sun made its way over the horizon.

Their tracks were easy to follow; there was only one trail up the mountain. About ten o'clock the hairs on the back of my neck stood up and did a little dance. They were bristling something awful. Jed was in the lead, and I called for him to hold up. When I got up to him, I slid my horse and suggested he do the same.

We drank from our canteens and filled our hats so the horses could have a drink. We were getting low on water, but with many streams in the mountains, we had no fear on that count. But I did have a fear on another count; I felt someone was watching us.

Jed agreed and said that the trail we were on was the perfect place for an ambush. I asked him how they would do it. He said if it was him running things, he'd leave a man behind to get us on the trail and then meet up with the other two later.

"Well Jed, there's nothing for it but to go on. We're the law in Redemption. If we let these geezers get away with robbing our bank and killing our citizens, then every no-good saddle tramp in the territory will be comin' to our town tryin' their hand at bank robbery or anything else they thought they could get away with."

"Reckon that you're right. I'll take point."

"Sorry Jed, I'm the marshal and that's my job. But if they get me, you keep going. You don't have to bring them back if they're dead, only if they surrender. But either

228

way, bring their guns and horses back, sell 'em, and give the money to Missus Baxter. I reckon she could use it now with her husband gone."

With nothing else to say, we got back on our horses. Jed tied the mule's lead line to his saddle horn so as to keep his hands free. With our Winchesters out and lying across the bows of our saddles, we proceeded on.

We hadn't gone far when a bullet smashed into a boulder I was riding by, splashing up bits of rock. A second later, I heard the sound of the shot. That meant that whoever shot at us was a fair ways off.

We both dove for cover, and smacked our horses on their rumps to get them going and out of the line of fire. Seeing as how the mule was tethered to Jed's horse, he wisely followed along.

We were lying among some good-sized boulders, and Jed asked me where I reckoned the shooter was.

"I reckon he's two hundred yards up that slope," I said, pointing off to the left. "It's a good thing the sun was to our backs. I think it must have got in his eyes, elsewise he's a lousy shot."

Jed was smiling as he checked his Colts to make sure they were loaded. They were always loaded. I think it was just a nervous habit with him. I had me a Smith and Wesson Schofield I had picked up a year back.

When Jed had his guns back in their holsters, he said, "Alright Huck, how are we gonna play this? You wanna charge up the hill at the sonavabitches or do it Indian style and come up from behind 'em?"

"Well Jed, there was only the one shot, so I reckon you called it right when you said they'd leave one man behind to finish us off. They must have seen there were only the two of us around the fire last night. Probably figured one man in ambush could take care of a couple of jaspers like us. But I don't like the idea of chargin' up the hill. One of us is bound to take a bullet or two. No, you stay here and keep him busy with your Winchester. I'll circle 'round and get above him. I'm gonna stand now and draw his fire, you watch to see where the muzzle flash comes from."

Jed grabbed my arm and said, "That ain't too smart Huck."

"Don't worry. We know he's not a good shot, and I'll move fast to give him a very little target. You just see where the shot comes from."

When I was back down safe among the rocks, Jed pointed out where our friend was. I nodded and told him to count to three hundred because that's when I expected to be behind and above him. "Then hold your fire because it might be me you hit, and that would be kinda embarrassin' for both of us."

I got up to where I wanted to be just before I hit three hundred, and I saw our man. His horse knew I was there before he did. When his horse whinnied, the man spun around in a panic. He didn't see me, so I had the chance to take him alive. "Throw down your gun, and put your hands up if you wanna see the sun come up tomorrow," I yelled down to him.

But as Jed said, these weren't the brightest boys in the choir. He did a half-turn and fired where he thought my voice had come from. I sighed and shot him just above the heart and a little to the center. I was aiming for his heart, but he moved on me. He was now on his knees and raising his gun for another shot. I knew he was as good as dead, and I didn't want to put another bullet into him if I didn't have to. I wanted to let him say his last words, and maybe give him a little water.

"You're shot bad partner, and you're gonna die, but do you wanna die alone? Throw down your gun, and I'll come to you." He must have been hurting pretty bad because he dropped the gun and fell over backwards. I walked down and kicked his gun a little farther away from his hand. Then I called to Jed, telling him to bring up a canteen.

While I waited for Jed, I knelt down on one knee and asked him his name. But he wasn't talking; he turned his head away. I could tell he was in bad pain, and he was breathing rough. It made me wish I had killed him outright to spare him that. He was young, about Jed's age.

Jed walked up and handed me the canteen without saying anything. Losing blood makes you thirsty and when he saw the canteen, he ran his tongue over his lips. I uncorked it, raised his head a little, and put it to his lips. After he drank his fill, I saw a red froth coming from his mouth. That meant he was shot in the lungs or at least one of them.

I eased his head down and asked him his name.

"It's Samuel."

"Well Samuel, you got any kinfolk we can contact for you?"

He told me there was no one that cared a hoot if he lived or died. Then he tried to smile, but couldn't quite make it. "Maybe a whore down Sonora way, if she's still alive."

I smiled at him and asked, "Who were the men with you, and where are they headed?"

"I cain't peach on my friends, mister."

So I asked him if he was the one who shot Baxter.

"No, there was to be no shootin'. But that Ned, he's a crazy one. When he shot that man, Dan and me couldn't believe it." Then Samuel asked if he could have some

232

more water. But before I could get the cork out of the canteen, he died.

We collected his guns and rounded up his horse. Before riding out, I went through his pockets. All he had on him was twenty-five dollars. Jed asked me if I thought that was his take from the robbery. "Maybe, those teller cages couldn't have held more than sixty, seventy dollars total."

"Not much to die for," said Jed.

"It ain't," I agreed.

We didn't bury him; we didn't have a shovel, and we didn't have the time. I took point leading the horse; Jed followed leading the mule.

After a short spell, Jed asked me if I thought Cantry would try any funny business while we were away. "I don't think so. We cost him half his men in just two days. I think he'll lie low while he figures a way to get us, McNally, and the homesteaders outta the picture for good."

"You think he's getting replacements for the men we ran off and the ones we killed?"

"I don't see how he can. It's not as if he can come into town, pick up a couple gun slicks at Niles' store, and call it a day. No Jed, he's down to ten gunnies, and he'll have to make his play with them." I believed it at the time, but I was wrong. Cantry would round up some more guns.

"Yeah," said Jed, "but one of those gunnies is Tuck Cole. He'll do for two, maybe three."

"What's the matter Jed? You think he's faster than you?"

"Won't know that 'til I face him."

I nodded, and just then we came to a bend in the trail. Before us lay a small valley, and in the valley was a town of sorts. There were a few buildings on its one street and a few houses scattered about, but the town consisted mostly of tents. On the trail down, nailed to a tree, a sign announced that the town below us was named Bisbee.

Coming in, we passed a smelter, and Jed remarked that they must be doing a little mining. I couldn't disagree with him, so I said nothing. It was just after noon when we made our way up the street; we cast no shadows.

We came to a large, white cotton tent with a three-foot-by-two-foot board over the entrance. On the board, painted in black, was the solitary word, SALOON. In front of the tent, ground-hitched, (there was no hitchin' rail) were Ned and Dan's horses. Jed knew the hoof prints.

There was no grass around the tent, so we walked our horses about a hundred yards back behind the street where there was a little grass and some shade from a few trees.

We picketed the three horses and the mule. All four of them were happily grazing as we proceeded to the saloon.

We went inside and once our eyes became adjusted to the dimness, we saw that the place was lively for the middle of the day in the middle of nowhere. There were men sitting at most of the tables. Four men stood at the bar—two at the far left by themselves, two more at the other end. The bar itself was a plank set upon two barrels. The back bar was three cracker barrels turned upside down.

Jed leaned over and whispered to me, "Which ones you reckon they be?"

I didn't know, but I knew how to find out.

"Jed," I said loud enough to be heard by the men at the bar, "let's you and me get a drink. It's been a long dusty trail."

We settled in at the middle of the bar between the two sets of men and ordered our poison. When the barkeep poured our drinks and placed the bottle on the bar, I asked him if he'd seen any strangers in town. I was wearing my tin star, so he knew I was the law. He didn't turn his head, but his eyes flicked to his right, my left. Without meaning to, he told me all that I wanted to know. It was obvious he was trying hard not to get involved, so I let him off the hook.

"Don't worry about it; the men we're after are probably long over the mountain by now." Out of the corner of my eye, I saw the tension go out of the two on the left.

I winked at Jed and invited the two men to our right to join us in a drink or two. They readily accepted. I did likewise to the two on our left. They declined. When we were joined by our brethren from the right, I poured healthy portions of whatever it was we were drinking into their glasses. It tasted like turpentine.

We downed our first drink and one of the geezers said, "Couldn't help but overhear, Sheriff, that you're hunting some men. What'd they do, if I might ask?"

"First of all," I said as I poured them another shot, "I'm a marshal, not a sheriff. But as to why I'm looking for them, I want them because they are back-shooting, murderin' sonavabitches. They shot down an unarmed man back in Redemption." I said it somewhat loud to see how they'd take it down at the other end of the bar.

What they did was down their drinks and turn to leave. I let them get halfway across the room before I said in a raised voice, "Where ya goin' Ned? Don't like to hear 'bout back-shootin' murderers?"

They froze right where they were; they did not turn around. The two that were drinking with us moved off as far away as the tent would allow. Jed took three steps to my left. All the noise and conversation in the place came to a halt, and time slowed down as it always does in those kinds of situations.

"Okay boys, shuck them gun belts, and be gentle about it. I'll give you the same chance I gave Samuel. If you want to live the day out, don't do nothin' stupid."

At the mention of Samuel's name, the one on the left straightened and put his hands up in the air. The other one, still facing away from us, kept his hands where they were, the right hand hovering near his gun. That had to be Ned. The one with his hands up was tall and skinny; he wore a blue checkered shirt.

"You, in the blue shirt, if you don't want any part of this fight, move away from your partner and shuck your gun belt." He did so without turning to face us.

Now, I've never shot a man in the back and it didn't seem like a good time to start. So I ordered Ned to turn around slowly, advising him that any fast moves on his part would result in his death. When he was facing me, I could see he was itching to draw, but his eyes kept flickering between me and Jed.

"What's bothering you?" I said. "You think that if you draw on me, my deputy will cut you down?"

He didn't answer.

To Jed I said, "If he outdraws me, you let him walk outta here, the other one too. Do you understand?"

Jed hesitated, but finally I heard a soft "Yes" to my left. I hadn't taken my eyes off of Ned.

When that was settled, I said to Ned "What's the slowdown? I hear you're hell-on-wheels when it comes to shootin' bank managers. Come on gun slick. Draw on a man that's facing you with a gun in his holster."

I always look at their eyes. The eyes tell me before their hand does when they're going to go for it. Ned was no exception.

He blinked and went for his gun. Unfortunately for him, he was a mite slow. I had a bullet through his jaw by the time he cleared leather. I have to admit though, he had sand. He didn't go down, but instead tried to raise his gun. If we had been outside that would have been the end of it, but I was afraid that if he got off a shot, an innocent person might get hurt. So I put a bullet right between his eyes. His gun went off into the dirt floor of that seedy saloon in Bisbee, Colorado Territory, and he dropped for the last time. We then hauled Dan back and locked him up until the circuit judge could get to town.

Tom had not had any trouble while we were away. Maybe it was the shotgun he carried everywhere or maybe it was just his pleasant personality. I'm not sure which, maybe a little bit of both. Jed was happy that we wrapped

238

things up and were back so soon. The big barn dance was only three days away.

TWENTY

Hollister wasn't a homesteader. He was a rancher who ran two thousand head of beef. He knew the day of the open range was ending; there were just too many emigrants flocking west. In an effort to broker a peace between the sodbusters and the cattlemen, Hollister was throwing a dance.

All the people in the county were invited: the town folk, the nesters, the ranchers and their hired hands. It was Hollister's desired hope that if he could get them all together in a social situation, they would come to realize that they were neighbors and not adversaries.

Hollister had gone to considerable trouble and expense to host this get-together. He had a special barn for his hay that had no stalls; it was a wide-open space. The barn now stood empty; he would not cut his hay for another month. In the last few weeks, his hands had laid a wooden dance floor in the middle of it.

It was probably the only structure in the county that had room enough for the number of people he hoped would attend. He slaughtered two steers, and his wife had been cooking for three days so there would be eats enough for all. There were lanterns, their globes painted red and blue, hanging from the rafters. Strung from support to support were crape banners of red, white, and blue. In addition, every man in the county who owned or could play an instrument was pressed into service. For some of them, it did not take that much pressing.

The dance was the talk of the county for weeks beforehand. At length the big day arrived. It was early October; the weather was cool, the sky cloudless, and there would be an almost full moon. It was as though God Himself was helping out so that the people on this one small part of His earth could come together and find peace. The entire county would be there, even Bob McNally and his outfit were coming. All the residents of the town and the prairie were to be there. All, that is, except Cantry and his men. Cantry had declined the invitation to attend.

• • • • •

Tom and I were sitting outside the office at the jail enjoying the weather when Jed pulled up on a rented buckboard. Jumping down, he tied the reins to the hitching rail, then came and stood next to where we were sitting. He leaned against the building and looked at the buckboard not saying anything. Tom and I didn't say anything neither.

After a few minutes Jed said, "Well?"

Tom looked at me, and I looked at him, then we continued saying nothing. We knew Jed was wanting us to remark on the rig, but we thought we'd have some fun with him first.

When he could stand it no longer he said, "What do you think?"

I looked to Tom, and he looked to me, and we both shrugged our shoulders at the same time. Then I turned to Jed and said, "Oh hi Jed, didn't see you come up."

Jed rolled his eyes and said, "Very funny Huck. But what do you think of the rig?"

As though I hadn't seen it before, I stood, walked over to the edge of the boardwalk and examined it very carefully. "I think Jed's got something here. It looks a lot more comfortable than riding a horse."

"You know what I mean. Do you think Jenny will mind riding in it? It's all they had left at the livery stable."

I figured that the ribbing had gone on long enough, so I put Jed out of his misery.

"Looks fine to me Jed. I'm sure Jenny will be proud and pleased to sit up there on the driver's seat beside you. Don't you think so Tom?"

Tom nodded his agreement.

"Well," said Jed, "I've gotta go over to Aaron's and pick up my suit and then take a bath. I'm gonna leave the rig here because I don't want no more dust on it than has to be." Aaron Meyer is the town's tailor. Jed had himself a new suit made just for the occasion.

When Jed had been gone a minute, I started to say something stupid like, "Must be nice to be in love like that young fella," then I remembered about Kalei.

We sat there in the shade of the ramada not talking. I did not know what Tom Sawyer was thinking, but I was thinking about Jed and Jenny. I was wishing that they could get on that buckboard tonight and just ride out of this country to a place where there were no Cantrys and no gun hands.

After a spell, Tom asked me if we were going to make an appearance at the dance. He said it would be a good time to talk to McNally and see what his plans were. He was right of course, but I still couldn't figure why he jumped into this mess to begin with. So I decided to ask him.

"Tom, you know I'm happy you're here helpin' out and all. I only wish it was under happier circumstances. But you know what I can't figure is, why? You're no gunny, but you're sure acting like one. If I didn't know any better, I'd think you were trying to get yourself killed. That ain't it, is it?"

He drew from his pipe and blew out the smoke before he answered. "Huck, you've known me a long time, and I can't lie to you. After Kalei was taken from me, I decided I wanted to die, but I didn't have the courage to jump off the mountain back there on Hawaii. I also wanted to see you again. So I came back to the States to see you and to die. From reading about you in that dime novel, I thought all I'd have to do was walk into a saloon and bump into someone, and he'd pull out his six-shooter and dispatch me to a better and finer world. A world where your wife is not torn from your grasp never to be seen again."

He was quiet after that, but I knew he had more to say, so I waited. After a moment, he went on.

"However, when I got here and saw what you were up against, I decided to stick it out and watch your back. When this is over, if I'm still of a mind to leave this world, I'll find a way to do so. But for now, I've got a job to do. Anyways, I want to be here to see how Jed makes out with Jenny. I wouldn't miss that for anything." He laughed and I joined him.

I finally answered the question he had asked earlier. "I reckon we'll hang around town for a while. It's a Saturday night, but with the whole county at the dance, things should be quiet. If that's the case, then we'll mosey on out to Hollister's and see what's transpiring." Tom had to remind me that the whores weren't going anywhere. Mister Hollister wanted to invite them, but his wife said that if he did, the whores would be the only females at the party.

After a while, Jed came back sporting his new black suit *and* a new store bought white shirt. The collar looked uncomfortable. And he wasn't wearing his guns.

He started to climb onto the buckboard, but I asked him to hold his horses for a minute. As I said before, I'm no great shakes with womenfolk, but in comparison with Jed, I look like Don Juan. So I thought I should give him a little friendly advice before he called on Jenny.

"Jed, you know that there are five men for every female in this county?"

"If you say so Huck, but I've got to be moving on. Jenny's expecting me."

"It's just this one thing. I know you are her escort, the one taking her to the dance, but she will be asked to dance by all the young Turks and maybe some of the older ones. So don't get your nose outta joint because of it. Let her be the Belle of the Ball. When you're standing there watchin' her dance with all those other fellas, just remember that out of all the men in and around Redemption, she chose to go with you."

"It's funny you should mention that Huck, because I was just thinking on the same thing. I don't reckon I'll be doing much dancing anyway because I don't know how to dance. And I sure as hell ain't gonna make a fool of myself in front of Jenny."

That's when Tom stood and told Jed to follow him into the office. Jed hesitated, but Tom gave him a stern look and Jed went inside. Not knowing what else to do, I followed.

When we all were inside, Tom closed the door and said to Jed, "I wanted you in here because I didn't want to embarrass you. I'm going to give you a five-minute dance lesson. It's all you're going to need. Now watch me."

Tom moved about some, it looked crazy to me, but he seemed to know what he was doing. Then he said, "All they play at these shindigs is the Waltz and quadrilles. With quadrilles, you just follow everyone else. And with the Waltz, if you can do these few steps, you can fool anyone into believing you've been doing it all your life.

"First of all, place your right hand slightly beneath Jenny's left shoulder blade with your right arm held at a ninety degree angle to your body. Your left arm should be raised so that Jenny's hand can rest lightly in yours and it should be held at her eye level. You got that?"

Jed didn't look like he had got it, but he nodded in affirmation anyway.

"Now come over here," said Tom, "and pretend I'm Jenny."

Jed looked to me like I might be of some help, but all I could do was shrug. So, resigned to his fate, Jed went to Tom and allowed his hands to be put in the appropriate position. He must really have wanted to dance with Jenny. Then Tom counted out the steps again. "Left foot forward, right foot side, left foot close, right foot back, left foot close and right foot side."

246

It was a sight to behold! The Laramie Kid swirling around the jail office with Tom Sawyer in his arms. After a minute of that, I think they both had enough; they dropped their hands and separated.

Jed looked a mite sheepish, but Tom had a big grin on his face and said, "That's all there is to it. Just remember: left forward, right side, left close, right back, left close and right side." Then with my blessing and I suppose Tom's, we bid the youngster on his way. Jed left mumbling the dance steps to himself, trying to commit them to memory.

When Jed had gone and was on his way, I asked Tom when he had learned to dance the Waltz.

"You weren't around then, but for a while my Aunt Polly sent me to refinement school on Saturdays where they taught you manners and dancing and things like that. I hated every minute of it, but over the years, I've found some of it useful. Like today."

Tom never ceases to amaze me.

TWENTY-ONE

It was the quietest Saturday night in the history of Redemption. Even the whorehouses were empty. Well, practically empty. After two hours of walking a very quiet and almost empty town, Tom and I saddled up and rode out toward Hollister's.

As we started, the moon came up out of the east and we rode in the cool October night onto the prairie. The soft white light of the moon illuminated the prairie grass as I had never seen it. The grass looked a silky, greenish-white. The scene was beautiful and all was peaceful. Tom and I spoke not a word as we made our way: the only sound . . . the clip-clop of the horses' hooves as they touched the ground.

A quarter mile out from Hollister's, we heard the music. Then we crested a rise and saw the lights. As we came into the ranch yard, we observed men outside the barn passing bottles around. From the looks of them, they were mostly cowhands from the ranches. We slipped our horses and went into the barn where right off we saw Jed standing by himself, looking forlornly at the dance floor.

I approached him and said "Howdy Jed, enjoying the dance?"

He looked at me and shrugged his shoulders, "It's alright, I reckon."

The music stopped and the people left the dance floor. Jenny walked up and said, "Hello Marshal, hello Mister Sawyer."

In unison we replied, "Evening, Ma'am." Then I added, "Are *you* enjoying the dance?"

"Oh yes Marshal, it is ever so much fun. Only I wish I could get Jed here to dance a mite more. He's really a fine dancer."

Jed looked pained. "Yeah, I'm a fine dancer alright. I only stepped on her foot about a dozen times."

"That just means, Marshal, my foot was not where it was supposed to be," responded Jenny.

Jed still looked pained.

One of the musicians announced the next dance was to be a contra and that it was ladies choice. That meant the ladies would pick their partners. Of course, Jenny grabbed Jed's hand and started to drag him onto the dance floor, but he was resisting.

"Jed," I said, "it's not polite to refuse a lady's offer of a dance."

With that same pained look on his face, he said, "Huck, I don't even know what a contra is."

"Don't worry none, just follow what the caller says to do. If he says for the men to take two steps forward, you take two steps forward, and if he tells you to step to the side, you do that. Isn't that right Jenny?"

"It sure is, Marshal. Now you come with me, Jed Bevins. You are my choice for this dance, and I will be mortified if you refuse me."

As he was led away, and just to have a little fun with him, I said, "If the caller tells you to dosado, then you dosado." The abject fear on his face shrieked, *"What the hell is a dosado?"*

Tom said he wanted to get something to eat and left to rustle up some of Hollister's food. I saw Hollister talking to McNally and went over. As I walked up, I heard McNally exclaim, "Damn it, Lew, this don't seem to be workin' out. Look, all the cowpunchers and ranchers are on one side of the barn, and all the homesteaders are on the other. The only time they come together is when a puncher works up the nerve to ask a nester girl for a dance."

They saw me coming, and stopped talking long enough to greet me like a long lost relative. Hollister said, "Glad you're here, Marshal. Bob has been tellin' me he wants to quit this shindig and go home. Thinks it's a waste of time. He says nesters and cattlemen can never live side by side."

Right then the music started up and it was kind of loud. I suggested we go outside where we could hear ourselves think. Once outside, I noticed that there was a murmur going through the crowd, and some of the men were pointing over to the southwest. There, up in the black sky, was an orange glow. It could only mean fire!

McNally saw the direction the men were pointing and shouted, "That's my place!" By then the music had stopped, and the people in the barn were coming out to see what all the excitement was about; some of the men were rushing for their horses. I could see if I didn't do something soon, the entire place would empty out.

I yelled "STOP!" as loud as I could. Once I had their attention I said, "We'll go and see what's going on, but I need some of you men to stay here to protect the women and kids. This might be a trick to lure us away." I went to my horse, pulled my Winchester from the saddle boot, and tossed it to Jed.

"Jed, you stay here. I want you in charge. It could be Indians that set the fire as a feint to draw us out. Get the women and children into the barn, and have the men surround it carrying whatever weapons you can dig up for them."

Hollister spoke out, "I'm going with you, Marshal; I've got four rifles and two shotguns up to the house. My wife will get them for your deputy to distribute."

Next we decided which men would go and which would stay. It took less than a minute, and we ended up with half homesteaders and half ranchers and their punchers. I led the way with Tom riding by my side.

It didn't take us long to get to the fire. McNally's house and barn were ablaze. The livestock had been let out. We saw a few horses at the edge of the firelight grazing on grass. It wasn't Indians that set the fire; they would have taken the stock.

McNally knew what the stock being around meant, and hissed, "Cantry!" In a clearer voice, he said, "He's been tryin' to run me off since I got here. I'm the only rancher that shares the range with him, and he can't stomach that."

McGuiness was with us, he was the first to suggest a bucket brigade, but there was only one bucket sitting next to the pump. His offer of help did not go unnoticed by McNally. We sat our horses away from the heat and watched McNally's house and barn burn. There was nothing else to do; the fire was too far gone by the time we got there.

Then McGuiness said something that would change everything; he offered his home to McNally until he could rebuild. "You ain't never done nothing agin me or mine, and even if you did, the Christian way is to forgive and help our neighbors in their time of trial."

"I thank you McGuiness. I can tell you're a true Irishman and a Christian, but Hollister is my brother-in-law. I will stay with him. Tomorrow is Sunday. Right after services, I'm gonna start to rebuild, and your help would be mighty appreciated," responded McNally.

All the men, both nesters and ranchers, pledged their help in the rebuilding of McNally's ranch. If it was Cantry that set the fire, it had the opposite effect than what he had intended. For the fire at McNally's ranch had united the small ranchers and the homesteaders.

We returned to Hollister's and the men started to gather up their families, getting ready to go home. When McNally saw what was happening, he jumped up on a buckboard and said, "As you all know, I've lost my house tonight, but that ain't nothin'. I'm still alive and kickin', and tomorrow I start to rebuild. I'd sure appreciate it if you all did not cut the evening short on my account. I see there's still plenty of food left, and if you men that were playing the music would resume, I'm sure there's plenty here that would like a few more dances before we call it a night. Anyways, I ain't danced with my little sister yet." Looking out over the crowd that had gathered he continued, "There she is! Whatcha say, Missus Hollister, care to dance with your older brother?"

That was all that was needed. No longer was the barn divided in half with the nesters on one side and the ranchers on the other; everyone mingled.

Before Tom and I left, McNally cornered me and told me that first thing in the morning, before services, he and some of his hands were gonna pay Cantry a visit. "Ain't no man gonna burn me out and git away with it."

I took a tick or two before replying. I wanted Bob to fully understand what I was about to say. "We ain't even sure it was Cantry. And he's got Tuck Cole and nine other gun slicks backin' him. How many of *your* men are gun slicks? Do you wanna get your men killed?"

That kind of took the wind out of his sails. Then I went on, "Me and my deputies are gonna pay Cantry a visit first thing in the morning. If I even think he had something to do with the fire, I'm gonna tell my deputy, the one you know as the Laramie Kid, to put a bullet in his head. You have my word on it. Is that good enough for you?"

"I reckon," he said, "it'll have to be. But take mind, Marshal, that after tonight, this range ain't big enough for both Cantry and me."

I didn't bother to tell him that Jed was eventually going to put a bullet into Cantry no matter what.

TWENTY-TWO

We left Redemption early, Tom, Jed, and me. Being a Sunday morning, the street was deserted. We rode northwest toward Cantry's ranch, each one of us lost in his own thoughts. I'm not sure, but I reckon Jed was thinking that at long last he was going to be set free from his vow, and then he could get on with his life. Tom, from the look on his face, was contemplating the next life. I think he was sure he'd get his wish from either Cantry or one of his gun hands this morning. But I knew Tom Sawyer; he would not step in front of a bullet until the business at hand was settled. We moved slowly. There was no need to hurry; death is forever.

I looked at my watch as we rode into the yard; it was just ten o'clock. There were a few hands hanging outside the bunkhouse, but we paid them no mind. At the front of the house, I slipped my horse and told Tom and Jed to stay where they were.

The Chinaman eventually answered my knock on the door. He was wearing his white housecoat and had an inscrutable look upon his face. When I said I wanted to talk to Cantry, he informed me that Cantry had left for Denver the day before with Cole. I didn't think Cantry was the kind of man to hide behind a Chinaman, and I knew Cole wasn't, so I asked how long they'd be gone.

255

"Mister Cantry say he be back in seven, maybe eight days, and say I should have plenty of food on hand. Say he bringing back more hands."

I could only infer from what the Chinaman said that Cantry had gone in search of more gun slicks, though he'd be scraping the bottom of the barrel. Contrary to what most people think, especially those who read dime novels, most gunnies are back shooters. They are the scum that come to any new land to take advantage of the honest folk who came in search of a new life, a new beginning.

There wasn't much we could do if Cantry wasn't around. Or was there?

I walked my horse over to the bunkhouse. Jed and Tom followed. There were now five of Cantry's men hanging about, and they seemed real interested in us.

"Howdy boys, going to services this morning?"

None of them laughed at my attempt at humor. So I asked another question, "See the big fire last night?"

One of the men took a step forward and said, "If you mean the McNally ranch, then we didn't see it, Marshal. None of us left the ranch last night." He grinned and turned to his friends, "Ain't that right boys?"

Along with the general agreement, there were a few laughs, and one man snickered, though I didn't see who it was.

About then my temper was getting the better of me. I turned to Tom to tell him to pull his shotgun from its scabbard, but I need not have bothered. He was sitting tall in the saddle with the shotgun's stock resting on his thigh; the barrel pointing straight up. Tom was learning fast.

Then to the jasper that had spoken I said, "How did you know it was the McNally ranch if you didn't leave here?" Well, that wiped the grins right off their faces real fast. Without turning from them, I advised Tom to lower his gun and point it at the man I had been talking to. At that point, his friends started to move away from him, but I warned them that my other deputy would kill the first man who took another step.

It's one thing to meet a man in a fair fight. This is a tough country, and most men wear a gun. It's a useful tool out here. There are animals to be protected from, and some of those animals are men. If the good people did not fight back, then this country would be run by bad men, men like Cantry.

I had waited long enough, maybe too long. I was hoping to avoid an all-out range war. I thought maybe Jed and I (and Tom) could scare Cantry into acting decent; I reckon I was wrong. It was now time to fight back.

"Shuck your guns and let 'em fall to the ground, boys. I ain't playin' with you home burners no more. I oughta hang the lot of you from those trees over yonder," I said, while pointing to a small grove of oak trees.

For once, I was glad I had a reputation. And I'm sure they were all well aware of Jed's. Tom, he didn't need a reputation . . . not holding that four-shot cannon of his.

When they were rid of their guns, I ordered them to move over against the bunkhouse wall and sit on the ground. One man started to say something, but I interjected, "I will kill the first man that tells me I have no sway here or that I'm off my range." That stopped all further attempts at conversation.

Once they were sitting down in the dust, I told Jed to go into the bunkhouse and gather up any guns that he could find. In a few minutes, he was back with a couple of six-shooters, an old Sharps .50, and a new Henry. He laid them on the ground next to the other guns, and without me having to tell him, he went into the barn and retrieved the long guns from their saddle boots.

Before he got back, I slipped my horse and walked up to the five men. Standing over them I said, "The only reason I'm not gonna hang you gents is that I'm tryin' to keep the killin' to a minimum, that and the fact that you were just takin' orders. Collect your kits, saddle your horses, and get outta this country fast. If you don't, I'll tell McNally where to find you. He wanted to come over here this morning and if he had, it would have been with fifty riders, both nesters and cattlemen. By now all five of you, and anyone else he could find working for Cantry, would be kickin' air with stretched necks. Now ride!"

They stood and started to go into the bunkhouse, but one man held back and said, "It's bad enough losing our guns, but Cantry owes us two weeks' pay."

I shook my head at the stupidity of some men. Here he was getting out with his life, and he was worried about two weeks' wages. Then I thought of something. "What does Cantry pay you? I figure it's double a cowpuncher's pay because you were hired more for your guns than to punch cows. What is it, eighty dollars a month?"

The man nodded.

"Alright, you can take some of Cantry's cows for what's owed you and a few extra for your trouble of having to herd them to a place where you can sell 'em." They liked that idea just fine. "Just one more thing," I said, "where's the rest of the outfit?"

I was informed that there were only four others, and they were rounding up strays from the arroyos to the north. I told Jed and Tom to get these five on their way, then go and see to the other four. "Get their guns, tell 'em to grab some cows and get moving. Tell 'em not to come back for their kits. Then meet me back here." I figured they'd take a lot more than a few cows, but that was fine by me. I don't normally condone cattle rustling. However, in Cantry's case, I was willing to make an exception.

After everyone had gone, I walked back to the house and knocked on the door. When the Chinaman answered, the first thing I asked him was his name. "It is Hu Chang," he said. Then I asked him where he slept. "In a room off the kitchen," he answered.

"Alright Hu Chang, go and collect your things, you're movin' into the bunkhouse. But don't worry none, you'll have it all to yourself." He didn't say anything; he just bowed and went off to do as he was told.

As soon as he had transferred his belongings to the bunkhouse and was sitting on one of the bunks, I instructed him to tell Cantry that it was me who had run off his men and set fire to his house. "The name's Huck Finn."

Chang's eyes did widen a mite when I said I was going to burn the house, but only momentarily. I then added, "I'm not gonna burn the barn. It would only inconvenience the animals. However, I want you to feed them and take care of 'em until Cantry returns. Do you understand me?" He bowed in his inscrutable manner. I took that as a yes. At the door, as I was leaving, I turned and asked him why he worked for a man like Cantry.

He stood and drew himself up to his full height of five-five, and in perfect English said, "I was cooking for the railroad until they drove the Golden Spike. Then I needed a job, and Cantry needed a cook." He hesitated for a moment before adding, "I have a wife and a son back in China that I have not seen in three years. I am working to bring them over here. I would work for the devil himself if it would hasten the day of our reunion." Where the Pidgin English had gone I had no idea.

I thought for a moment and then asked, "How much to get 'em here?"

"Four thousand dollars. There are debts in China that must be paid first, and then they can leave."

"How much you got saved?"

"Almost seven hundred dollars."

"Tell you what, Chang. As soon as you deliver my message to Cantry, you come into town. I've got some money sittin' in a bank in Missouri that ain't doin' me no good. I reckon I can spare five thousand dollars to get your people here. The extra thousand is so you can have a decent home waitin' for them when they get here."

I didn't wait for a reply. I went into the house and went from room to room spilling lantern oil, making a trail of it out to the front parlor. It was a handsome house, and it would be a shame to burn the books in the study, but I had a message to send. With the strike of a match on my britches, the house went up in flames.

I stood and watched the house burn. Presently, Chang joined me. Together we stood and watched the flames consume the house, not speaking. At length Chang said, "There were a few books in there that I would have liked to save." He hastily added, "Not for Cantry, but for me."

261

About the time the flames were dying down, Jed and Tom came riding back in. I had not told them what I was going to do, but they didn't bat an eye. In fact, Jed smiled at me and nodded his approval.

"Get everyone on their way?" I asked.

Tom answered me, "Yeah, them and a lot of cows. They each got about a year's wages coming to them when they make Abilene or wherever they're going."

As I mounted my horse, I reminded Chang of my message to Cantry and not to forget to come in for the bank draft. Then the three of us rode out heading for town. Along the way, I thought we should tell McNally that Cantry was not around, just in case he wanted to do a little night riding in Cantry's direction. I also thought the news of Cantry's house accidently catching fire would brighten his day. But we never did make it to McNally's.

Along the way, Jed noticed buzzards circling a spot about a half a mile to the west of us. Thinking it might be an injured animal and that we could put it out of its misery, we headed in that direction. What we found was a wounded man lying on the ground. He had lost a lot of blood; his shirt was covered with it. At first, we weren't even sure if he was alive, but as we rode up, he blinked his eyes open. I was the first on the ground, and I knelt next to him. He tried to speak, but only a hoarse whisper escaped his lips.

"Jed, toss me your canteen." I cradled his head in the crook of my arm and let him drink his fill.

As I withdrew the canteen from his mouth, he said, "My family, my family."

By now Jed and Tom were on the ground standing over us supplying shade to the man's head. He was pretty well burnt. He must have been lying out there most of the day. How he was still alive was a mystery to me.

I laid him back down and started to remove his shirt to examine the wound. But he weakly swiped at my hand and said, "Don't bother 'bout me. Get on the trail of my family. They was taken by three men."

I swore we'd get his family, but first I was going to look at his wound. I would have washed it out, but it had stopped bleeding and I didn't want to open it up again. I didn't think he could stand to lose too much more blood. I tore a piece off my shirt to make a bandage just in case the wound started to bleed. As I was attending to that, he told me what had happened.

"We was coming out from Kansas going to California. We had planned to wait out the winter in Denver where I hoped to find some work. We was camped about a mile back. This mornin' while my wife and daughter was in the back of the wagon puttin' things away, and I had just finished hitchin' up the horses, three riders came up—two Mexicans and a white man. Without saying a word, the big

Mexican took out his revolver and shot me. Then he jumped from his horse into the driver's seat and drove the wagon away. He was followed by his two partners, one of them leading his horse. I followed them for as long as I could until I collapsed. Then you found me."

"At what time did you get shot?" I asked.

"About an hour after sun-up."

"What is your name?"

"Roy Price. But why are you hanging here asking me fool questions? You should be out after 'em!"

I told Tom to ride into town and get the doctor and a buckboard. To Price I said, "We're gonna wait with you until my deputy gets back; it won't be more than an hour. Those *hombres* aren't going anywhere fast in a wagon. They'll have to stop for the night, and we'll be there well before they can get their coffee on. They left a trail a blind man could follow."

"But you don't understand what they could do to my wife and daughter while you're standing here."

I was tired of talking and asked Jed if he'd like to explain it.

He asked Price the age of his daughter.

"She's sixteen."

Jed took off his hat, mopped his brow and said, "The way I figure it is, they stalked you and your family like you were game. And when they were ready, they made their move. I can see their trail from here. After you fell, they headed south. They plan to sell your women down in Mexico or maybe to some Indians along the way. They won't molest them because then they'd be damaged goods. White women bring a lotta money in Mexico. Some are worth their weight in gold, and they're a mite easier to transport. But don't worry none. Those men will be dead, and we'll have your women back to you by sunset tomorrow. We will bring them to you in Redemption. You have my word on that."

"Redemption?" he asked.

"The name of our town," I answered, "When that boy gives his word, ain't nobody gonna stop him from keeping it."

We got Price onto the buckboard after Doc had looked him over. He confirmed what I already knew; the bullet had passed through, missing the lungs. All that was needed now was to clean out the wound, patch it, and leave nature to do the healing. Maybe if Jed and I got his wife and daughter back, that might help too.

I said to Tom, "After you get Mister Price situated, go and see Niles and tell him that you're in charge again until we get done with the kidnappers. If he has a problem with that, you tell him he can talk to me about it when we get back. I reckon we'll be back tomorrow about sunset."

Jed and I set out at a good clip and gave the horses a good workout. We kept a decent pace until just before dusk; then we walked our horses. By then the trail was fresh, no more than an hour old. We had to be careful because we didn't want to blunder into them unawares.

Just before full dark, we found a dry wash where we hid the horses. Taking our long guns from their boots, we proceeded on foot until we saw their fire. Crawling on our bellies, we got close enough to their camp to hear the conversation. First off, we were surprised to see not only the two women and the three bandits we expected, but also four Indian braves. The braves were speaking Spanish and there seemed to be some dickering going on. I don't understand Spanish, but it was plain to see that the Indians were dickering for the women.

Jed whispered to me that the Indians were Arapahos and when he was with the Pawnee, they had traded with them a little. He added, "I speak a few words of their language."

We quickly came up with a strategy. Jed stood and walked into the bandits' camp. Him coming out of the darkness and into the flickering firelight got everyone's attention. Speaking to the Indians in their language, he said, "These women are mine. They were stolen, and I plan to kill these men, but I do not want to harm you."

Then to the Price women he said in English, "I am a friend; I have been sent by Mister Price. Now if you ladies will please come over here by the Indians, everything will be all right."

Our plan was simple. Get the women out of the line of fire, and let the Indians know they were not under attack. The Indians were sure to have a camp nearby and if we killed them, it would be sure to dust up more of a ruckus than we wanted to—or could handle—at the time. Besides, we didn't want to kill innocent men, be they Indians or not.

Jed's appearance was so unexpected that the bandits were momentarily caught off guard. By the time the bandits rallied, the women were out of harm's way. That's when I opened up. The big Mexican that had shot Price was the first to go down. By the time I levered my second round, Jed had killed the other two.

The Indians were now standing and talking excitably among themselves as I walked out of the darkness. Before they could do something decisive, I directed Jed to tell them that they could have the men's horses and guns and anything else that they wanted. But the team, the wagon, and the women were ours. That seemed to mollify them. After all, to their way of thinking, a horse or a gun was much more valuable than a woman.

While Jed was talking to the Indians, I spoke to Missus Price. "Howdy ma'am, my name's Huck Finn, and I'm the marshal of Redemption, a little town east of here. We found your husband, and he's all right. But now we've got to get you and your daughter outta here before those bucks over there or some of their friends cause any trouble. If you and your daughter would climb up on the wagon, I'll hitch up the team, and we'll be on our way."

Not only did the Indians take the horses and the guns, they took the bandits' clothes as well. When I was finished hitching up the team, I turned to call to Jed and saw that two of the bandits were as naked as the day they were born; the third was dressed in a red union suit.

After Jed saw the Indians on their way, we started out; me in the driver's seat and Missus Price and her daughter next to me. Jed walked with us until we got to the place where we had left our horses. He tied my horse to the back of the wagon and then rode alongside as we headed for home. The night was lit by a full moon, so there was no trouble seeing the trail. Along the way, I learned the daughter's name was Susanna.

After two hours, I suggested to Missus Price that she and her daughter get into the back of the wagon and try to get some sleep. I don't know if they slept or not, but after what they'd been through, I thought that they should have some time alone. I planned to roll all night.

As the sky lightened in the east, I pulled up to rest the horses and ourselves. It had been a long, hard twenty-four hours for Jed and me. We unhitched and ground-staked the horses, then we crawled under the wagon to get a couple hours of sleep. Before we fell off, Missus Price was there with some blankets. We thanked her, and I asked her to wake us in two hours. Then I promptly fell asleep.

I was awakened by the smell of frying bacon; it's a good way to wake up. I shook Jed awake and crawled out from under the wagon. Missus Price was kneeling before a fire turning bacon and Susanna was pouring water into a coffee pot.

"Mornin' Missus Price, mornin' Susanna."

"Morning, Marshal," they responded. Missus Price added, "I was just about to wake you boys. The coffee will be ready in a minute, and as soon as this bacon's cooked, I'll make some biscuits in the grease."

We ate quickly and were soon on our way. There wasn't much talk; the women were lost in their own thoughts, and I reckoned Jed was thinking of Jenny. Me, I was thinking how lucky we were that the Indians had not put up a fight.

I rolled the wagon up to Doc's house an hour before dark. The women went inside while Jed and I unhitched the horses. He took them over to the livery stable and paid to have them rubbed down and fed.

Figuring Missus Price and her daughter would be needing a place to stay while Mister Price recuperated, I headed to the Excelor Hotel and made arrangements with Missus Simms, Jenny's mother. She ran the hotel. Her husband had been killed in the war. Then I went to the boarding house to take a long, hot bath. I was going to let Tom keep the peace in town for one more night because after the bath, I was going to get into bed and sleep for at least twelve hours. I was dead-and-buried tired.

All I had to do now was wait for Cantry to show.

TWENTY-THREE

The next day saw me up before dawn and down to the eating house before it opened for business. We all call it the eating house because that's easier than calling it by its rightful name: The White Goose Restaurant. It's part of the Excelor Hotel and has two entrances; the one on the street and one from the side, off the lobby.

Because the street door was locked, I went into the lobby to wait for the restaurant to open for business. While I was sitting in a very comfortable chair, reading a month old newspaper from St. Louis, Missus Simms approached me.

"Good morning, Marshal. You're up kinda early this morning."

"Yes ma'am. Got to bed early. I was plum tuckered out after two days in the saddle."

"Yes, that was a mighty fine thing what you did for those people."

"I didn't do it alone, I had Jed with me. In fact, if it wasn't for him being able to talk Injun' talk, we might have had us a real problem."

"If you don't mind, I'd like to talk about that. I mean him."

271

"Him, ma'am?"

"Your deputy, but let's go into the restaurant. I'm sure the coffee's ready by now."

She unlocked the side door. We went in and seated ourselves at a table, she sitting on the bench opposite me. Jenny wasn't in yet, but the cook stuck her head out of the kitchen door to see who had come in, and Missus Simms asked her to please bring us some coffee.

We made small talk until the coffee arrived, and as I took my first sip, Missus Simms said, "I want to talk to you about your deputy."

"Yes ma'am, what about Jed?"

She seemed kind of nervous and little hesitant, but I figured she would spit out what she had to say in her own good time. At length she did. "You see, Marshal, Jenny's my only child, and it wasn't easy raising her alone. I know she's a growed woman and knows her own mind, but I want what's best for her. . . "

There she faltered, so I thought I'd help her along.

"And you think Jed might not be good for her?"

"Look Marshal, I let her go to the dance with him because she told me no one else had asked her. I didn't believe that for a minute, but I didn't want to make a fuss. Now I'm afraid she's sweet on him."

Sipping my coffee and looking at her over the rim of the cup, I said, "You mean Jed?"

"Of course I mean him!"

"You mean who?"

"Your deputy!"

Taking another sip of coffee and placing the cup on the table, I smiled and said, "Do you know that you have not once said his name? It's Jed Bevins, in case you don't know."

For a moment, she was taken aback. Then she said, "His name is the Laramie Kid. He's a killer, and the whole town knows it. For God's sake, Marshal, he's killed thirty men!"

I sighed and picked up my cup; it was empty. I asked if I could have some more coffee. After the cook poured me a cup and I sugared it, I said, "Ma'am, I don't think it was thirty men, although you're close. But there is something you should know." I then told her about Jed taking sick and the Pawnee saving him. I told her about Cantry raiding the Pawnee village and killing sixty men, women and children. I made her aware of Jed's promise to his dying friend, and at the end I added, "Jed came here to kill Cantry, but when I asked him to hold off, he did so. He's been a help in trying to prevent a range war where innocent homesteaders and ranchers like McGuiness and

McNally could be run off their land or killed. Instead of us killing the sonavabitches, we ran off those that we could. Those six we killed over at The Silver Dollar came into town to kill us by ambush. If they had succeeded, then Cantry would own this town. And if Cantry owned this town, your business would dry up and blow away. There would be no more homesteaders or cowpokes eating in your restaurant except Cantry's men. And there ain't enough of them to make it worth your while to keep open. Besides, they're all hired killers. There would only be Cantry buyin' things in town, and he could dictate his own prices. Is that the kind of town you want to live in?"

It was not the kind of town she wanted to live in and I knew it. I just wanted her to understand that we lived in a harsh land, and sometimes a man had to do things that went against his grain. She understood. Without another word, she got up, smiled at me, and walked out the side door, passing Jenny as she came in.

As I drank my coffee and waited for Jenny to come and take my breakfast order, I heard a rapping on the glass behind me. I turned around and saw Jed standing outside. Someone had forgotten to unlock the street door. I started for the door, but was brushed aside by Jenny as she rushed to Jed's rescue. The poor boy may have had to stay out in the cold another few seconds or so.

When Jed was seated at the table, I asked him what he was doing up so early.

"Went to bed early," was all he had to say on the subject.

We both ordered flapjacks and said nary a word until the plates were empty. Then Jed asked me what was next. He meant what was next in relation to Cantry.

"All we can do," I said, "is wait for him to get back. But we never did make it out to McNally's. I think I'll ride out there today while you keep an eye on the town. I'll tell him about what happened at Cantry's place. You know . . . the accident that burnt his house to the ground?"

Jed nodded, and I stood. "I'll be over to the jail. I've gotta bring some food to our prisoner. Come on over when you're finished here." Meaning when he was finished mooning over Jenny. Then I went to the kitchen to get a plate of flapjacks for Dan.

About an hour later, I was sitting outside the office enjoying the warm sun on my skin when McNally rode up.

"Howdy, Marshal. Nice day ain't it?"

"Sure is, Bob. Why not light a spell and enjoy the sun with me. It'll be snowin' before you know it."

"Thanks, Marshal, but I didn't come into town to sit; I came to talk. I expected to hear some word about Cantry. And here I find you sittin' there without a care in the world. Did you confront him like you said you would?"

Just then, Jed walked up and I could see Tom down the street going into the eating house.

"No Bob, I didn't confront Cantry, though I know he burned your house or had it done."

Still sitting his horse, I thought Bob was going to have a fit. He turned five shades of red and then sputtered, "I told you if you didn't take care of him that I would. You had your chance, Marshal, now I'll take it from here!"

I couldn't hold my laughter in any longer and let loose. He looked at me as though I should be certified. I said, "Hold on Bob, me and my deputies went out there the next morning like I said we would. He's in Denver, so all we could do was run off all his hands and some of his stock, and burn his house clear down to the ground. When he gets back, we'll either run him outta the country or plant him in it."

Bob looked at me and then at Jed. Then he looked up the street and then down the street before saying, "If you don't take all, Huck Finn. Reckon I could sit a mite, but not in here the sun. Let's go across the street to The Silver Dollar. I'm buyin'."

Sitting at a table over beers, Jed and I filled Bob in on what had happened on our visit to Cantry's. When we were done with our recitation, he had a grin on his face, as I knew he would.

"So what's next?" he asked.

"We wait for my other deputy to find us, and then we make a plan of war. But in the meantime, we're gonna have us another beer," I answered.

Before we got to our third beer, Tom walked in holding his ever-present shotgun. Seeing the beer and the empty glasses he said, "Some marshal." Then turning to Jed, he added, "And some deputy." He laughed and ordered himself a beer. When Tom was seated, I informed all at the table that this was our council of war.

I said right off, "Bob, you're not gonna be in on this. The fight, when it comes, is gonna happen here in Redemption. Tom, Jed, and me are the law here. You've got a house and barn to rebuild; you best be doin' that, and let us take care of Cantry."

He got mad like only an Irishman can. However, being of Irish descent myself, his words and maledictions just flowed over me like water off a duck's back. And him being an Irishman, he ordered himself a whiskey from the barkeep when he came to realize that I couldn't be moved and he was out of it. I warned him that if he showed his face in town again before we took care of Cantry, I would arrest him and hold him in jail until matters were settled. He downed his whiskey, told me I could pay the bill, and stormed out. As we watched him push through the swing doors, Jed said, "He's got bottom—he's a man to ride the river with."

"Yes," I said, "he's got grit, and he's a good man. *And* I wanna keep him alive. You and me, Jed, we know this business. And you Tom, I wanna keep you alive also, and I aim to do just that."

"Are you going to arrest me?" asked Tom.

"No," I answered, "you're in. But I don't want you taking any fool chances."

Now that we had that settled, we got down to business. I figured Cantry and his men would come at us in the morning because Denver was a two-day ride, two *full* days. They'd hit his ranch at dusk and would be too wore out to go on the warpath. They would wait until morning and then come in from the west, which would put the sun to our backs. It was a small advantage; however, we would need all the advantages we could get.

We didn't know how many men Cantry would have, but it was a safe bet it would be about ten. Cantry always kept twenty hands, and he had no idea that we had run off the nine he left behind. So he'd be coming from Denver with about ten men . . . if he could find that many men willing to fight and maybe die in another man's war.

I laid out the plan that I had come up with the day before while driving Missus Price and her daughter into town.

TWENTY-FOUR

That afternoon, as I was walking the town, I saw Chang coming out of Niles's store and approached him.

"Howdy Chang, what brings you to town? Cantry ain't back yet, is he?"

"No, Marshal. It's just that except for what was in the smoke house, I have no food out there. It was all consumed in a fire if you'll remember. Mister Cantry and his men will be expecting to eat when they arrive, so I came into town to get some supplies."

"Well, I'm glad I ran into you. I was thinking of riding out there, and this saves me the trip. I need a favor."

"Sure, Marshal, just ask."

"When Cantry gets back, and after you feed him and his men, can you slip away and come to town? I need to know when he's back and how many men he has so that we can be ready."

"Sure Marshal, it'll be my pleasure."

As long as he was in town, I took him over to the bank to get that bank draft I promised him. I also sent a letter to Potter to make sure he honored the draft when it was presented. Chang tried to thank me, but that sort of thing is embarrassing. I pointed out that the best way to thank me would be to let me know when Cantry got back so that I could set up for him.

Chang assured me that it would be done. He said he was only staying on to give Cantry my message; now, he would have a second reason—to warn me of Cantry's return. We shook hands, and I stood there and watched him through the dust he kicked up as he drove his buggy out of town.

Turning to go back to the jail, I came face to face with Jim Niles, and he did not look happy.

"Did I just see you talking to Colonel Cantry's chink?" he asked.

"Yes, Mister Niles, you did."

"All I can say is that you've got your nerve. I was just coming to see you. Bob McNally was in this morning and said that you set fire to Colonel Cantry's house. Burnt it right down to the ground! I don't believe it; you wouldn't do such a thing."

It wasn't a question, so I said nothing, which riled him up even more. Then he raised his voice and said, "Well, did you set fire to Cantry's house or not?"

I was getting a mite tired of explaining myself, but he was my boss, so I reckoned I owed him something. "I did it because he burnt out McNally. I did it because he wasn't around for me to put a bullet into him. He's gonna be riding in here any day now with some gun slicks from Denver, and when he does, I want you to stay off the street and tell the rest of the town to do the same. There's gonna be gunplay, and the ones I want dead are Cantry and his men, not innocent town folk."

His mouth gaped open and he tried to speak, but nothing came out. Finally he said, "Finn, you're fired! You were hired to keep the peace, not to have gun battles in the street with one of our leading citizens. Cantry's my best customer, and I'll be damned if I'll allow you to act in this high-handed manner."

I could have told him that Cantry planned to kill McNally and the nesters if they didn't move off the range. I could have told him that would bring in the army and martial law, and Cantry would be gone anyway. The only difference being that there would be families driven from their land, and maybe a father or a husband would die defending his land. I could have told him that if anyone had to die, then let it be Cantry and his gun slicks, not good, God-fearin' people. But as I said, I was tired; I told him nothing of that. Instead, I looked him in the eye and said, "I'll give you this badge when I'm damn good and ready. But if you think you're man enough to take it from me, then do so now."

He closed his gaping mouth, looked me up and down, and finally he said, "This ain't over."

"Damn right it ain't over, but keep outta my way 'til it is." I left him standing there gulping air like a landed fish.

The next morning, Tom and I were sitting outside the jail smoking our pipes and watching the street traffic. Jed was walking the town keeping the peace, or maybe he was visiting with Jenny; I'm not sure which. We had made our plans and there was nothing for it but to await Cantry's arrival. We couldn't go to him; we were too far outnumbered to fight it out in the open. We had to wait for him to come into town, which is what we were doing.

Presently, Tom cleared his throat and said, "Huck, do you remember when we were back in camp right after we signed up, and we were doing all that marching and not getting anywhere?"

"Sure," I said, "I remember. How could I forget? Remember how we used to soak our feet at night?"

Tom smiled at the memory and said, "I remember, but I wanted to talk about something different. Do you recollect one night we asked each other why we joined up? You said it wasn't about slavery; you were just looking for some adventure. Do you recall that?"

"Sure Tom, I recollect that I do." He was leading up to something, so I kept my answer short and waited for him to continue.

"I told you I wasn't fighting for slavery either; I was fighting for the Cause. But that wasn't exactly true; the Cause *was* slavery. I told you I didn't think badly of colored folk, but I didn't think they were the same as us."

I said nothing, so he went on.

"It's just this, Huck. I want you to know that I've changed my way of thinking. You notice that I don't use the word nigger no more, I mean anymore. I think it's hurtful to colored folks." He stopped speaking for a moment; he had a faraway look in his eyes. It was like he wasn't there. He could have been on the other side of the world.

In time, Tom came back from wherever he had gone and said, "Huck, you're the best friend I ever had, next to Kalei that is, and I'd like you to know my thinking just in case anything happens in the next day or so."

"Besides Cantry, what brought that on?"

"A lot of things, Huck. First of all, Kalei's uncle was as black as Jim. Well, maybe not black, more brown, but if he were to get on a train, he wouldn't be allowed to sit with the white folks. Yet, I never met a kinder or more educated man. Kalei was half white and half Hawaiian, and I loved her more than anything. Being with them taught me so much. A man is a man no matter the color of his skin. I don't know, Huck; I just want you to know that's the way I feel. I want you to know that I've changed."

"I'm glad you changed. I read in a book once that life was all about change. It would be kinda pointless to go out the same as we came in. I came to your way of thinkin' a while back when I spent so much time with Jim. You can't help but see the humanity in a man when you spend time with him. But I still say nigger. And I call a chink a chink. I never thought about it hurtin' them. So maybe I won't do it no more. But to me, it's what's in a man's heart that counts, and you've always had a good heart Tom, so don't let it worry you none."

About suppertime, the three of us were moseying up the street. Tom and I were going to eat at The Silver Dollar because we wanted a little whiskey to work up an appetite, and Jed was going over to the eating house for some reason or other. We were about to separate when I saw a lone rider coming into town from the west. The sun was low, almost touching the horizon, and we couldn't make out who it was. The only thing we could tell was the rider wore no hat and looked kinda small. I thought it might be a woman.

We stood, shielding our eyes from the sun, waiting for the stranger to get close enough so we could make him or her out. And wouldn't you know it? It was Chang. He walked his horse up to where we were standing and after nodding at us, he simply said, "Evening, Marshal . . . Deputies. Cantry's back."

At that news, Jed decided he could visit with Jenny another time and came into The Silver Dollar with us.

Being suppertime, The Dollar was almost empty. Most people ate at the eating house or at home. There were just a few saddle tramps at the bar that had no place else to be. Mike wasn't there either; he was probably home with his family eating supper. Henry was behind the bar wiping a glass when he saw us come in with Chang.

He put the glass down and said, "Sorry, Marshal, but you know we don't serve chinks in here."

Chang stopped in his tracks with Jed and Tom right beside him. I continued walking until I was opposite Henry at the bar. I took off my hat, and sadly, slowly shook my head. "Henry, you're not a bad fella, and I'd sure hate to have to arrest you for being stupid. That man is not a chink; he's a Chinaman. At least that's what my deputy Tom says. He is a friend of mine and he's probably smarter than you and me put together. So he's gonna sit with us and if he wants, he's gonna drink with us. Are we gonna have a problem, Henry?"

"No sir, Marshal, just doin' my job. What would you gentlemen like to drink?"

When we were seated around the table with a bottle of some good stuff in front of us, Chang told us about Cantry.

He rode in with Cole and eight new men. Chang said they didn't look like much, but you can never tell with gun slicks. Of course, Cantry was enraged when he saw the remains of his house, and was further irritated when he learned that his hands had been run off. But Chang said the thing that bothered Cantry the most was that his Confederate uniform was destroyed. For that desecration, he swore to hang me from the highest tree in the county.

It seemed I was right in my surmise that they'd come in the morning. Chang told us that he cooked them a meal over an open fire, seeing as he had no kitchen stove anymore. The plan was to kill me and anyone else that got in their way, meaning Jed and Tom. Then they were going to pay McNally a visit and then the sodbusters; they had a full day planned. It looked like Cantry was going to start his range war tomorrow.

Chang said he'd stay in town and help out if I wanted. I didn't know how good he was with a gun, but it was my intention to keep the innocents from being killed, so I declined his offer. Instead, I asked him to eat with us. An offer he accepted.

After we had all gotten outside some thick steaks with all the trimmings, Chang said he had to go. Leaving Tom and Jed at the table, I walked outside with him. When we were standing next to his horse, I asked if he was riding back out to Cantry's.

"No, Marshal. If you don't need me, then I'll be riding north up to Promontory Point where I'll catch a train to San Francisco. But before I go, I want you to know how much I appreciate what you have done for me and my family. If I am ever fortunate enough to have another male child, I will name him after you. His name will be Hu Huck Finn."

I grimaced at the thought and told him it was bad enough there was one Huck Finn in the world and that a Chinese baby with a handle like that would have a hard time of it while growing up. He just gave me that inscrutable smile of his, got on his horse, and rode out.

While Chang and I were talking, Jed and Tom had settled themselves on the bench outside the saloon. When I walked up, Tom was smoking his pipe, and Jed was cleaning one of his guns. Leaning against an awning post I said, "Alright boys, from now on we're on a war footing. We've got a big day tomorrow, and we'll need some shuteye; so we'll take turns walking the town tonight. Three shifts of three hours each. Even with Cantry comin', we still have to keep the peace. But seein' as how it's a Tuesday night, things should be quiet. Tom, you take the first walk around, and I'll relieve you. Jed, you take the last, then come and get us when you're done. We have things to do before sunrise, 'cause we don't know when Cantry's gonna ride in, and I wanna be ready for him."

Two hours before first light, the three of us gathered in the front parlor at the boarding house. From there we proceeded to the livery stable because, as I had told the boys the night before, we had things to do.

Later, I was sitting outside the jail with my chair tipped back, my feet on the rail, and my hat pulled down so low that it looked like I was asleep. But from under the brim, I could see up and down the street in both directions. The morning was cool and crisp; to the east, the morning star hung low in the gray sky. To the west, a sliver of a crescent moon was just touching the mountains.

If Cantry was going to rid the range of McNally and the homesteaders, he was going to have to be rid of me and my deputies first. They came in from the west, as we knew they would. I saw the dust swirls first, then an indistinct black shape that, at length, turned into individual riders. Eventually, I could make out Cantry in the lead with Cole right behind him. They rode slowly up the street as though they owned it. When they got abreast of the jail, Cantry halted, and the rest fanned out on either side of him. There were ten of them lined up on the street—all of them facing me. Cantry was in the middle with Cole next to him. No one spoke, but Cantry was giving me a hard stare.

Finally he said, "Marshal, I want you to come with us."

I had to smile at the man's nerve. "I hear you want to hang me, Cantry. You figure it will take the ten of you to do it?"

That surprised him; I could see it in his face. He probably reckoned on giving me some cock-and-bull story to get me out of town and then stretch my neck from a tree in an out-of-the-way place. But now that I knew of his plans, he was thinking on what to do next. Even Cantry had to know that it's bad business to kill a lawman in his own town. Then again, Cantry was a pretty downright arrogant sonavabitch.

After taking a minute to think, he said, "You burned my house and for that you will pay."

I could have reminded him of my promise that whatever he did to the nesters, I would do to him. But the ball was about to go up, and nothing I said was going to stop it. Abruptly, Cantry said, "Shoot him, Cole!"

There it was. And it was a good thing that I was anticipating Cantry saying just that because Cole was fast, but that day, I was faster by a second. Though it didn't do me any good. His horse stepped sideways just as I squeezed the trigger. My bullet nicked his ear, but that was all. His shot plowed into the awning post next to me. Before he could get off a second shot, I dove through the open door of the jailhouse. Then all hell broke loose.

Tom was in there, ready with his shotgun, and before I even hit the door, he broke the window, stuck the barrel through and started blasting away. Jed was in the Silver Dollar across the street, and he let loose at the same time as Tom. We had them in a crossfire.

After what seemed like an hour but was less than a minute, they broke and raced down the street. We had planned for this. We reckoned they would either leave town or find shelter from our bullets until they could finish the job they had come to do. And they did just what we hoped they would. Halfway down the street stood the livery stable with its big, wide double doors inviting entry. It also had double doors in the rear for escape, if need be. That's where they took refuge.

Earlier that morning, we had gone to the livery stable and removed the horses, taking them to a private barn at the edge of town. Then we persuaded the hostler to be our guest at the eating house when it opened. We told him to stay there until one of us came to get him. After he and the horses had been taken care of, we nailed two-by-fours across the outside of the rear doors so there would be only one way in and one way out. Now Cantry and his remaining men were just where we wanted them. I say remaining men because four of Cantry's men were lying dead in the dust outside the jailhouse. Two of them were hit with Tom's shotgun blast, and the other two had bullet holes right where their hearts should be. That was Jed's shooting. I was so busy diving for cover that I got off no more shots. By the time I raised my head, the shooting was over, and Cantry and his men were holed up in the livery stable.

Jed walked over from The Silver Dollar, and Tom and I went out to meet him. After looking over the dead (they were just young cowpokes, not hardened gun slicks), we walked on down to where Cantry and his men awaited us. On the way, I decided I didn't want to kill any more of those men from Denver than we had to. Hell, I didn't even want to kill Cole and Cantry. The more you kill, the easier it gets. I'd been fighting that killing urge for a while by the time that crisp, cool morning rolled around.

When we got within sight of the stable, we saw one of the Denver men peering out, his body concealed by the right side of the door. I told Jed to put a bullet into the wood just above his head to drive him back inside. No use letting the enemy know your numbers.

I sent Jed to the left, Tom to the right, and had them flatten out against the building, one on each side of the door. Me, I stood in the middle of the street where I could be seen and called out to the men inside. I never said that I was smart.

"You men in there, my name is Huck Finn and I'm the marshal of this here town. Four of your number are lying dead up the street, and we don't want to kill any more of you than we have to. I don't think the job pays enough to die for. It's pretty hard to enjoy your money when you're lying up there on Boot Hill."

I felt kind of exposed out there. I wanted to say what I had to say and move off to the side a mite so I wouldn't make such a nice target. So I quickly continued, "Anyone that wants to put up his gun will be allowed to leave. Anyone, that is, except Cantry. The backdoor is nailed shut and in five minutes we're coming in shooting. If you want out of this, come out leading your horse with your right hand on the bridle and your left hand high in the air." I figured that was enough and walked over to stand beside Tom, out of the line of fire.

Tom asked me if I thought any of them would take the offer. I couldn't answer him. Any sane man would know that we could starve them out. They were bottled up and they knew it. However, one thing they didn't know, but I did, was that the longer this drew out, the more of a chance that some of the leading lights of the town, Cantry's friends—or I should say people that made a living off of his trade—would try to interfere. I wanted to wrap this up within the hour if we could.

As it turned out, we didn't have long to wait. Two of them came out leading their horses with their hands in the air, just as they had been told. Before they cleared the door, we heard from inside, "Oh hell!" and a third man followed them out.

Keeping them covered, we led them to the side of the building where we took their guns. Then I asked what Cantry had offered to pay them to run peaceful homesteaders off their land.

The oldest looking of the lot answered for all of them. "The Colonel said he'd pay us a hundred dollars for two weeks' work driving squatters off his land. He didn't say nothing about no homesteaders, and he didn't say nothin' about attacking a town marshal. It seemed like good money until you boys showed up."

I had one more question to ask. "Who's your friend in there?" I meant the last of the Denver men.

"That's Billy Dixon; he fancies hisself a gunfighter. But he ain't nothin' but a cowpuncher like us."

"Alright, you boys drift, and if you're still in this country come sundown, I'll arrest you for somethin'. Now git."

One of them asked for his gun back saying that it cost him a month's wages. My answer was that next time, he should be more careful who he signed on with.

When they were gone, I yelled into the barn, "You ready to give up, Cantry? Come out now, and I'll arrest you for attempted murder on a lawman. You get yourself a good lawyer, you just might get off."

I could have guessed his answer. "You go to hell, Finn! You want me . . . you come in here and get me!"

"That go for you too, Cole? You can ride out of here if you want; I only want Cantry."

I didn't expect an answer because Tuck Cole wasn't known as much of a talker. However, he fooled me by saying, "I ride for the brand, Marshal. I take a man's money, I stick it."

I looked across the way at Jed and shrugged. He smiled and shrugged back at me.

I could tell from their voices that they were all the way in the back, but I wanted to pinpoint them a little better than that. I took a quick look around the side of the door into the gloom of the stable, hoping I wouldn't get my fool head shot off. The only thing I could see was the barrel of a gun sticking out from behind the slats of a stall. The hand holding the gun was shaking. That was Billy Dixon.

Turning to Tom, I told him what I saw and where, and asked him if he could blow a hole in the slats off to the side of where Dixon was. "I think he's ready to give up; he just needs a little prodding." Tom took a quick look himself and assured me he could do so without hitting the boy.

I traded places with Tom and he took a deep breath. Then he swung around the side of the door, let off a blast, and was back next to me before there could be return fire. Then we heard a voice yell out, "Don't shoot! I'm coming out unarmed!" And Billy Dixon, ex-gunfighter, came running out; he left his gun and his horse inside. I couldn't tell him to ride, so I ordered him to wait for us at the eating house. Then we got down to business.

Cantry and Cole were waiting for us. Cantry wanted me dead; Cole was just a hired gun, paid to kill anyone that Cantry pointed him toward. Jed came to Redemption to kill Cantry. Tom, he came to Redemption to get himself killed. I came to rid the range of Cantry, one way or the other. In the next few minutes some of us were going to get what we wanted, what we came to Redemption looking for, and some of us were going to die.

There was nothing for it but to do it. I told Tom we'd go in shooting on the count of three. Jed was across the way; I held up my hand and pointed inside, then held up three fingers. He nodded. One by one I folded in my fingers. Jed went in from the left; I took the middle with Tom to my right.

I had asked Billy Dixon where Cantry and Cole were situated, so I knew that they were both at the back, on the right in the last stall, and that they had put their horses in the opposite stall. I was glad to hear it because they both rode fine horses, and I would have hated to harm a good horse.

We went through the door shooting as fast as we could pull the hammers back and squeeze the triggers of our guns. It wasn't that we thought we'd hit anyone; we were just covering ourselves. Four steps in, we all fell to the ground. They were ready for us and hurling lead as rapidly as we were firing at them. Jed rolled to the left and found cover behind a water trough. Tom went to the right and into a stall. Me, I had a bullet in my leg and crawled over to where Tom was.

It was a clean wound; it didn't hit bone. The bullet went through my thigh, and it was bleeding a mite too much. But this was no time to worry about that. I ripped my shirt for a bandage and wrapped the wound as best I could, but it didn't do much good. The blood still flowed. Any other ministrations would have to wait.

We were in a kind of Mexican standoff. Between Tom and me, and Cantry and Cole, were a number of stalls. None of us could get a clear shot. Jed was across the barn and had a better angle for shooting, but Cantry and Cole were pretty well hunkered in back there. So there we were. Me bleeding and no one shooting. I was getting a little light-headed from the loss of blood and was trying to think of a way to move things along when Cole shouted, "Marshal, this ain't getting us nowhere. I wanna make a deal."

I had offered him a deal earlier, but that was all right. If he wanted to walk, he could. That would leave only

Cantry to deal with. But then he surprised me by saying, "I want to stand and draw against you or your deputy; I don't care which. I heard of both of you, and I think I'm faster than either one of you. If I win, Cantry and I walk out of here. If not, then I won't care one way or the other what happens to Cantry."

I couldn't stand, and my vision was starting to blur. I was about to tell him no deal when I heard, "Alright Cole, but Cantry has to stand and throw down his gun. I don't trust him. It will be just you and me. The marshal will honor the bargain." It was Jed talking.

I yelled to Jed that I was the marshal and that I was running things, but he paid me no mind. He stood and walked out to the center of the barn and waited. Presently Cole stood up, his gun in his holster. He did a half turn and made a motion, then Cantry stood up. Cole held out his hand, and Cantry handed him his six-shooter, which Cole promptly tossed onto the dirt floor. There they stood facing each other . . . Jed and Cole. I didn't like it and if Cole killed Jed, I'd kill the both of them, Cantry *and* Cole. Bargain be damned! But right then, there was nothing I could do. To do or say anything would only distract Jed.

Slowly, Cantry moved away from Cole. Tom and I were standing now, with me leaning on a stall door for support. I could hear no sounds out on the street even though it was a Wednesday morning. People were either obeying my order to stay inside or the earlier gunplay kept them indoors.

Cole and Jed stood fifty feet apart. Cole's hands hovered over his guns. Jed had two guns also and could shoot with either hand. His arms were folded, his hands nowhere near his guns. That seemed to anger Cole. He thought he was the best, and he wanted no advantage. When word got around that he had killed the Laramie Kid, he didn't want people saying it was because the Kid gave him a break. But seeing as how there was nothing he could do about it, he made his move.

I have to say Cole was fast, maybe even faster than me. But Jed, well, he was something else. His arms unfolded and then his gun was in his right hand. I didn't even see him draw, he was that fast. Jed got off two shots before Cole had his gun level. Both shots hit Cole's heart. There's only the quick and the dead. That day, it was Tuck Cole's turn to die.

Jed stood a moment looking at Cole's body, and then approached Cantry, his gun still in his hand. He raised the gun, pulled back the hammer, and pointed it at Cantry's heart. Tom took a step forward, but I motioned for him to wait. It was Jed's play, and I was going to let him have his head. Time slowed; the four of us stood in that barn waiting for Jed's gun to cough death.

I was watching Jed's trigger finger and as I saw it start to tighten, Cantry fell to his knees and covered his face with his hands. He started to bawl like a baby. In between sobs, he pleaded for his life. It was a sorry sight to see, but then I didn't expect much more from the man. Jed looked at him for a moment with disgust. He eased back the hammer of his gun and holstered it, saying as he did so, "I've hunted you for six long years, and I've hated you every minute of every day of those years. I lived for the day that I could kill you, but you're just not worth it. My killing days end right now."

After finishing with Cantry, Jed turned and looked at me. I nodded my approval, and he smiled. We were walking toward each other (I was limping) when I heard the shot and then Jed fell into me. It was as though he had been pushed from behind. I fell with him on top of me; he was dead weight. Just before I passed out from the lack of blood, I heard the roar of Tom's shotgun.

TWENTY-FIVE

It was dark when I awoke; the lamp was lit, and I was alone. I did not remember lighting the lamp, but I didn't let it bother me. *I better get to the eating house before Tom and Jed finish off all the flapjacks.*

When I attempted to get out of bed, I found I had no strength and I had to lay back down. Then the memory came to me. *Cantry and Jed. Jed! He was shot!* I had to get moving and go see about Jed. I must have made some noise, because as I was fumbling with the covers, Jenny came in . . . without knocking. I was embarrassed for her to see me in the altogether and pulled the covers up to my neck. Then I had the presence of mind to ask her what she was doing in my room, and more importantly, what had happened to Jed.

She informed me that Jed had been shot, but he would live. And that she was in my room because she had been nursing both Jed and me since we had been carried in that morning. I had a lot of questions, but right then, I was too weak to ask them. As long as Jed was all right, I could . . . I could . . . That's as far as my thoughts got before sleep claimed me once again.

The next time I opened my eyes, it was daylight and Tom was sitting in my chair reading a newspaper. When he saw that I was awake, he put the paper aside and shook his head saying, "I'm the only one of us who wanted to catch a bullet, but you and Jed hogged them all for yourselves." He laughed and asked me if I was hungry. I hadn't thought about it, but yes I was. And thirsty too.

He excused himself and left the room, but was back within a few minutes carrying a glass of water. "Jenny was in looking after Jed, she's gone to get you something to eat."

More than eating, I wanted to know about Jed. So Tom filled me in on what had happened.

"You couldn't see it because Jed was blocking your view. But when he turned his back on Cantry, Cantry scrambled for the gun that was lying on the ground in front of Cole's body. I didn't realize what was happening until it was too late. By the time I had my gun up, Cantry had already shot Jed in the back. But it was the last act of his life. I shot him twice from twenty feet away; there was hardly enough of him left to scrape up."

It was like pulling teeth to find out Jed's condition, but eventually, I learned that the bullet had entered him low and gone upwards because Cantry was on his knees when he fired. That was lucky for Jed because it went up and out without hitting his lungs or anything else of importance. Then Tom told me about my condition. "The doctor says you've lost a lot of blood and you'll be weak for a little while, but you'll live." Well, that was good to know. It's always good to know that you're not gonna die anytime soon.

Two days later, I was strong enough to get out of bed and went to see Jed in his room. I knocked on the door, and a female voice invited me in. I found Jenny fluffing a pillow. Jed looking somewhat embarrassed. I asked if I could sit and visit a spell. Jenny made it clear that it would have to be a short spell, seeing as how Jed needed his rest.

"Yes Ma'am," I acquiesced.

I was allowed a few minutes before being ushered out. *That girl sure has taken charge*, I thought as I walked back to my room.

The next morning, after looking in on Jed, I sat outside the boarding house enjoying the fresh air. Jed was coming along fine, but it would be a while before he could get out of bed. It was pleasant sitting outside after being shut up in my room. In a while, I would go over to the eating house for some breakfast, but right then, I did not want to move.

I was lost in thought when I heard someone clear his throat. I looked up to see Roy Price standing before me.

"Mind if I sit a spell, Marshal?"

I pointed to a chair, then waited for what he had to say. In his own time he got to it.

"Just wanted to thank you for what you did for us. As you know, I've been laid up, and this is the first chance I've had since you brought me into town."

I told him, as I had told Missus Simms, that I didn't do it alone. I had the help of Jed and Tom. He nodded and said he had already thanked Tom, and as soon as Jed was up and around, he was going to thank him also.

I asked about his wound. "It's almost healed, Marshal." Then he asked about mine. Finally, he said that he and his family were going to stay the winter in Redemption and head for California in the spring. I suggested that he might want to hook up with a wagon train because it would be safer than traveling alone, which of course, he already knew, but I told him anyway.

About the time I was ready for breakfast, Tom came along, and we went over to the eating house together. Tom's been acting as marshal while I've been laid up, so he sleeps late. It was mid-morning, and we had the place to ourselves. Jenny wasn't serving; Susanna was. Susanna was hired to help out because Jenny was spending all her time looking after Jed.

Over coffee, Tom pulled out an envelope from his pocket and handed it to me. I noticed some dried blood on it, but I didn't say anything.

"I took this off what was left of Cantry," said Tom. "I've been waiting for you to get on your feet before I gave it to you. It's from his brother in Chicago. It has his return address on it. I thought you might want to write him and tell him what happened to his brother. And there's still eight thousand head of beef out on the range that someone has to take care of; winter's coming on fast." He averted his eyes and then went on. "I would have written him myself, but seeing as how I killed his brother, I didn't think it proper."

I didn't say anything for a minute. I slowly sipped my coffee and thought on how to put into words what I had to say. At length I said, "Tom, even if you don't know it, you're a lawman. In fact, you're more than a lawman; you are the new marshal of Redemption, Colorado. I gave over my tin star to Jim Niles yesterday. Him and me had some words, and in the end, we both thought you'd make a better marshal for this town than me. I asked him to let me tell you, so now I'm tellin' you."

He looked shocked and said, "I'm not taking your job, Huck. I didn't come here for that."

"What did you come here for?"

He hesitated a moment, "You know . . ."

Yeah I knew what he meant, and I knew that in time he would change his mind. I didn't want to embarrass him and make him admit that things had changed. So I said, "Do you remember me telling you a few days ago about reading a book that said life was all about change?"

He remembered.

"Well it's not just us that change; times and places change too. You are a different man than you were when you left Hawaii. And this is a different town than when you first got here. The way you spoke of Kalei, I know you will always love her. But do you think she would want you to throw away your life when you have so much of it left? I'm sure she's in heaven preparing a home for you, and you will be with her soon enough. Eternity is for a long time, but there are people here on earth who need you. Jed and I are two of them. If you hadn't been here to help out with Cantry and those Slash C boys in the saloon, Jed and I might both be dead. And because of you, Mister Price is alive; you're the one who went and got the doctor and the buckboard that brought him into town.

"I guess what I'm really trying to say is that this town needs you, and the people here like you. I'll be moving on as soon as I'm sure Jed is all right. So it looks like you're the marshal, and as marshal, it's up to you to write the letter to Cantry's brother. You'll find that as marshal, you'll have to do some things that you'd rather not.

"Now, I'll help you out this one time. You tell the brother what Cantry was doing to the nesters and how all his hands were gunnies. Then suggest that he hire some drovers to take the cattle to Abilene and put them on a train to Chicago.

"I looked it up; Cantry never filed a *Right of Use Claim* on the land he built his ranch on, so he didn't own it. All the brother has claim to are the cows. Then go out to McNally, and tell him to round up his cattle off the range because anything out there will be swept up when the drovers hit. They're not going to take the time to separate brands or to brand the calves. They'll have the snows to beat. Tell McNally if he wants to take a few head in payment for the new house he has to build, you'll look the other way."

By the time I was finished talking, my coffee had gotten cold. I raised my cup to Susanna to get a refill. She's not as efficient as Jenny, but she's young yet.

Tom was quiet until Susanna had gone and then he said, "Reckon you're right, Huck. I do like the town, and now that I think on it, being its marshal might be just what I need to give me a purpose in life. Oh, and there's just one more thing. I forgot this," and he handed me five one thousand dollar bills.

"You just *forgot* this?" I said while waving the bills at him. "It sure is something to forget! So tell me about it."

Looking a little embarrassed, he said, "It's nothing. I mean I took them off Cantry. You can see a few flecks of blood on some of the bills. Should I send them to the brother?"

I had to think on it for a minute and then said, "With your permission, Marshal, why don't you let me handle this?"

Tom was momentarily taken aback at being called "Marshal," but he rebounded with a big grin and told me to do with the bills as I liked.

A week later, Jed and I were sitting outside The Silver Dollar in the late afternoon, just two retired lawmen watching the world go by. We were trying to work up a thirst. Usually that was not a problem, but since we were wounded, Doc has limited our drinking. He said we could have nothing before sundown and then no more than three shots. Of course, normally, we would have been inside working up a thirst and maybe even helping it along with a shot or two. But Jenny's hell-on-wheels when it comes to having Jed obey Doc's orders. So I stayed outside with him just to keep him company.

Just to make a little conversation, thinking that it would make the time go by faster, I said, "Seems like more and more people are movin' to this neck of the woods. Yesterday, Niles told me there were five new families homesteading out on the range. You ever think of filing for a section?"

Jed didn't look at me when he answered, but stared straight ahead. "I figure I might go on to California. You know I never did make it the first time I set out."

"Thinking of going by yourself?" I asked wryly, knowing full well the answer.

"Not exactly. I was thinking of taking Jenny with me."

I acted surprised and shocked. "You cannot take a young, single girl away from her mother and traipse out to California with her."

"Of course not! We'll be married."

Still acting surprised and shocked I said, "I didn't think you'd ever get up the nerve to ask her. You *have* asked her, haven't you?"

"Well . . . not exactly."

"What do you mean by *not exactly*?"

"It's more like I was told the news. The other night when Jenny brought me my supper, she told me that we were going to be married, and we were going to live in California. She says she wants to get me out of this wild country so I won't even be tempted to go back to being a gunfighter."

I knew all that. Jenny had communicated her plans to her mother. And the night before, Missus Simms had come to me and asked if I thought Jed would make a good husband for Jenny. She knew what my answer would be, but she wanted to be reassured nonetheless.

Just then, by prearrangement, Jenny walked up.

"I hope you boys are being good and waiting for sundown before you start your carousing."

Jed said nothing, but he was smiling! He always had a lopsided grin on his puss when Jenny was around. I winked at Jenny and said, "Jed's tried to drag me into the Dollar three times, but I keep tellin' him I won't go against Doc's orders." They both laughed because they knew if anyone was trying to drag anyone into the saloon, it would be me doing the dragging.

I took out the five thousand dollars I had in my shirt pocket and handed it over to Jed. He reached out and took it, asking, "What's this?"

"That is a wedding present."

He tried to hand it back saying he could not accept it. "I still owe you money from twelve years back."

"So you do, my young friend. Then take this money and with it you can afford to pay me back."

That stopped him for a minute, but still he held out the five bills between us. Then I said what I was going to say to begin with. "The money's not mine. It was Cantry's, but seeing as how he has no more need for it, I thought it could be put to some good use."

I knew it would be a hard sell to get Jed to take the money, and would be even harder once he knew where it came from. That's why I arranged to have Jenny there. She

309

took the bills from Jed's hand, smiled at me and said, "That's right nice of you, Marshal. We'll use this to buy us some land when we get to California." She kissed me on the cheek and Jed on the lips and started to walk off before Jed could say anything else. But she stopped after a few steps, turned and said, "Why don't you boys go into the Dollar a little early tonight: I'm sure Doc won't mind."

That was not by arrangement, but it should have been.

TWENTY-SIX

Two weeks later, after having said good-bye to my friends, I was riding north. I thought I might head up to the Dakota Territory, but hadn't made up my mind yet. When I came to the tracks of the Union Pacific Railroad, I turned east and followed them until I came to a station. It wasn't really a station, just a boxcar with its wheels taken off, sitting next to a water tower.

With a fifty-dollar bribe to the conductor, I booked passage for me and my horse to ride in the mail car. I was damn lucky that they had a ramp they used to wheel heavy boxes up into the car.

I had decided to go to New York. I had had enough of living by the gun. For a change, I wanted to walk around without a gun strapped to my leg. I wanted to see one of those New York shows. You know the ones with all them pretty girls. I had plenty of money, and I thought it about time I enjoyed some of it. I was tired.

The first thing I did when I hit New York was find a stable for my horse and a place for me to hang my hat. I had a local bank arrange to have my money transferred up from St. Petersburg, and then I was in business.

After a month of seeing shows and hitting saloons, I was getting a mite restless. I thought maybe I had made a mistake in thinking that I could live in a city as big as New York. But on the very night I was thinking those thoughts, I ran into the gent who would alter my future.

I was standing at the bar in the Alhambra doing some drinking after a show, when I accidently jostled the man next to me, spilling his drink. He was good-natured about it, and I offered to buy him another to replace the one I spilled.

As the barkeep was pouring his drink, the man introduced himself as James Bennett, managing editor of the New York Herald. He also told me that the paper had the largest circulation of any newspaper in New York City, which meant that it had the largest circulation in the country. I introduced myself. His eyes widened, and he choked a little on his drink.

"You don't mean to say that you're *that* Huck Finn? Huck Finn from Buntline's dime novels?"

"Yes I am," I answered, "but put no stock in them; there's very little truth in what he writes. And if I ever see him, I'll punch him in the nose!"

He laughed and said, "You may very well have the chance. He's over there sitting alone at that table in the corner. He's the rather stout gentleman wearing the brown coat."

I turned to see what looked to me like a fat old man. "He's older than I thought he would be. It wouldn't be sporting to hit him."

Bennett suggested we go over and have a drink with him so that I could tell him my thoughts on his novels. Well, I had nothing better to do, and Bennett was the first person I had met in New York. I would enjoy telling Buntline exactly what I thought of his novels, at least the ones that used my name.

When I was introduced, Buntline grabbed my hand and pumped my arm as if it were a pump handle.

"Very glad to meet you, Mister Finn. This is indeed fortuitous; I just started a new book about your exploits in Colorado. Please sit down, and let me buy you a drink."

To say I was staggered by what he said would have been a massive understatement. How did he know what happened in Redemption? It had been only two months since that day. Or was he talking about some other shootout in Colorado? There'd been a few. Maybe he was talking about that dust-up in Durango three years back.

Buntline explained to me how he knew about what happened in Redemption. A newspaperman passing through town right after the fight with Cantry had heard talk about it. When he got to Denver, he telegraphed the story to his paper. Then other papers picked up on it and printed it.

"That's right," said Bennett, "we ran it a month ago. Tell me, is it true that you faced down twenty armed men all by yourself. That, when the smoke had cleared, there were nine dead, and the rest were running for the hills? That you were mortally wounded and only the love of a good woman pulled you through?"

I could only shake my head in astonishment at such foolishness. If that was the story being repeated all over the country, I could see that there was no way I could correct the misconceptions. So I said, "No, it was thirty armed men."

They didn't know if I was funnin' them or not, and I let them ponder it while I helped myself to Buntline's very fine liquor. I could see that I wasn't going to talk Buntline out of writing his new book, so I enjoyed his whiskey and answered the questions (not truthfully) that were asked of me.

At one point, Bennett suddenly slapped his opened hand down hard on the table. "I've got it!" he shouted. "Huck, you could sell papers!"

I know we were drinking a mite—the bottle was almost empty—but if he thought I was going to stand on a street corner and hawk newspapers for him, then he was drunker than I was. Then he explained what he meant. "Your name will sell a lot papers. You'll be a reporter with a byline."

I thought he was touched in the head, or maybe it was just the liquor talking. I couldn't be a reporter; I could barely speak proper English, never mind write it. However, I kept my musings to myself because Bennett ordered a new bottle to celebrate his great idea.

Buntline filled our glasses and raised his, "Here's to the western hero," he said.

As we left the saloon late that night, I promised to come to his office the next day. I might have had a bit too much whiskey myself to have promised anything like that.

The next afternoon, I went to the newspaper office, mainly because I had nothing else to do, and saw Bennett. He had been giving a lot of thought as to where to place me. "Then it came to me," he said "the sports desk! You would be a natural with the way you speak. You have that downhome nomenclature." I didn't know what nomenclature was, but if I had it, maybe I should see a doctor.

I told him that I could not write well enough to be a newspaperman, and that I knew next to nothing about sports.

"What's to know? Just come back with the right score, or who won the fight. You'll get the hang of it. What I want from you, more than accurate reporting, are your impressions of the event. I want you to tell our readers about it in your own words. Don't worry; anything written by Huck Finn is going to be read."

He wanted to trade on my name, but what did I care? I was bored.

And that is how I became a newspaperman.

TWENTY-SEVEN

I've been doing this newspaper writing for nigh on twenty years now. One good thing about being famous and writing a newspaper column that is printed in various newspapers around the country is that your friends know how to reach you. I receive over one hundred letters a week and every once in a while, I get one from an old friend.

Ten years ago, I received a letter from Mac Conroy, the man that killed Ed Trask down in Lamesa. He became a preacher and lives in San Diego. He's married and has four children. I don't recollect how many boys and how many girls, but by now, they're most likely married. He told me the last liquor to touch his lips was what I gave him the night I arrested him.

Two or three years back, I got a letter from Chang telling me his wife and son got over here all right. He also told me that in the first four years after reuniting with his wife, they had three more children. They must have been making up for lost time. Anyway, the first child was a boy and true to his word, Chang named him Huck Finn . . . poor child. But what I wanted to tell you is that, at the time I received Chang's letter, Hu Huck Finn was entering that new college Leland Stanford started down south of San Francisco. He's going to be an engineer. He's going to

317

build bridges and railroad tunnels, big things like that. And I am very proud to say that I am his honorary godfather. Imagine that!

Jed's not much for letter writing, but Jenny writes me quite regular, about once a year when they send me my crate of oranges. You see, every year at Christmas time, a crate of oranges arrives at the newspaper office and in the crate, every year, is a letter. I'm not much on oranges, so I hand them out for people to take home to their children. Fresh oranges are hard to come by in New York City in the wintertime.

Jenny's first letter, however, did not come in a crate of oranges; it came by regular mail. She wrote that she and Jed had settled in a little town called Los Angeles and bought a small piece of property with an orange grove on it. It seems Jed has an affinity for plants and trees. After a few years, they bought more property, and Jed planted it all with orange trees. Every year after that, they bought more land, and Jed planted more trees. It took a while for all those trees to mature, but now Jed and Jenny are the fourth largest producers of oranges in the state. They have two daughters; the oldest one, Sally, is married. The younger daughter, Lanie, wants to go into the family business, and Jed wants her to. But Jenny wants her to marry a good, respectable man. She tells me that Jed and Lanie spend hours together out in the groves inspecting and caring for the trees, and if it was up to Jed, Lanie would take over the business today, she knows that much about it. Jenny writes that she's fearful Jed will insist on Lanie coming into the business. She says Jed doesn't put his foot down very often, but when he does, it stays down. They are very happy and have a good life.

Tom and I exchange letters about twice a year. He keeps me abreast of the news concerning Redemption, and I tell him about life here in New York City. He doesn't seem very impressed. Roy Price and his family never left for California. When spring rolled around in '74, they filed for a homestead, and they're still there. Susanna married a cowpoke and lives up in Wyoming.

There were so many nesters moving onto the range that it was decided a county sheriff was needed. Tom was offered the job, but thought it would entail too much time in the saddle, so he declined. The county held an election, and Bob McNally beat out Bob McGuiness for the job. Then McNally turned around and hired McGuiness as his deputy.

Tom took up with Missus Simms after Jenny left. He moved out of the boarding house and into the hotel, but they have never thought of getting married. The whole town knows about their arrangement and does not care.

In one of the first letters I received from Tom, I learned that Makaio had passed. A letter Tom had mailed to him came back marked, "Deceased."

Tom and I are nigh on sixty years of age now. He tells me he'd like to retire and sit on the hotel porch for the rest of his days, but he knows Missus Simms, Mary, will never allow it. She keeps him pretty busy doing repairs around the hotel and restaurant.

I've never married, probably because I spend too much time in saloons. I too am thinking of retiring. You can only attend so many boxing matches and baseball games before they all look the same. Anyways, it's getting harder to come up with different ways to say the same old thing about the same old thing.

I don't think I'll be writing about any more of my adventures. Nowadays, the only adventure I have is trying to get a good table at Delmonico's Steak House. Though sometimes in the winter when it's real cold outside and the heating in my room is not doing its job, I think of Molly Lee. You remember her, the girl down in Virginia who wanted to run away with me all those many years ago? Well . . . on those cold nights, I think of Molly Lee and what might have been.

Huck Finn

New York City

1895

Thank you for reading **Redemption**. I would like to hear from you and get your thoughts on the story. Good or bad. Please go to http://huckfinn76.com and click on the "Contact Us" button. If you would like to read a short except from *Molly Lee*, the sequel to **Redemption**, please turn the page.

Andrew Joyce

That's the way things stood for the next month. Business increased a little, partly due to my promoting myself as *The Spicy Lady* and partly because the snows had come. The miners could not work and had to sit on their claims throughout the winter or someone would take them over. I heard that the previous year a few miners had left for the winter, and when they returned, someone was sitting on their claims. It led to a little gunplay, with the one that was faster on the draw ending up with the mine. With the miners not mining, there was nothing for them to do but go to a saloon and warm their insides with whiskey or their outsides with one of the whores . . . or both.

I had made no progress with John Stone. He was always polite enough, but that's as far as it went. It was on a Tuesday night—not that the day of the week matters—that I finally worked up the courage to make a play for him. As usual, he was sitting in his chair watching the room. Over the last few weeks there had been a few minor altercations, but John always kept things peaceful. Sometimes it took a blunt knock to someone's head with the stock of his shotgun, other times it took pointing the ten gauge in someone's face. Both methods seemed to work equally well.

I walked over to John, and with a slight nod to the shotgun on his lap, I asked, "Won't you hurt innocent people if you ever have to discharge that thing?"

He didn't say anything for a minute, then he let fly with a stream of brown tobacco juice out of the side of his mouth, and I'll be damned if he didn't hit the spittoon sitting next to his chair dead center. Without taking his eyes from the room, he answered me. "It's just for show. If you point a ten gauge at someone, most of the time they'll do what you say. If I ever have to shoot someone, I'll use this," he said as he touched the Dragoon Colt holstered on his hip.

I had just asked him if I could buy him a drink at the end of his shift when a ruckus broke out over at the faro table. When I turned around to see what all the commotion was about, I saw a man holding a revolver on Chan Harris. "You've been cheating me all night. I've lost my poke to your double-dealin' ways and now I want it back!"

Chan shrugged and started to count out some gold coins. After all, it wasn't his money, it was mine. He'd give the man his money back and let me worry about it. Smart thinking on his part. I reckon he wasn't counting fast enough to suit the man holding the gun. The shot, when it came, made all those within the room jump. All, that is, except John Stone.

Chan started to fall to the floor while the other two men at the table dove for cover, as did everybody else in the room except John and me. Before Chan hit the floor, John had the Colt out of its leather, and from his hip put a bullet into the gunman's heart. Of course, it entered from the back, but no one was complaining, least of all the dead man bleeding onto my floor with two twenty-dollar gold pieces clutched in his right hand.

When the smoked cleared, John said, "I reckon I *could* use a whiskey after work."

I ran over to where Chan lay and knelt down to see what I could do to help him, but he was already dead.

The place cleared out fast. A few men stayed and formed a circle around Chan and me. Still kneeling next to him, I looked up into their hard faces. I saw nothing. To them, death on a Tuesday night was just another night out on the town. Maybe a shooting added a little excitement, but that was all . . . unless you were the one shot.

I had seen dead men before. There were the two Yankees back at the farm. And Mister Fellows died in my arms. I wore his blood on my shirt until the shirt was taken away from me by Crow Mother. I don't know why, but Chan's death affected me more than the others had. Maybe because after finding the gold and buying The Spicy Lady, I thought my life would calm down some. Now here I was kneeling over another dead man. A man I didn't even know that well. But he worked for me and I thought I should have done better by him. He should not have died making money for me.

I stood up and wanted to tell those still present to leave, but the words would not come. I started to shake and I felt like I was about to scream when I felt a strong hard arm around my shoulder and heard a voice, a surprisingly gentle voice seeing as who it belonged to, say, "You boys best be getting on, we'll be closing up early tonight." No one ever argued with John Stone unless he was drunk, and no one was drunk after seeing Chan Harris killed.

John took over. When the place was empty except for those that worked there, he told Dick and Dave to carry Chan into the back room and lay him out. He told me to go to the bar and have Abe pour me a water glass full of rye and then drink it.

I couldn't stand up much longer, so I took my rye to a table and sat down. John was standing over the man he had killed. I don't know what he was thinking, but at that point I didn't care. I was supposed to be a hard woman, but here I was going to pieces. If we hadn't been snowed in, I would have gotten on my horse that very minute and headed back to Virginia to be held in my mother's arms, Hunts Buffalo be damned!

We didn't have any law in town. There was no marshal or sheriff. We didn't even have a mayor. When Dick and Dave came back from laying out Chan, John told them to pick up the other man and throw him out onto the street, then go to Chan's digs and see if there were letters or anything to tell us if he had any next of kin. He directed Abe and Gus to leave by the back door and lock up as they usually did. As I've said, no one ever argued with John Stone. They all did as instructed.

John got the place closed up and came over to where I sat. He was holding the cash box. "I reckon you'll want to put this in the safe before you go upstairs."

I looked up at him and started to laugh. I was getting hysterical. John nodded and went into my office. When he returned he said, "I put it on your desk, it'll be safe enough." He held out his hand and I took it. He pulled me to my feet and without saying a word, he walked me upstairs.

That night John Stone held me as I cried for Chan Harris . . . and maybe a little for myself.

Made in the USA
Lexington, KY
21 July 2019